F
WATER
A
L
L
I
N
G

Stories for Travelers
by
David Mohrmann

Printed and bound in the United States of America

Library of Congress Cataloging-in-Publication Data
Mohrmann, David.
Water Falling: short stories by David Mohrmann

ISBN 978-0-9969922-3-7

Front and Back Cover Paintings by David Mohrmann
Cover design by David Mohrmann and Jesse Ostrowski

Note: The story "After The Ruins" appeared as a chapter
in the novel "XOCOMIL, The Winds Of Atitlán."

Also:
The author welcomes comments on these stories about traveling,
and how they might compare with yours.
Feel free to contact him by email: mohrmannd@gmail.com

ACKNOWLEDGMENTS

Since this is a book about traveling, I first need to acknowledge the many thousands of people who—because of political persecution, war, poverty, or ecological devastation— are forced to leave their home. That is a kind of travel not included in these stories. Touristic adventures, no matter how challenging, cannot compare with the plight of displaced people. I support their determined struggle to survive, and I highly respect those who comfort them along the way. Every traveler longs to be welcomed. That is what all good people want, to meet the goodness in others, to feel safe and at peace.

I am thankful to those who helped these stories find their form. My weekly writer's group, TGI (John Daniels, Nancy Wheeler, Jeanie Gale, Wanda Naylor) has been a constant source of support and direction. My wife, Lee, is always a trusted advisor. And my daughter, Zan. I also want to thank Bernadette Cheyne for a careful early reading of the material and some important notes. My thanks as well to Nancy Carlsen-Paige, Doug Kline, Rich and Joey McCutchan, Marshall Kane, Larry Fried, Theresa May, Peg Anderson, Steve Ladd, Robin Retherford, Erik Linblom, Fhyre Phoenix, Jim Hight, Janet Patterson, and good ol' Uncle Kurt, who probably said, "If you don't know where to go, best sit back and look at where you are."

A special thanks to Jesse Ostrowski for all the design help.

Of course I am most grateful for my editor, John Heckel. His in-depth analysis guided these stories throughout their long hard journey.

WATER FALLING

LASTWORD BOOKS

CONTENTS

Man cannot discover new oceans unless he has
courage to lose sight of the shore.
-Andre Gide-

The gladdest moment in human life
me thinks
is a departure into unknown lands.
-Sir Richard Burton-

A mind stretched by a new experience
can never go back to its old dimensions.
-Oliver Wendell Holmes-

I haven't been everywhere
but it's on my list.
-Susan Sontag-

Doctor Seuss said, "Oh the places you'll go."

But I think he'd agree there's more to it than that. It's the things you see in those places. It's who you meet, what happens, and how you are changed.

This is a book about people traveling.
Not going from place to place, but *traveling*.
To clarify, I turn to an expert in the field: Coyote.
Asleep in the desert he once dreamt of a wide and mighty waterfall. Though having no idea what it was, he knew what it meant. He was part of that cascading flow, a single drop of it tumbling through space, on his way to who knows where.

He woke up smiling, then set off like every step was new. There is no other way to travel.

SACRED GROUNDS
-a fable for today-

A beautiful long-eared rabbit and an old withered coyote sit across from each other at the Sacred Grounds Cafe. Both wonder why the waitress doesn't stop to take their order, or even bring a glass of water.

She is a skinny blond girl whose dark steely eyes and thin pale lips contradict the *happyface* button that smiles above her nametag: **GAIL**. She has never seen animals sitting in a coffee shop. She doesn't know what to do.

Why me, she thinks, *on my first damn day at work?*

Gail's training was yesterday. It did not amount to much. The regular waitress, Meredith, showed her how Fred, the cook, liked his orders written. She also talked about what a sexist pig he was. "Same as my ex-husband," she said.

"Is there anything special I need to know?" Gail asked.

"Nah," Meredith said. "Nothing special ever happens here. People drinking too much coffee, that's all you get. Hell, if some guy doesn't like how his eggs are cooked, just bring 'em back to Fred. That's the only problem you might have. Don't worry, kid, you'll be fine."

But Gail isn't *fine.*

She busies herself from table to table, writing orders, filling half-empty cups of coffee, delivering food, bringing extra napkins, and asking if everything is okay...or if there is anything else...anything at all she can do?

1

"No," the customers tell her, "we're *fine*." Some of the older women call her "hon." One of them pats her on the hand and says, "Oh, hon, thank you so much."

That, for the moment, makes Gail feel better, but eventually she will have to go see what the animals want. She knows it, dreads it, and will avoid it as long as possible. Maybe if she keeps ignoring them they might leave? Gail goes to a table she's cleared, wipes the remaining crumbs into her hand, sponges the surface clean, then sponges it again. Feeling watched by the animals, feeling nervous, she scurries to the kitchen for fresh plates and silverware.

"Like a chicken," says a smiling Rabbit, "with her—"

"Yeah," interrupts Coyote.

Both laugh at Rabbit's intended, and appropriate, cliché. For Coyote the mirth is forced. He loves when their minds merge, yet today is irritated by the cause. *Why must such precious time be wasted?* It is hard for him not to be grumpy, especially now, having just returned from a long and arduous journey in the desert. To survive the afternoon heat he slept in caves. Mornings and evenings he climbed the highest ridges, scanning the open landscape down below, connecting in his mind the scattered *hoodoos*, ordering them like stars of an unnamed constellation. That is his job, his life's work. It takes a lot of energy, a lot of concentration, and every time the effort costs him.

More withered than usual, he slumps on his bench seat. His once shiny fur hangs from tired bones like a worn-out rug. *As it should.* That's how he thinks. Like others of his kind, Coyote is both blessed and cursed with ancient wisdom. He sees things that others do not. He sees, for instance, that his traveling companion is not merely a rabbit with long ears—and perhaps, indeed, not a rabbit at all. He looks again into her sparkling eyes, her glorious being. He remembers her elusive dance as he chased her for hours over hills of cactus and sage, her moves so unpredictable, so baffling, so divine, that he could not help falling in love. Coyote now understands how inevitable it was. She is such

2

a beauty. And he sees how fate has managed to bring them here. Everyone, including the harried Gail, is captivated by their presence. Some appear as upset as the young waitress that animals are sitting at a table like normal everyday people. Others, though, appear upset at her for not taking care of the furry strangers.

Lots of upset all around—that's what Coyote sees.

At the next table over is little Andy Furtado. The two-year-old cannot take his eyes off Coyote. The boy stares at the long whiskered face. Andy hears his mother say, "What a shame, what a shame." He gives her a quick glance, certain that they share the same feeling: *Something is wrong here. Why are the animals being mistreated?*

The boy, of course, is too young for that actual thought, but knows how he feels. He senses that something profound is about to happen. He has no idea what.

Coyote looks Andy in the eyes. He blinks with obvious intent, then turns to Rabbit, reaches out a paw and touches her shoulder. "Sweetheart?"

"Yes?"

"Will you dance?"

"Oh," she says. "Yes, Sweetheart, I'd love to."

That's all it takes. They leap from their confining seats. "Ah hah!" Coyote calls out. He mimes, with twirling paws, several slight-of-hand bits of illusion while Rabbit does her wild desert dance around a frozen, dazzled Gail.

It is a dance of forgiveness. In the desert it forgave Coyote's instinctual need to hunt her. Now it forgives the poverty of human judgment, the sad fact of how misinformed beliefs lead to bad behavior. Coyote keeps pretending to do tricks, as if distracting the crowd, but he knows that everyone will look past him...will silently watch, with new eyes, his scintillating lover...watching as she hops, she bounds, she spins in all directions.

Before long the magic works, compassion settles in, and Gail smiles.

Coyote and Rabbit return to their booth. A warming calm has filled the room, a transparent haze of grace.

Coyote blinks again at little Andy. Andy blinks back.

Though the boy will never understand what happened, it has changed his life forever.

Gail is also changed. Ashamed of herself, and wishing to make amends, she goes directly to the animals. "Sorry for the wait," she says. "Please, can I help you?"

By then, however, having danced the dance and blinked the blink, there is nothing else they need to do, or anything they want. Both of them feel full. Completely full.

"No thanks," they say, and just like that they're gone.

WATER FALLING

"The great, the magnificent, the one and only Niagara Falls!" Kane barked like a demented carny. "Drove all night and half the day to get here. Too bad we have no idea where it is. Too bad there's no time to find out."

"So sue me," said Jerry.

Jerry was the boss—because his dad bought the truck— but more importantly he was Kane's best friend since grade school, so they said whatever they wanted.

"Fuck it," Kane said, to make clear he was done complaining. He was embarrassed to act like some spoiled brat. "Sorry."

"No sweat," Jerry said. "Hey, if it's light enough once the trailer's loaded, we'll give the falls a drive-by."

The boss must've figured that would get his friend motivated, which it did.

After splitting a sandwich they got to work. The house had lots of nice furniture, and a backyard full of kid stuff. The owner, Mrs. Stevens, was not pleased to leave "such young guys" on their own, lamenting that she had no choice, that she was late for some meeting. "Lock up when you're finished and put the key under here," she said, pointing to a pot with a dead plant in it. She said all of that without a smile, with barely a glance.

5

Between her and it, Kane would take the dead plant.

He was heading down the ramp for another load, wheeling the dolly ahead of him, when he saw two young women walking by, and a cute little girl in between, her tiny hands holding tight to theirs. He smiled.

They smiled back and stopped to say hello.

Jerry came out of the house with a portable TV set. He put it on the ramp and started talking to the women like he'd known them for years. Gone was his hurry to get the trailer loaded. Niagara Falls? What Niagara Falls?

Of greater concern, they both knew, was their need for genuine female attention. Whatever they could get. They'd been on the road for five months, back and forth between the two coasts. *Global Van Lines,* read the sign on their truck, *you'll love the way we move!* Sounded good, except how about a bit of adventure once in awhile? Wasn't that the deal? Though the sixties were now two years gone, in Kane's mind the world had changed in essential, mysterious ways, and his main job was to figure out what that meant for him. For instance, sex. He'd grown up too late for the *sexual revolution* train. He needed to catch up. So why not be bummed out by day after day of work? Not yet a single female hitchhiker, or foxy waitress, or horny unappreciated housewife. In fact, this was the first time that good-looking women had spoken, with interest, to either of them.

For Kane it was a great surprise. He was happy, and hopeful, and nervous he might say something wrong, might somehow screw things up. But Jerry was as cool and confident as ever. Right away he got the name of the one with a short skirt and impossible-not-to-notice breasts.

Gretchen.

"I'm Jerry," he said, giving her hand a tender shake.

It seemed he'd forgotten Linda back in Carbondale. Fiancée? What fiancée?

"And this," Jerry said, "is my partner, Kane."

The prettier one shook Kane's hand. "Hi, I'm June."

"We're heading for McDonalds," said Gretchen. "Time to preach under golden arches."

"Preach?" said Jerry. "Why's that? Something wrong with eating hamburgers?"

Gretchen showed a slight grin. "No. Or French-fries either. And we don't usually have to preach."

June frowned. "It's not *preaching,* it's—"

"It's called *Giving Testimony,*" said Gretchen. Her tone seemed a touch sarcastic, a little poke at June's correction. "We stay under the arches because it's impolite to talk to people while they're eating. But they see us waiting, and most of them, when they're finished, come to listen. They give us lots of food along with their good advice. Sometimes they give us money."

"No kidding," said Jerry.

"I kid you not," she said.

"Hey," said June, "you guys hungry? Want some McDonalds?"

"Sounds good to me!" said Jerry.

"Sure," Kane said, "why not?"

Why not? Well, because he hadn't eaten McDonalds since graduating from high school, a full year ago, and though he was not completely vegetarian, and probably never would be, he considered himself far beyond McDonalds.

Obviously it was time to re-consider. Otherwise they might never see these young women again...so yeah, okay, obviously, *why not?*

He and Jerry worked extra-hard while the women were out preaching, or whatever it was they did. By the time they came back, a few hours later, the forty-foot trailer was close to packed. Some things got dinged up in the rush, including two porcelain lamps, an oak table, and an antique maple rocking chair. Jerry would be paying damages on the other end, but for now he didn't seem to mind. "Oh well," he'd said every time it happened, *"c'est la vie."*

7

"You two must be starving," said June. Though a lot less curvy, Kane liked her best. She was the little girl's mother. Though twenty-four years old, she dressed like a little girl herself in one of those old-fashioned frilly kinds of skirts that never did a thing for him before. Incredible how fast things could change. "Here," she said, and handed him a hamburger. Along with the mustard he got a whiff of her, which made him think of roses.

The five of them sat next to the trailer, scarfing down cold burgers and fries.

June asked Kane his age and where he was from. She asked about the things he liked to do.

He could have told her a lot, but had a hard time answering, distracted by her lovely face, her eyes holding his, her lips slightly parted as she listened, and nodded, and took in every word. Kane thought of Niagara Falls. It was a passing thought which passed, in fact, quite quickly.

After a lot of talk, Jerry said, "I guess we should get back to work."

"Gotta do whatcha gotta do," said Gretchen.

June said, "Maybe we can help."

"Against regulations," said Jerry.

"Bummer," said Gretchen.

"Yeah," he said, giving her his special grin. "Good thing I never cared for regulations. Hey, if you want to grab some small stuff and set it by the trailer, be my guest."

"Lead on," Gretchen said, and followed him into the house.

The little girl started fussing. "You'll get done faster," said June, "if I stay here with her."

Kane nodded, grabbed the dolly, and went after the stove, the last heavy piece. He'd been waiting to do that because he knew it would look impressive. As he muscled it out to the ramp, June watched him from the lawn.

"Need some help?" she said.

"Nah, I got it."

An hour later, as the sun dropped behind the house, they locked it up and hid the key under that dead plant.

They stuffed a Doughboy pool into the trailer. Then a few remaining garden tools. Last came a Ping-Pong table to close the whole deal off. Kane tightened the final strap and pulled the door down as carefully as he could, but the tongs of a rake kept getting in the way. He tried to gently twist them inside.

Jerry said, "Excuse me," and threw open the door. He grabbed the rake and jammed it into a tiny crack up under the roof. A few of those tongs needed to bend, that's all there was to it. *"Voilà,"* he said, slamming the door shut, "three houses in a box."

Gretchen sang, "Ta Dah!"

Jerry sat on the grass. So did everyone else.

"Where you taking this stuff?" said June.

"Los Angeles," said Kane.

"Los Angeles," she said in the Spanish way. She closed her eyes, like she was trying to find it on a map inside her head. *"Los Angeles,"* she said again, as if the name itself inspired her, making the place sound a whole lot better than it was.

"Yep," said Jerry. "Be there in three days."

"Bullpucky!" said Gretchen. Her leg was touching Jerry's when it didn't really need to.

"We go straight through," he said. "One of us sleeps while the other drives."

"They make you do that?" Gretchen said.

"No, darlin'," said Jerry, "we make ourselves. The faster we get there and unload, the sooner we get a refill. The more houses we move, the more money we make."

"Ah," she said to him, kind of sparky, "it's all about money, huh?"

"Not *all*. Just *mostly*. I want to be retired when I'm thirty."

"Then what?"

"Then who knows? I guess you'll have to ask me then."

"Wait," said June. "You mean you're leaving for Los Angeles tonight?"

"Real dern soon," said Jerry. He took a deep breath, blew it out, rubbed his stomach and went full-on cowboy: "Soon as I'm finished digestin' them scrumptious viddles."

Dumb as he looked, all puffy and self-satisfied, it got June and Gretchen laughing, which got the little girl laughing even louder, which got the rest of them laughing at her. As it began to die down the kid let loose again and it started up like new. That went on for a while. By the end, the five of them might have been mistaken for friends.

Kane said to the little girl, "Sorry, sweetie, I forgot your name."

She ducked her head and shook it like a rattle.

"Her name is Angie," said June. "She's my angel baby." Angie made a face and June reached under her chin for a tickle. "Aren't you my little *angel, baby?*"

Angie squirmed loose, giggling, nodding her head as fast as she'd been shaking it.

Kane said, "How old are you, Angie?"

Her face turned serious, like he'd asked the meaning of life. She shot up three fingers.

"Can we go with you?" said June.

Gretchen laughed. "Yeah, uh-huh," she said, as if the idea of them riding with these guys all the way to California was beyond her wildest belief.

Exactly what Kane was thinking.

"I mean, if it's okay," said June.

"Against regulations," said Jerry, real stern, and looked at Kane. "Which means why the heck not, right buddy?"

"Your call," said Kane.

Gretchen said to June, "Why Los Angeles?"

"Because I'm tired of being here. Tired of living in a shelter."

"We wouldn't need a shelter in Los Angeles?"

"Who knows? It's a new place, right? Besides, in Los Angeles there's an ocean. Angie's never seen the ocean."

10

"What's ocean, Mommy?"

It was the first thing the kid had said.

Jerry leaned in for the little girl's attention. "Water and sky, honey. Water and sky as far as you can see."

"I like water and sky, Mommy."

"I know," said June. "Me too."

"Well yeah, uh-huh, sure," said Gretchen, "I mean, who doesn't like water and sky? I'm also fond of pyramids. Maybe we should go to Egypt instead."

"As fond of pyramids as you are of oceans?" said Jerry, nudging her knee with his, trying his coolest to let her know how fun this trip could be.

"What's pyramids, Mommy?"

"C'mon," said June, "*why not* go to Los Angeles?"

Jerry grinned at Gretchen. "Yeah, *why not?*"

She grinned back at him. Kane was astounded. It was a mystery how Jerry knew what to say and do.

"Well," Gretchen said, frowning, as if ready to give a final objection—but that was just her playing around—"sure…heck…*why the heck not?*"

First they went out of their way to drive by the falls. The sun had dropped beyond the far trees. There was nowhere to park their monster truck and trailer combo. Kane heard a loud oscillating drone, much louder than their engine, like zillions of croaking toads. He was in the passenger seat, his head out the window same as every other tourist. But he could barely see the beginnings of it. Weird, to watch tons of water falling through space and not know where it landed.

Jerry said, "That's it, Poncho, vacation's over. Time for you to sleep." He shot a glance at Gretchen, who was sitting on the double bed, no doubt hoping she got the hint.

She tapped Kane on the shoulder.

"Okay," she said, "I'll trade."

It was sometime after midnight and they were someplace in Ohio, their second run through the *Buckeye State*, a state

11

they'd never seen except as headlights on asphalt. Jerry was driving and Kane was still trying to nod off. He was on the bed with June, with Angie in the middle. The space was small and stuffy, but Jerry had closed the curtain, which meant that's how he wanted it. He and Gretchen were up front, sharing life stories. From what Kane could hear there'd been no mention of the fiancée.

That was Jerry's problem. Kane didn't care, he had problems of his own. To begin with, this kid, Angie. From the second she'd stared into his eyes and held up those three fingers he'd had a strange feeling. It got stranger when she slid between him and her mother on the bed. Right away she cuddled up, her tiny arms wrapped around his elbow. At first it felt nice, then less and less nice as the hours wore on, as she began rubbing and kneading and pinching his skin until he somehow imagined that Angie was an extension of her mother, that it was secretly June with her hands on him, which got him fantasizing, against his better judgment, about his once steady girlfriend, Gail, who would let him touch her breasts but only with her clothes on. Thinking of all he'd missed got him hard, which made him feel like a pervert lying next to this little kid. He tried to think of other things. Any other things. Like his dream of someday traveling to Australia, or South America, or wherever. He pictured himself on a long white sandy beach, baking in the sun. Parrots squawked from the palms above his head. The big blue sky was full of puffy clouds.

He'd softened up, and was beginning to doze off, when Angie started kissing his shoulder. *Oh, please, stop.*

There he was, with nowhere to go, and it would be weird to push the kid away, maybe start her crying. He slowly lifted the arm she was kissing, held it in the air and stretched it out above her head. But there was no place to put it. Worse, his missing arm allowed her to cuddle closer. She burrowed her head into the side of his chest.

"Nighty night," she whispered.

That was when it happened. That was it. When he heard the little girl say that, say it with such innocence, such sweetness, his fear of her suddenly vanished. At once certain of the child's goodness, he lowered his arm and gave her shoulder a gentle squeeze. Though it was the slightest of squeezes...*Oh My God*...it felt, well, necessary. *Natural*.

Yes, that was it. *Natural*.

His childhood had been so miserable that he'd never once imagined having a kid. But now he felt slapped into consciousness, like a newborn parent.

"Nighty night," Angie said again.

Kane gave her shoulder another squeeze. He kissed her on the forehead, exactly like a father would, like nothing could be more natural. "Nighty night," he said.

And they fell asleep.

He knew they fell asleep because he woke with Jerry shaking his leg, saying they were in Indiana, saying he needed a cup of coffee and did Kane want anything?

Kane asked if it was his time to drive.

"Nah," Jerry said, "I'm okay"—which was definitely okay with Kane.

Kane was happy just the way things were.

The next thing he knew, Jerry was shaking him again, saying they were in Iowa. Everyone else was up and laughing. At him. At his snoring. Angie made loud honking sounds to show how bad it was. He growled and turned over, too exhausted for a sense of humor. Kane was glad to hear them get out of the truck. He enjoyed the quiet for less than a minute, needing to pee and aware that he was hungry. He shook himself free of the covers, put on his boots, and trailed them into the restaurant. Everyone must have thought they were a bunch of first-time campers. It was after noon and they looked like crap.

The place was full, the service slow. Jerry didn't seem to care. He paid for breakfast, said good-bye to the grouchy waitress, and, showing off, left her a big tip.

Kane took over driving. They got less than twenty miles before Angie needed a toilet. For them, hauling around a forty-foot trailer, a toilet was not an easy thing to find. And a bit farther down the road it was Gretchen. Then June. Then Angie again. Kane was pulling into every truck stop, every rest area, and every time, like it was his job, Jerry made a big deal out of getting promises, before they left, that everyone was finished peeing.

"Promise?" he would say, a big scowl on his face.

Even Angie knew it was a joke.

It was clear to Kane that his friend had lost all interest in hurrying this trip along. Los Angeles could wait. His fiancée could wait. The whole damn world could wait. At one rest area, with the stuff Jerry bought at the last truck stop, the boss decided they should have a picnic. He laid down the blanket from the bed and opened a half-gallon of red wine.

Kane made a toast to Niagara Falls.

"To water falling," he said.

After eating, everyone stretched out like there was no tomorrow. *Yeah, okay, why the heck not?*

Kane woke up blinking, confused by the starry sky. He could hardly believe that the day was gone, that it was ten o'clock, that they were sprawled out on a blanket somewhere in Iowa.

"You ready?" Jerry said.

But he wasn't. Kane felt groggy, had a stiff neck, and none of that mattered because it was still his turn to drive. "I can go another few hours."

Jerry pinched Kane's cheek, took one last chug of wine, handed him the half-full bottle and followed Gretchen up onto the bed. She pulled the curtains closed.

June raised her eyebrows. "Okee-dokee."

She hoisted herself to the passenger seat.

Kane lifted Angie up into her mother's lap, then got back to driving.

After a couple of hours the little girl scooted over, beyond the gearshift, onto the edge of his seat.

14

"No, honey," said June, "it's not safe."

"It's fine," Kane said. "The good thing with these trucks is the bigness of everything, including the seats." He shifted to the side, to show all the room he had. "See Mommy?"

Angie mimicked him, "See Mommy, see?"

"You sure?" June asked.

"No problem," he said, meaning he hadn't felt this happy in a long long time.

Somewhere in Nebraska, as Jerry and Gretchen began making noises in the back, June turned up The Kinks and asked Kane, please, for a sip of wine. She joked that Angie shared things a whole lot better than he did.

Kane started singing *Lola*. June chimed in.

Angie turned her head back and forth between them, watching and giggling.

After *Lola* came *Top of the Pops*. Then *Moneygoround*.

Kane advanced the tape to his favorite song.

"Apeman," he said. "My anthem."

And he sang it with gusto until Jerry stuck his head through the split in the curtains. "Hey, man, you mind turning off the music so we can sleep?"

June made a face.

"Okee-dokee," said Kane, smiling at June, pushing the appropriate button. He checked the clock. Two in the morning. The Interstate looked like an empty runway.

A few minutes later Angie said, "Mommy, I'm tired."

June opened up the curtain and laid her on the bed. Then re-closed the curtain.

Without skipping a beat, she scooted to the inner edge of Kane's seat, where Angie had been. He gave as much room as he could, making sure he could reach the gearshift. She put her arm around his neck and held onto his shoulder.

He never would've thought any of this possible.

"Praise the Lord for big seats," she said.

"Hallelujah," he said. Feeling giddy, he could not help singing it: "Hallelujah, Hallelujah, Hal-aye-aye-looo-yah!"

"No, I'm serious. I praise The Lord for everything good."

15

Okay, serious. So Kane got serious too. "I was wondering about that."

"What?"

"You and Gretchen. You don't *seem* religious."

"Oh? Why not?"

"I guess it's the McDonald's thing. Hard for me to imagine either of you preaching."

"No, she said that wrong. It's not like you're thinking. We tell people what led us to God. I guess to Gretchen that sometimes sounds like preaching."

Kane nodded, and considered keeping quiet, then said, "What is it you say?"

"What?"

"I mean, when Gretchen thinks you're preaching."

"You making fun of me?"

"No, honest, I'm just curious. I have no idea what it means to...what did she call it?"

"*Giving Testimony*. It's like a confession, okay? I say what's in my heart. I confess how lost I was and how I found God. I talk about how I've learned from my suffering. I've learned to make sacrifices, to do what needs to be done. I say what I believe, that there are signs. Clear signs."

Yeah, Kane thought, *like water falling into nowhere*. But he was mindful not to say it. He used to laugh at her kind of God-fearing, religion-following, fantasy-making bullshit. Blind faith seemed stubborn to him, and intentionally blind. Since falling for June and Angie, though, being *Lord Almighty Certain* didn't seem the least bit funny.

"I tell people how I've suffered," she said. "I admit that I'm paying for my mistakes. I've learned from God I can't live reckless, not ever again. Not with a child to raise."

It occurred to Kane that what they were doing right this minute could be seen as reckless. But he decided to keep his mouth shut...decided that God, *if there is a God,* must know better than him.

16

She said, "I tell them the Lord's truth is right in front of us. Right here, for each of us to find. God will guide us if we pay attention. We have to figure that out for ourselves."

Kane smiled. He might not believe in God, but trying to figure things out was something he did every day.

"Yeah," he said, "which can be hard."

"I see you do your best. I've been watching the way you are with people. You're wonderful with Angie."

"Well, yeah, but Angie's easy, she's an angel."

"She's usually shy. Especially with men. She trusts you, Kane, and I see why."

They talked for hours. Time and space passed by, unnoticed, through the rest of Nebraska and into Colorado. THE ROCKY MOUNTAIN STATE. Kane saw that sign clearly. The sun had not been up long but it was already getting warm.

Or maybe that was June, her body pressed next to his.

Kane had never felt this wide-awake. It felt like he could drive forever. He would have kept on drinking, too, if the bottle weren't empty.

They were near a town called Ovid. It was desolate country—a landscape without people—only barbwire fences, dried-out grass, lots of crows and cows. But the Rockies were off in the distance, towering over the plains: snow-capped peaks shining like the lights of a promised land.

As the motor rumbled its deep guttural chant, Kane was having incredibly wondrous thoughts. Thoughts of him and June and Angie. He told his warning mind to try and be supportive. *I mean look! Look at what's happening here!* June also wanted to live in the country, in a wooden house, with a big garden. They both wanted dogs and cats, chickens and goats. *Talk about signs!* Here she was, right here, her arm around his neck and the two of them looking straight ahead, like they were thinking this stuff together.

As if in total agreement, she gave his shoulder a squeeze.

He put his hand on her knee.

Oh My God, is this for real?

Kane heard a horn, and caught sight of movement to his right. He saw the nose of an old blue pickup on the frontage road.

June said, "What's he doing?"

"No idea."

The pickup pulled ahead, honking and honking. Kane saw the driver staring his way. Maybe the guy wanted to race? Maybe he was drunk? Kane took another glance, then another. The guy was steering with his right hand, trying to watch where he was going, while waving his left arm out the window and behind him.

June said, "What's going on back there?"

"Where?"

"Behind us. That's where he's pointing."

Kane checked his right mirror. Couldn't see a thing. No...wait. Wait. Straining his eyes, he noticed something by the back wheels, what looked like...looked like...*sparks.*

"Oh shit!"

He started braking.

"What?" said June.

"I don't know, I don't know."

Usually he'd downshift, one by one, through all thirteen gears. No time for that. The brakes squealed while he steered the truck as far as safely possible off the road.

Jerry's head shot between the curtains. "What the fuck's going on!"

"I don't know," Kane said, the truck screeching to a halt. "I saw sparks by the—"

Jerry, naked, pushed past June, over the empty seat and out the door. "Everybody out!"

June grabbed a crying Angie and handed her to Kane. She got down behind them on the driver's side.

Gretchen went the other way, then came running around the front of the truck, pulling up her skirt, her shirt wide open.

18

Jerry finished disengaging the truck from the trailer. "Get them on the other side of the road!" he hollered, climbing back into the cab. He pulled the truck forward as they ran to the median strip.

Flames shot out from underneath the trailer. In less than a minute the whole back end was on fire.

Kane sat on the rocky ground and watched.

Unbelievable.

His mind was stuck right there, right on *Unbelievable.*

June sat next to him, Angie crying in her arms. She was trying to comfort the child, saying, "Shhh, shhh, it's gonna be okay, honey, I promise. Shhh."

Jerry ran toward them across the road. He'd managed to get his pants on. His naked torso was white as a shell. He looked into Kane's eyes and said, "The CB isn't working, I don't know why, I have to find a phone."

"Okay."

"I have to find a phone," he said again. "You stay here in case someone comes."

"I don't know what happened, man, I—"

"No!" Jerry said, his voice sharp and insistent, "forget it! You stay here, all right?"

"All right."

He handed Kane the empty wine bottle. "Get rid of this."

He meant *now.* Kane walked to the far side of the median strip, across the eastbound lanes and up against a barbwire fence. He squeezed the neck of the bottle, wishing he could strangle it. Tears made a blur of the sky. "No God, please," he said, and threw the bottle as far as he could.

On his way back he saw them talking. June was listening to Gretchen, then she said something and shook her head. When he got close they went quiet.

Decisions had been made.

"They can't be here," Jerry said to Kane. "I'm taking them with me, to a truck stop or, I don't know, whatever I can find."

"Yeah. Okay."

19

June was staring at the ground. She didn't say a word but Kane felt her sadness.

Then she hugged him. A strong, lasting grip. She gave him a soft kiss on the cheek before letting go, taking hold of Angie's hand and walking off. He could tell what was happening without having to look. He didn't want to see anyone's face.

Once they were gone, Kane slumped down on the rocky median. No, this was not his world anymore, this could not be happening to him. He watched as the trailer full of other people's lives went up in flames. He tried his best to figure it out. It was like a puzzle with a missing piece, a piece that, could he find it, might fix everything. Might give him some bit of hope.

A few people stopped and asked if they could help.

No, he told them. That's all he said.

That's all it took to make them go away.

Kane was lying on his back, looking at the sky, when Jerry, kneeling next to him, said they had to leave.

"I screwed up," Jerry said. "I should've called the office first, I...*Jesus, never mind.*"

"The girls," said Kane. "What did you—?"

"They're okay. I gave them money, they're on a bus. Listen," he said, reaching over and squeezing Kane's shoulder, "the dispatcher told me we can't be here. Anyway, not you." Then he said something about alcohol, and liability, company fire insurance and some official report he had to make. He was talking fast.

Kane stared at his friend. He understood the words, but not what they meant.

"Let's go," Jerry said, and helped him to his feet.

Kane's head was pounding. His eyes burned. He followed Jerry through the billowing smoke. They climbed into the cab and roared away as a big red fire truck came over the hill in front of them. Soon it flew past, sirens blaring. To Kane it felt like screaming in his mind.

He closed his eyes. He would not ask where June and Angie had gone. Though somehow knowing he'd never see them again, he could not believe it. How could something so real, so undeniable, disappear so fast?

How was that possible?

Desperate, he tried to hold on, tried to keep her near. *I know, you need a sign. You need to see I'm worth it. You need to understand...that fire was not me.*

Jerry said, "You okay?"

But it was June who Kane heard. He heard her wanting to help, and was grateful she stayed quiet while he fought back tears. He had to convince her how strong and dependable he could be.

"Please," he whispered, "please let me show you."

"What?" said Jerry.

Kane opened his eyes. He looked out at rolling hills, distant snow-peaked mountains and a clear open sky. The beauty felt overwhelming. So did the thought of asking his friend's forgiveness. Or June's understanding.

Things he did not deserve.

"Never mind," he said.

ALMA

Mexico Mexico Mexico. Sara was tired of hearing about it. It was the same thing every time Roger came to visit— Mexico this, Mexico that—and Jack, her husband, getting restless.

Then one night, after his friend left, Jack found her in the bedroom and said, "You know, honey, maybe we should go."

Sara was listening to the radio and busy folding clothes, so could act like she hadn't heard. She did not want to have this conversation. After finishing the laundry she would prepare new activities for her fourth-grade class. In addition to teaching every day, or preparing to teach, or wishing she never had to teach again, Sara cleaned the house, and cooked, and made sure that she and Sam, their fourteen-year-old son, had some quality time together. And Jack was busy too, as a freelance carpenter. Jack was no slouch. After he got home each night, and on weekends, there were things to fix, or firewood to split, or the lawn to mow, or who knows what? They were working people. Family people. All of which meant that they had little time to fantasize about foreign places. Their dream of *someday traveling* stayed right where it belonged, at a comfortable distance.

But Roger kept pushing it closer. He was a friend from Jack's childhood, a guy Jack hadn't seen for thirty years. They'd run into him at a St. Paul bar in 2000, where he'd bought them drinks, round after round, and filled their ears with useless chatter. The guy was clever, oh yeah, and wanted them to know it. At one point he'd lamented the "bogus hype" of Y2K. "Broke my heart," he said. "I was hoping for modernity's last gasp."

For some reason beyond Sara's understanding, Jack got a kick out of this guy, and kept encouraging his weirdness by laughing at his jokes. Then, as they were leaving, he invited Roger to their house for dinner. The very next night. *Huh?*

"That okay, hon?" Jack asked.

Well, what was she supposed to say?

"Yes," she said, smiling at Roger, "if you can make it."

"Consider it made," he said.

Of course Sara was the one who had to shop for food and prepare the meal. And Roger must have liked it because now, every summer, he was certain to show up for more. He was the main reason she didn't want this conversation.

Jack turned off the radio.

"Well," he said, "what do you think?"

"Of what?"

"Mexico! Acapulco! Roger keeps inviting us. We could get out of town, honey, have a real vacation, stay at his place by the beach for free."

Sara pictured the Mexican coastline, tried to see it without Roger. She imagined walking with Jack along the shore. Just the two of them. "That would be nice."

"Yeah, right? Wouldn't that be great!"

Luckily, Jack's cell rang, a call he had to take—a problem with some job—and she knew the whole Acapulco thing would get dropped. Not because of the call, or any other work responsibility. More important than any of that, his mind would remind him, was his lack of respect for Roger. He didn't like the guy either. She knew that because of things he'd told her about when they were kids.

"Roger thought his copper hair was cool," Jack had said. "He got everyone to call him *Red*. The guy loved any kind of attention. We were friends, yeah, but he was usually such a dickhead."

Knowing how Jack felt, she figured that by bedtime he would let Roger, and Mexico, fade from consideration. Which he did. By the next day they were back to their normal lives, safe and snug and happy.

But time passed quickly, and there, again, was Roger. Though Jack might not respect this *dickhead,* he welcomed every visit. And the more they drank, and discussed his place in Acapulco, the less his faulty character seemed to matter. Sara could see how much Jack wanted a vacation from Minnesota. Not a week off to do needed chores around the house, but something different, something exciting. He thanked Roger year after year for the friendly invitation. Then, every time, he let it go. Sara could see he was torn. Though longing for an adventure, he must hate the idea that Roger, of all people, would be the one to make it happen.

In 2007, after Sam went off to college, Jack bought a map of Mexico. He bought a used guidebook too, and most nights stayed up reading it. Then he switched to the Internet. In general, like Roger, he was no fan of computers, avoiding them whenever possible, but suddenly he could not resist, sometimes staying up long after Sara went to bed.

She began to worry. His dreams, until now, had been tempered by common sense. He used to talk about spending a month on the Boundary Waters, just him and a canoe. But his work and need for family would not allow it. He loved the Vikings, would go to every game if he could, but season tickets, especially with the cost of Sam's tuition and housing, were more than they could afford.

Unfortunately, this Mexico thing was different. Jack was a nonfiction kind of guy, a factual guy, and with Sam now gone the facts had changed.

In spite of his problems with Roger, a free place by the beach was getting harder to pass up.

Sara dreaded what that meant for her. In addition to Roger's looks—his bushy copper hair and artsy horn-rimmed glasses—she disliked his attitude, his manner, his way of making everything difficult. Even his simple "How are you?" was a trap. No matter what she said, it would be challenged. If she said "Fine," he'd grin and say something like, *"Fine, is that all? Oh, my dear, I'm sorry."*

Once they were sitting on the back deck, drinking wine, while Jack was busy at the grill. It was a beautiful summer night. A full moon. Feeling relaxed, and that for Jack's sake she should give this guy a chance, she let down her guard and confessed to Roger how sorely she missed Sam.

"Oh yes," he said, "I expect you do. But consider how happy he is to be out of his parent's reach."

What a dickhead, she thought. It felt like he was poking at the soft spot in her heart—the tender, private, sacred place she tried to keep safe from others.

Contrary, that's what Roger was. *Contrary on purpose.*

Pure and simple, she did not trust him.

And she didn't trust his girlfriend either, a Mexican woman named Maura. She'd only met the woman once. That was plenty. Maura was a queen bee type: attractive, yeah, in a heavyset, pompous sort of way. She had deep, hazel, penetrating eyes. Her strong Spanish accent and slow calm delivery made every word sound regal. The queen had looked around their house and said how "clean and orderly" it was, meaning *suburban and boring.*

Sara had been glad when Maura and Roger left. She'd wished that Mexico were leaving too, and hoped to never hear of it again.

Roger didn't visit in the summer of 2008, the first time in years, which was not lost on Jack. The map of Mexico got promoted from his desk drawer to the garage wall. He was getting downright antsy. In early October, on her fifty-first birthday, they went downtown for sushi, were on their second round of sake, when he said he thought they should go to Acapulco.

Sara nibbled at some ginger. "The place I'd love to see is Utah."

"For godsakes, Sara, we're in our fifties! Aren't we ever going to get out of this country?"

She managed to change the subject and again the moment passed. It wasn't until the following year, in the summer of 2009, that Sara had no choice but to think of Mexico. It was because of Jack's health, because he hadn't been sleeping well, or been too interested in sex, and none of that was normal. One night she found him snoring at his desk. His head was on top of the blank Remodel Bid that had to be finished, he'd told her, before he went to bed.

The next day Sara insisted he get blood tests.

A week later she went with him to his physical.

Their doctor, Harry Phillips, was a fat jovial type, prone to silly jokes. He stuck his finger up Jack's butt and said, "Ooh, I think I struck it rich." Jack laughed and seemed to relax, as the doctor must have intended. Harry scowled at the glove and threw it away. "Prostate is a teensy bit enlarged," he said. "That explains the extra peeing." He lowered his head to eye Jack from above his bi-focal glasses. "Other than that, my friend, you are quite a remarkable specimen. Fifty-five, I suppose, is the new thirty."

"Then why the trouble with sleeping?" Sara said, having little faith in him or any other doctor.

"Who knows? My guess is he's been working too hard, perhaps worrying too much."

She was not convinced. "And his blood tests?"

"All exceptional," said Harry, "except for a slightly elevated PSA."

"Which means?"

"Oh, probably nothing. It's one of many diagnostics for prostate cancer, but please, Sara, *please don't worry*. The number is meaningless unless it continues to rise. We'll keep an eye on that. In the meantime, Jack, I suggest you learn the game of golf, and how to lose."

"Thanks doc, I'll try."

"Good," said Harry. "Just don't try too hard."

They left the office and went out to breakfast.

Jack laughed when Sara insisted on getting another opinion. "Opinion?" he said. "Of what?"

"I don't know," she said, refusing to say the *C* word, "that's what we're trying to find out."

He held her hand and dismissed her concerns.

"Fine," she said. "Whatever you say."

But she couldn't let it go. Something had to change.

The following week, when Roger showed up, as expected, Sara brought out a pricey bottle of wine, served a nice dinner, and announced that she'd booked airline tickets for Mexico City: a two-week trip during her Christmas vacation.

Jack, as expected, was suspicious. "You should have checked with me."

"Never mind him," said Roger, clinking her glass, "Fantastic idea! Better yet, fly directly to Acapulco!"

Sara had thought of that, but wanted to spend some of the time away from him and Maura. "I also want to see the city. The murals and museums, the parks and—"

"Okay," he said, *"if you must.* Maura has a house there, too. We can pick you up."

Damn, thought Sara. "Great!" she said.

Once Roger left, Jack got a beer and sat next to her on the couch. "Well?"

"It's not what you're thinking."

"Oh?" he said. "Then what is it?"

"Look, Jack, I changed my mind, okay?"

"Why?"

"Because your prostate deal made me realize I've been selfish. If you're willing to put up with that dickhead, honey, so am I."

In Mexico, Roger was known as *Rojo*. *Red*. He and Maura were waiting at the Mexico City airport. He drove them, in his Volkswagen van, up into the hills, past two gates with armed guards. "Maura and I would be dead," Roger whispered, "if they could read our minds."

Sara did not bother to question that. Roger trying to be funny, that's all it was. And it was no surprise to hear that Maura had come from a rich Mexico City family. She'd been raised with a personal maid and gone to the best private schools. But entitlement had not suited her. Or so she said. She was estranged from her father and brothers, was a professor of psychology at *UNAM* (The Autonomous University of Mexico), where she taught seminars on "feminism" and "self-empowerment."

They pulled into a driveway and up to a two-story house, twice the size of Jack and Sara's. There were well-tended flowerbeds being doused by sprinklers.

"My grandfather left me an inheritance," Maura said. "Lucky, because we needed a place to live."

"Wow," said Sara. "You must have a gardener."

"And a maid," said Roger, as if embarrassed. "And a cook."

"Well, yes," Maura said. "Because, unlike some of us, *Rojito,* I am busy working."

Roger glanced into the rearview mirror and grinned at Jack, apparently pleased by the insult. Sara expected a witty comeback. It never came.

In the morning Roger drove them around the city. In the afternoon they went to the famous Zócalo, then to Chapultepec Park. The next day they visited Frida Kahlo's home, and again, coming home, got stuck in bumper-to-bumper traffic. "Is it always this bad?" said Sara.

"Ah," said Roger, "truth at last. Ready for the beach?"

They were off at dawn, a five-hour drive on the toll road from Mexico City. Their place, Maura said, was on the northern edge of Acapulco, on a long slender peninsula between the Pacific Ocean and a large estuary. She'd bought the land in 1998, after the devastation of Hurricane Pauline made the coastline affordable.

Once reaching that peninsula, Sara saw, to her left, flashes of ocean between huge unfinished buildings. "New hotels going up, I see."

"Actually no," Roger said, "you don't."

"No?"

"*Newly abandoned* hotels. The local economy, I'm afraid, is in the toilet."

Before she could ask why, he stopped at a grocery store. They all went inside. Jack and Roger headed for the beer while Maura talked to the clerk.

"*Ay, Dios!*" she kept saying, shaking her head and sighing as he spoke. "*Ay, Dios!*"

Once back in the car, Maura shared what the clerk had told her: that headless bodies were being dumped every day into Acapulco's town square. In other places just the heads. It seemed that Roger had failed to inform Jack and Sara of the drug cartels that were fighting for control of the Mexican coastline, that they murdered anyone who got in the way. Two days ago, some new gang shot up a restaurant in Acapulco. Seven people were killed.

"No wonder there are no tourists," Maura said. She'd bought the local newspaper and began translating the lead article, entitled: *Who would not prefer Bali?* "Acapulco's chief of police, Benito Alvarez, was found in a burlap sack outside his home, chopped into little pieces, with a note stapled to his skull: a message from the Beltrán Leyva cartel that the new chief had better be more helpful."

"Bad guys killing bad guys," Roger said as he drove. "Good thing we're so good."

Typical Roger humor. Dark and dumb. Typical squinty grin, as if proud of his stupidity.

He took the next left, and there, beyond the end of a short street, was a view of the Pacific Ocean.

Sara had seen it twice in her fifty-one years. Her first time was as a small girl, three or four years old, on a trip to Oregon with her parents. She remembered sitting on her mother's lap, staring at the endless water. An impossible thing to understand when all she'd known were the small lakes of Nebraska. Her mother had tried to explain, saying how deep it was, and big, and that "people live on the other side who look different from us, and speak a different language." That had frightened Sara. She would not go play in the waves. Her mother held her close and gently stroked her hair. "It's okay," she kept saying. "I'm sorry I frightened you. It's okay, honey, it's okay."

It wasn't for another thirty-one years, after marrying Jack, moving to Minnesota and having a child of her own, that she got another chance. They'd gone on a two-week trip to the West Coast. Sam was four years old. By then Sara was familiar with the Great Lakes and the Boundary Waters, and should not have been awestruck by the ocean. But she was. It was the same—her feelings of wonder and disorientation. The little girl inside felt scared. She had to be comforted by Sara, the adult, who knew better, who felt excitement beneath the fear as she ran with her little boy out into the foamy surf.

In spite of her dislike for Roger and Maura, she'd been excited to see it again, to play in the waves, to watch the sun set over the water. How horrible that news of the cartel murders made the sea look cold and alien.

"Home sweet home," Rojo said as he pulled into a driveway on the left.

Maura unlocked a gate and swung it open.

Roger drove in. He parked and they got out of the van. "Time for a tour," he said to Sara. "I know Jack's interested in the building stuff. You probably aren't."

More of his knee-jerk judgment.

"Yes," she said, "actually, I am."

"Actually?" He smiled as if knowing she didn't mean it.

30

She glanced around, expecting a fancy house like the one in Mexico City. Instead, beyond a palm tree, she saw a simple building, its wooden siding faded by the sun. It looked like an enormous shed, maybe forty feet long by thirty feet wide.

"That," said Roger, "is the main house, where we stay. First, though, I want to show you our humble project." He led them to the left, toward what looked like a bunch of huts on stilts. "As you can see, there's a bit of work to do. We're planning this as a hostel for backpackers. In other words, cheap and simple." They walked around the collection of small ramshackle structures. Roger led them into two, which were basically the same. He laughed off the shoddy workmanship as "a sign of my rebellious nature."

As he was showing Jack a pile of recycled lumber, Maura whispered to Sara that the land, and high taxes, took most of her dwindling inheritance. Because professional labor was too expensive, Rojo had decided to do the work himself.

To look less like a *kept man,* assumed Sara. Instead, to her, he looked like a fool. What she saw was a mishmash of flimsy shacks. There were lengths of twisted boards—all types and dimensions—running between them, connecting them, holding them together like the web some demented spider. Halfway through the tour Maura got a call on her cell. She listened, walking away, then signaled Roger to come with her. Once they were out of sight, Jack winced.

Sara said, "Pretty bad, right?"

"Worse. Everything just slapped together. He told me that some carpenter friend helped him. If so, the guy was drunk."

Roger returned, and claimed to know what they were thinking. "Yes, rather primitive," he joked, "but hey, you know, it works." The lack of windows or doors he called "natural ventilation." Gaps, he said, were "necessary to appease the god of wind."

Because of the sloppy construction he may have been right, at least for the time being. And the time being was all that concerned *Rojo*. If a set of stairs was too steep, no problem. Or if a wall leaned, or a roof sagged. All that mattered was if what he'd done worked...well...well enough. In other words, did not collapse.

The look of things was irrelevant. That was his guiding aesthetic principle. That's what he kept telling Jack. Roger showed no signs of caring what Sara thought, but wanted Jack to appreciate his intentions, to understand how hard he toiled at not being "some anal materialist." Big deal if a floor creaked or a sink dripped. There were more important things for him to ponder.

Rojo was, after all (as he hinted more than once), a poet, a philosopher—a man of active intellect and spirit!

The whole deal was ridiculous, but Sara fought back saying it. That first evening, as they went to bed, Jack said to her, "Hey, it's none of our business."

Sara agreed. Not her problem. So she kept all negative thoughts locked inside her head, and soon began to enjoy herself. She and Jack took long walks on the beach, and played in the surf, and marveled at the sunsets. Though offered a room in the main house (which did have doors and windows) they'd decided to sleep in one of the raised huts, and each night were swayed by the evening winds.

It was romantic. No longer tired, Jack was always ready to make love. Sara had never seen him more relaxed. For that, within her own secret tender place, she privately thanked Roger.

Jack thanked him too, by helping rebuild one of the shakier huts. Because of its dangerous tilt, Roger needed Jack's expertise, and muscle, to stop it from falling over. They worked every morning. Most evenings, as the sun began to set, the two of them tried fishing from the shore. Though they never caught a thing, the beer must have eased their disappointment.

On day six, as Sara was passing by a room in the main house, she heard someone crying. It sounded like a girl. She stopped, then heard Roger's voice, low and soft and fatherly, as if he were speaking to a child.

Sara listened, but the words were all in Spanish.

The door opened.

A gorgeous young woman was sitting on a bed, sobbing, wiping at her eyes. She brushed aside her long black lustrous hair and looked straight at Sara, whose vision was then blocked by Roger coming out.

He closed the door and smiled at her.

"Oh," he said. "Hello."

"Sorry, Roger, I—"

"That's all right," he said, gently taking her elbow and leading her away from the room, out into the sunlight. "Alma is working out some difficult stuff."

"She looked miserable."

"Well," said Roger, smiling again, "that, I'm afraid, is part of the process."

She stared at him, wondering what he meant.

He said, "Now you must excuse me, I have a session with someone else."

Session? Process? What's going on?

Upset, Sara went looking for Jack on the beach. He was just getting out of the water.

She handed him his towel. "Can we talk?"

"Yeah."

They sat on the warm sand. She told him what had happened and what Roger said.

"Wow," said Jack, laughing.

"What's funny?"

"Roger. Always finding some way to be special. He mentioned that he's been working with Maura on 'experimental modes of therapy,' whatever that means."

"Is he trained as a psychotherapist?"

"In his mind, yes."

"Wait, I…I don't get it…I mean how can he—"

"Who knows?" said Jack. "It's because of Maura. Students of hers have somehow become their 'clients.' I don't get it either."

Sara hugged him and held on tight.

Jack said, "You okay?"

"I don't know. It gave me the chills the way that girl was sobbing."

"Just more *none of our business,* I guess."

"I guess," she said. But she could not stop thinking how trapped the girl looked in that dark little room. It didn't matter to Sara how Roger chose to live, but should he be trusted with other people's lives? *Damn...hell no!* She found Maura in her office, and politely, calmly, said so.

"Roger has his own methods," Maura said. "They are not mine, but he is good at bringing up emotion, at pushing buttons."

True. That much Sara could corroborate. "He has no formal training, right?"

"Has 'formal training' made the world a better place?" Maura said. "Not Mexico, I assure you."

"How do you know he's not doing that girl harm?"

"Harm?"

"She looked frightened," said Sara. "Like she was there against her will."

"You know nothing about Alma."

"Okay, tell me."

"No," Maura said. "Roger and I have no secrets about *our* lives, but I will not share hers."

"That's fair. That's right. But I still think what you're doing is wrong."

Maura smiled, leaned over and kissed Sara on the cheek. "Thank you, dear, for being honest." It seemed a calculated display of therapeutic modeling. "Honesty, for me and Roger, is of paramount importance. It is the core of our therapy and we demand it of our clients. It means having no defenses, no secrets, no unexamined faults."

Maura spoke with an air of authority, as if convinced she were a brilliant, revolutionary thinker. Her expertise, Sara had learned, was in the field of gender psychology. Her focus: "Patriarchal Suppression of The Feminine." She'd written two books on the subject. She was working on a third. Sara was impressed, but the fact of Maura's accomplishments made things harder to understand. How could such an intelligent woman be so deluded?

Though Sara wanted to say that, and more, perhaps for now she'd said enough.

Late that afternoon, as the two couples lounged in the garden shadows with glasses of wine, Maura made fun of Roger's "pretentious horn-rimmed spectacles"—bent on proving, perhaps, how *honest* she could be.

"Rojo," she said, "is my perfect mate."

"Oh," he said, hand on his cheek, pretending to blush, "how sweet."

"This man is my research," said Maura. "He embodies every corrupt aspect of the patriarchy."

Roger smiled as if it were a wonderful compliment.

"And," he said, "I know it."

"True," she conceded. "Self-effacement is one of your better qualities, though it often smacks of self-indulgence."

When he mugged a grimace she snuggled up and kissed him on the lips.

This kind of thing began happening every day.

Sara was struck by Roger's continued calm. He would listen to Maura malign him, grin his charming grin, and agree. He swallowed his pride, it appeared, because he had no choice, because he seemed to believe that an admission of moral weakness somehow proved his integrity.

It also, of course, gave him license to malign her. His attacks were usually goofy and prankish. Maura had no problem fending them off, which must have been his intention. He was playing with her, that's all—a skirmish he might win or lose, it did not matter, did not affect him in the least—and whoever failed to understand that was not worthy of his time.

Yes, Sara and Jack could have left, could have gotten on a bus to Mexico City, could have changed their plane ticket and flown back to snowy Minnesota. But that would have felt like surrender. With one week remaining, they agreed to spend as much time as possible away from their annoying hosts. They took longer walks along the shore. They collected lots of shells. They found a little bar down the beach and every afternoon drank a piña colada.

Hell, they were on vacation, right!

At the shared dinners each night they did their best to pretend that all was fine. Sara tried not to be judgmental, and as she changed her way of thinking, things got easier. She started to see the humor in this weird situation. Each day she grew more immune to Roger and Maura's caustic back-and-forth. It was clear that neither of them held a grudge. Often, along with the zinging barbs, came laughter, affection, and good-hearted joking. At times, Sara even admired them. It was strange how they elicited in her opposite sets of feelings: attraction and revulsion; pity and jealousy; exhaustion and exhilaration. Nothing was ever normal around these two. All beliefs—Sara's, theirs, or anyone else's—were challenged by Roger and Maura in a playful and forgiving way. Since they believed that humans were, by nature, fundamentally fucked up, no one was free of blame. Or, because of that fact, ever truly at fault.

"I am sorry," Roger said one day after a slashing Maura rebuke. His tone was diplomatic. "I see that my vengeful Hamlet has triggered your drowning Ophelia."

For them, Sara realized, life was a mysterious game, and the goal was to win it. That meant to neither be a player nor get played. There were no rules other than to stay open and vulnerable and, yes, *honest.*

Their "clients" were young female students from Mexico City. All of them seemed smitten with Maura. She'd begun conducting group sessions in the garden. The girls, three or four at a time, would sit at her feet, moon-eyed, and take in her wisdom like hungry chicks might gobble a big fat worm. Roger once caught Sara snooping. "Let me translate," he said. Obviously he'd been snooping too. "The focus, as usual, is the subjugation of Mexican women. Maura told that girl with the glasses to leave her jealous fiancé. Told that freckled one, with reddish hair, to loosen up, stop thinking like her mother, and find a good fuck."

Occasionally one of the female students spent the night. There were various spaces available in the main house for whoever showed up in need of counsel.

Alma, the young woman Sara had seen crying, was the only client with a designated room. Her name meant *Soul*, though she did not strike Sara as the least bit soulful. Brown and svelte, always wearing sexy clothes, the black-haired beauty flitted around the compound like an exotic butterfly. Either that or flew away for days on end. Men were often waiting beyond the gate. It seemed they were not welcome inside. Sometimes the girl went off by herself, in a rush, perhaps to avoid them. Sara had noticed.

Alma was impossible not to notice.

Day ten came. Hot. Windless and humid. As Jack and Sara were sitting, sweating in the garden, Roger and Maura joined them with a pitcher of iced tea. Then Alma came out of the house in ass-hugging Levi cut-offs and a skimpy top. Her body looked glazed. She waved and hurried toward the gate.

Roger let out a long dramatic sigh.

"How fitting," Maura said, "that a girl with that name should become our greatest test. She used to be a stripper in Mexico City. She has a lot of demons."

Roger said, "Alma did not turn out as her devout Catholic parents had hoped. Not a single religious bone in her whole scrumptious body."

Maura smiled and pinched his nose. "Pig."

"Guilty," he said.

Sara felt certain there was more to come…yet another calculated shock. But she no longer cared what these two said or did. If anything, she was curious how far their hosts might go, which she soon learned was pretty far.

"*Scrumptious Alma*," said Maura, "has become quite a problem for poor *Rojito*. She pouted at him. "I am afraid that he is obsessed with the girl."

"It's the hardness of her nipples," Roger said. "The softness of her ass."

"You see?" said Maura. "The boy cannot help himself."

"True," he said. "I'm pitiful. It's like an addiction. She can do things with her mouth that I never thought possible."

Roger cleared his throat, grinned, and stared at Sara.

Jack laughed, like it was all one big dumb joke.

Maura patted Sara's hand and said, "The little boy's naughty pleasure has led, as he and I both knew it would, to a great deal of well-deserved suffering."

"Oh yes," he said. "God knows how well I deserved it."

Oh yes, Roger was a pig. But Sara could understand the arousal of any man who saw that girl. Including Jack. She was glad there were only three days to go. Soon they would be heading back to Mexico City and the whole thing would be over.

Alma came for dinner that night. There was also Maura's eighty-three year old mother, who had been in the house since day one but was never seen except during the evening meal. She spoke fluent English. She'd learned it as a child at a private school in Mexico City, the same school where she later sent Maura. Sara did not know her real name. Everyone called her *Pajarita. Little Bird.*

The old woman, while a tad deaf and demented, was a vibrant soul who wanted to hear everything being said, and did not mind asking—over and over—that something be repeated. She also had her own stories to tell, which tended to get told, *verbatim,* every evening. No problem for Sara.

They were good stories, bright and funny, and it was interesting to watch her squeeze them into any conversation.

Twice that week a student/client of Maura's had joined them for dinner. Both times Pajarita was clearly pleased: a new person to hear her stories! What bothered the old lady was when anyone stayed more than a single evening. Then she wanted to know, in no uncertain terms, why this person was still there? Roger had to keep explaining Sara and Jack. For some reason, perhaps because they were older, and obviously tourists, Pajarita showed her most charming self.

"Yes," she would say after every introduction, "how nice of you to come again."

Alma, however, who'd been around far longer, was a continuous conundrum for the old lady.

Pajarita would look at her and say, "I don't understand, dear, why is it you don't leave?"

The rest of them would laugh. Pajarita laughed too, as if knowing that everyone agreed, that the young woman should go, she really should, yet for some baffling reason never did.

Sara also wished she'd go. Her initial concern for Alma had become an embarrassing kind of jealousy. She felt like an adolescent schoolgirl, lost in self-doubt and insecurity, intimidated by someone better than her. Sara worked against those feelings. She tried to be mature, tried to be friendly.

C'mon, it's not her fault she's so damn gorgeous.

But she changed her mind that night after dinner. They'd cleared the table and were all drinking lemongrass tea. Alma leaned over and whispered something into Maura's ear, then hurried to her room down the way. She smiled back at Roger as she closed her door.

"Well," Maura said, "it looks like we are in for a special treat."

"And what might that be?" said Roger.

Sara could see from his smirk that he already knew. Maura pinched his arm and both of them laughed. They rubbed noses. They kissed.

"What's going on?" said Pajarita.

"Alma is going to dance for us," said Maura.

Pajarita gasped and clapped her hands. The old woman's face was all aglow. "Oh no, you mean it?" she said, staring wide-eyed at her daughter as if assured that her prayers had been answered, that she would soon be on her way to heaven. "A dance?"

"Isn't that wonderful?"

"Oh my, yes," said Pajarita, "it's been such a long time since I've…will there be a proper band?"

"No, dear, it won't be us dancing."

"What?"

"It's the young lady, Mother, she—"

Alma came out of the room and all eyes turned to her. She had on black shiny shoes, knee-high white socks, and what looked like a schoolgirl's uniform. Well, not quite. The top was a fleshy pink, and the pleated white skirt was far shorter than any school would ever allow.

"Que bonita!" said Pajarita. "Oh, how Pascual and I loved to dance."

Alma was carrying a boom box. She set it on a chair and punched one of the buttons. Slinky Arab-sounding music played. She reached under the table and came up with a metal pole, about an inch in diameter and six feet long.

She climbed onto the table, held the pole vertical, and began to shimmy around it. After a quick flirtatious smile she hooked the pole with her right leg. She pulled it close, shut her eyes and moaned. Pajarita moaned too.

The music got slinkier, and Alma's moans louder, as with one fluid twist of her hips the white skirt fell to the table, revealing a black silk thong. She crouched in front of Jack and seductively wiggled her perfect ass.

Roger, from across the table, was smiling at Sara, waiting for her reaction. *More shock therapy.*

Defiant, she looked at Jack and laughed.

The girl kept wiggling her ass as she rotated slowly around the pole.

"Ay, Dios mío," said Pajarita, who did not stop watching.

40

Alma kicked her skirt away. Then she flicked off her pink top. Her breasts were small, firm, and bare except for the tassels hanging from her nipples.

"Oreeblay!" squawked a cringing Pajarita.

"She says that's horrible," Roger said to Jack. "I dare not imagine what's coming next."

Everyone but the old woman laughed. Even Sara.

What else could she do?

Alma moved in long curvy undulations that held them all in sumptuous disbelief. No one said a word. Pajarita stared up at the naked girl as if at an evil spirit.

The dance continued for several minutes. Alma twice swept over and down toward Jack, giving him the eye, that performance-style "fuck me" look. It was a standard stripper thing. Provocative but meaningless. As the music came to a dramatic end, drums beating and cymbals clashing, the girl let the pole fall to the table, ripped the tassles from her nipples, then gave a final dizzying spin before leaping off the table and running to her room.

"Bravo!" shouted Roger, applauding, rising from his seat.

Maura and Jack and Sara applauded too. Sara felt relief that it had ended. She looked at Pajarita, who was paled by the experience, her wrinkled jowls quivering.

"Oreeblay," the old lady kept whispering to herself.

Maura looked at Jack and said, "I think that dance was meant for you."

Jack laughed, obviously confused, certain she was joking.

"Really," he said.

"Yes," she said. "Really."

Sara laughed too. She could see Maura's little trap and was not going to fall for it. "Ooh," she said to Jack, snuggling close, "what a fantastic honor!"

But she tossed and turned all night, her dreams laced with pinkish hues. In the last was a small blond girl wearing a fuchsia-colored dress. Sitting on a hill, she stabbed at the browning grass with a stick. The girl looked like Sara as a child. She was singing a song, a song that Sara recognized but could not remember. Then, as if by magic, the grass turned white and fluffy, like the wool of a lamb. It was a lovely sight, soft and pure, but the girl did not seem happy. She kept singing, louder and louder, and stabbing until the wool turned red and started bleeding.

Sara woke with a start. Though Jack was lying next to her, she felt no comfort. And could not go back to sleep.

As soon as it got light she dressed, went to the beach, and walked farther than she'd ever gone. The tide was out. The waves were small. She found a dead whale, its eyes eaten away. Sara cried and kept walking.

After awhile she stopped, turned around, and walked back, past the dead whale. She would not look.

A long time later she sat on a piece of driftwood. She gazed out at the deep gray sea. She wanted to be home.

That's all she wanted, to be home.

The sun began to rise over the eastern mountains. Exhausted, Sara lay down on the sand and almost nodded off. She felt drugged, but was afraid of falling asleep, of having more dreams. She forced her eyes open, got to her feet and returned, slowly, to the house.

It was nearly ten o'clock.

She made coffee and sat in the garden.

Jack came out with a cup of his own and sat beside her. He held her hand, squeezed it, leaned over and gave her a long loving kiss.

She was beginning to relax when the gate banged open.

A man charged into the courtyard, shouting for Alma. He was tall and well built, with a thick red scar on his neck and a silver ring in his nose. He wore plaid shorts and a white wife-beater tee shirt.

"*Vení*, Alma!" he screamed, *"Ahorita!"*

Roger came out of the house. "I am sorry, Federico, but she's not here. She went shopping with Maura."

Federico went to look. Doors were opened and slammed shut. A few minutes later he came outside, walked up and

42

stuck an angry finger against Roger's forehead. "You tell her I was here, gringo. You tell her that."

"Okay. I'll tell her."

Federico smiled, his eyes locked with Roger's, his finger still stiff against the poor guy's skull. "Boom," he said. Then he laughed, turned away, walked to the gate and slammed it behind him.

"Asshole," Roger said. "Regrettably, Alma has terrible taste in men. Me included. But that guy, shit, that guy is real trouble. She should've known better."

"Who is he?" said Jack.

"Federico *Fuckhead* Fasso. He owns The Paradise. It's down the road a few miles, another failing restaurant and bar. But *Fuckhead* doesn't care because his money comes from selling coke. The guy is a total slime ball, a sociopathic wacko, but charming as can be, I'm sure, to Alma. He probably gives her anything she wants."

Sara said, "How long have they been together?"

"They're not. That's the problem. To her sex means nothing. Believe me, I know. But for Fasso it's a serious commitment. That's what Alma told me. He has lots of money, okay, and power, and he's used to getting whatever he wants."

It was an early dinner that evening. The sun had not begun to set. Alma showed up late and sat down next to Jack. Sara was on his other side, hearing, for the fourth time, Pajarita's story of first meeting her husband at the market in Cuernavaca.

Jack and Alma were talking. They could not have been talking about much since he spoke no Spanish and she knew only the simplest English. Nevertheless, Sara was trying to listen. She heard Jack mention Federico, and explain—by pointing at the table—that he had come here, to the house.

"Then he bought me flowers," said Pajarita. "My Pascual was quite romantic."

"Federico?" Alma said to Jack, as if there must be some mistake. "Come here?"

"He said he'd been watching me for weeks," said Pajarita.

From across the table, Roger said, "Yes, Alma, here."

"What?" said Maura. "When?"

"This morning," Roger said, "when you two were gone."

Maura grabbed him by the arm. "Why, *my dear,* didn't you tell me?"

"I'm telling you now."

Maura turned to face the girl. *"No lo pueda pasar, Alma! Me comprendes?"*

Pajarita looked back and forth between Maura and Alma. "Understand? Understand what? What cannot happen?"

"Nothing, Mother. Never mind."

The old woman indicated Alma with a flick of her wrist. "She's causing problems. I know it. Why is she here?"

Out front someone started shouting. Sara recognized Federico's voice.

"Ay," said Maura, hands covering her eyes.

Alma ran from the table toward the sound.

"Well," said Pajarita, "finally."

"Please, Mother, let Roger take you to your room."

"I can take myself," said Pajarita. The old woman rose, and without another word she limped away.

"I locked the gate," said Roger.

"Good," said Maura. "Let's see if the girl can handle this by herself."

Alma and Federico were now yelling at each other, all of it in Spanish. Roger, seeing his friends' confusion, translated as best he could: "She's trying to make Fasso go. Says she'll come to the Paradise and talk to him tomorrow. He says...says he's finished talking, says he...says he knows there's someone else, that he'll—*oh for chrissakes*—cut the fucker's balls off and stuff them down his throat." Roger glanced at Jack. "Alma's telling him no, it isn't true. She's begging him to listen, saying she loves only him, that she'll pack up her things and come to the Paradise." Roger closed his eyes and shook his head—in his mind, apparently, her agreeing to that was a big mistake. "Yes, Fasso says, you will, and you will stay! She says all right, all right! Now she's begging him to go, says she'll be there first thing in the morning."

It got quiet, then Alma came back inside, her face swollen from crying. Maura rose and led the young woman into her office. Roger followed.

Sara turned to Jack. "Good thing we get out of this nuthouse *mañana*."

"Yeah," he said.

She poured them another cup of tea.

Some minutes later Roger came back to the dining room, a cell phone in his hand.

"Bueno, Señor Pérez, hasta pronto," he said, and hung up. "Holy crap, I never expected that."

"What?" said Jack.

"Alma's father. She let us call him, and he's agreed to let her go back home. They live in a village a couple of hours from here. The plan is to take her halfway, to a town called Loma de San Juan. We're leaving in..." Roger checked his watch..."Fifty minutes."

"Sounds like a good idea," Sara said, relieved to be finally rid of her.

"Let's hope," said Roger. "Oh, uh, what that means is, we all have to leave."

"Yeah," said Jack, "right."

"I'm serious, *amigo*. Soon as Alma doesn't show up tomorrow at the Paradise, that wack-job Fasso will come here, probably with men and guns, looking for trouble. None of us want to be around for that. Vacation's over."

Sara could not believe this was happening, but knew it was time to pack.

It all happened fast. By seven o'clock, as the sun hovered above the horizon, they were on the road. Roger was driving and Maura sat with him up front. On the bench-seat in back were Jack and Sara. Alma was stretched out on a mat at their feet, hidden from outside eyes.

They drove south, to the top of the peninsula, then continued to the junction town of *Pie de la Cuesta*. At its outskirts they turned east onto Highway 95, away from the ocean and up into the mountains.

Sara noticed that Roger kept checking his rearview mirror.

Maura also must have noticed. "What is it?"

"I don't know," he said. "That car's been following us since somewhere before Cuesta."

"Probably going the same direction," Maura joked.

Roger didn't laugh. "I doubt it." A few kilometers later he turned into a gas station. The car pulled off and parked in the shadows at its entrance. It was a dark blue Isuzu Trooper, similar to the white one Jack and Sara used to own. Sara kept an eye on it while Roger filled the tank, washed the windows, paid the attendant and got back in the van. As he pulled to the edge of the road, the Trooper followed. "No doubt now," said Roger.

"What should we do?" said Maura.

"Keep going," he said, and with no other warning he bolted out ahead of a large red flatbed. The truck driver honked. The Trooper had to pull in behind him.

The road got steeper and curvier. Roger adjusted his speed, as necessary, to stay barely ahead of the truck. Maura, facing forward, spoke with Alma, loudly, in Spanish. Both of them sounded scared.

Then the talking stopped and it got far too quiet.

"What's going on?" said Sara.

Roger said, "Alma knows the guy who owns that Trooper. He works for Fasso."

They came over a hill and down into a small, narrow valley. The road straightened out for a few hundred yards. A yellow sports car roared up from behind, passing them all.

Roger pointed at a road sign. Loma de San Juan was six kilometers away.

"There's a bus station in this town," he said to Maura. "Maybe we're going to let Jack and Sara off."

"Huh?" said Jack. "You're putting us on a bus?"

"No, man, I'm just saying we might make them believe that. We could pretend to buy you tickets. For all they know, you might have wanted to drive through the mountains before going back to Mexico City. I'll park in front of the station and we'll hang out, take our time, like we're waiting for you to leave."

Jack said, "You really think these guys can be fooled?"

"That's what I'm hoping, yeah. You got a better idea?"

"No," Jack said, throwing up his hands. "Sure, man, whatever you say."

Maura explained the plan to Alma. Her head was propped on a pillow next to Sara's feet. She looked terrified, and that seemed right to Sara, who was glad that this young reckless woman felt the fear she deserved...that she was suffering, as she should, for the danger she'd brought to the rest of them. Alma looked up at her. Sara stared back, thinking, *Damn it, you must know this is all your fault!*

The girl's eyes brimmed over with tears.

Sara stiffened and looked away. She felt afraid to look back. She could feel the pain pouring from Alma; could feel an overwhelming sense of helplessness; could feel a deep aching sorrow inside herself, a void, as if her tenderness, her goodness, had been drained away. And she knew, somehow knew, Alma felt the same.

No, please, this is not what I wanted. Not this.

Without another thought, Sara leaned down and began gently stroking the girl's long black hair...like her mother used to do for her...like she used to do for Sam when he was small. *"Está bien,"* she whispered, over and over.

"It's all right...it's all right...it's all right."

The station was in the middle of town. It was a tiny building, nothing but a ticket office. A large space was marked off out front—enough room for a bus to turn in and park. Roger pulled past the empty lane, in full sight of the office window.

"Act normal," Roger said. He turned off the engine, got out of the van, came around and opened the sliding door.

Sara was leaned over, holding Alma's hand. Both of them were crying.

"Normal," said Roger. Then he put on a smile. "They're back there watching for christsakes, come on."

Sara and Jack got out.

Roger slid the door closed. He went to the rear hatch, retrieved the Americans' bags and set them on the ground.

Sara saw the Trooper parked behind the bus slot. She could not stop crying. She hugged Roger close, pretending her tears were for him.

She hugged Maura too, who whispered, "That's good, Sara, very good."

Bags in hand, they went inside the station. It was empty except for a woman behind the counter. Roger spoke with her for a couple of minutes, perhaps explaining what was going on, asking for the cheapest possible fare, not concerned with the destination.

Sara stepped up next to him. "Buy two for Mexico City."

"No," he said, as if Sara had not understood the plan. "That will be too expensive."

"I don't care what it costs," she said. Her long-restrained anger had risen to the surface. She took a calming breath. "This has to look real, okay. We're taking a bus to the city. That's what I want."

Though Roger seemed to understand, and agree, he looked worried. "You have any money?"

Jack dug into his wallet and handed Roger all of their remaining pesos.

"Good," Roger said, "Yes, that's plenty." He bought the two tickets and gave them to Jack, along with the change.

The ticket woman said their bus would arrive in fifteen minutes.

Roger's phone rang.

He answered it, listened, and said to Maura, "Her father is here. He's waiting by the post office." He got back on the phone, said something in Spanish, then put it away. "I told him half an hour. We might as well sit down."

There were three seats in the office. Sara chose to stand.

Jack said to Roger, "You locked the van, right?"

"Yeah," he said, "but that won't matter if they think she's in there hiding. Best we act casual and hope they don't go look."

Roger leaned over, took hold of Jack's shoulder, and thanked him for going on the bus.

Maura reached out and held Sara's hand, saying how grateful she was for the help with Alma. "And I must tell you," Maura said, smiling, "how much I enjoyed our visit."

Sara smiled back, and let go of the hand. The queen was trying to make the farewell look genuine. They talked of other things, it didn't matter what, and from time to time Sara glanced out at the Trooper. What would she do if some guy got out with a gun? What could she possibly do?

Luckily, the bus came early.

The driver stored their bags in the carrier space. He closed it, said, *"Listo,"* and climbed in behind the wheel.

Roger hugged them both. Then he stood back and quipped, "Ah yes...life."

"I know that you don't like us," Maura said to Sara.

"Yes, dear, honesty," Sara said. She smiled, gave Maura a kiss on the cheek, and started toward the bus. Tears filled her eyes. She turned around to face the woman. "Look, it's clear that you care about Alma. I hope you can leave her alone."

As she and Jack made their way to the back seat, Roger and Maura, with sad expressions, gazed up at them and waved.

Sara looked out the rear window as the Trooper pulled into the street. It drove past the bus, made a U-turn, and sped off in the direction of Acapulco.

Jack sat next to Sara. He held her hand. She took one last glance at Roger and Maura down below. They were finished waving. He leaned over and kissed her. Then, at once, they started laughing. For them the danger had passed.

Not for Sara. During the God-awful seven-hour trip to Mexico City, and the sleepless night in a cheap hotel, and the next morning at the airport, and throughout the flight home, she kept seeing that girl on the floor of the van, frightened beyond words, squeezing her hand.

And for many weeks afterward Alma's fear felt close.

Then one day Sara woke to find it gone.

She sat up in bed and looked around the room.

Jack was already off to work. She was alone.

She lay back down, lay absolutely still, shut her eyes and went to her most tender place. It was quiet there. A quiet that went beyond any possible sound. And it felt good. She felt at peace. Though she might wish for some deep and abiding comfort, some secret instruction on how to live, how to properly handle whatever sadness might come next, she knew that was not going to happen.

She thought of Alma, held her spirit tight and then released it. The girl was safe. Sara couldn't be sure of more than that, but that was enough.

SEÑOR GARBAGE

Ben was visiting his mom at Lake Atitlán, Guatemala, when she decided to go to the states. Her health had deteriorated during the past couple of years. No local doctor knew why, which was why she felt the need to leave. The announcement came one morning over coffee. "I'm going to see a specialist in New York, get a thorough examination, figure out what the heck is happening."

"Good," he said, "I'm glad."

"Yeah," she said. "Tomorrow."

"What?"

"Better late than never."

She seemed to love catching him off guard, to make fun of the most serious things.

"I'll go with you, Frances." He loved using her first name whenever she had him miffed.

51

"No, Hon, you need to stay and keep my house company."

Another joke. Her way of saying she'd rather go alone. Well, yeah, that he understood.

"I'm going," he said.

"You don't have a ticket."

"I'll get one, *Frances.*"

"Please, *Benjamin,* don't be such a pain in the ass. You think I want my grown-up son following me around New York City? I'll be with my friend, Helen. We'll have way more fun without you."

Ben gave up, which wasn't easy. For months his mom had kept saying not to worry, that her illness was "some damned hormonal thing." While hoping she was right, he feared it was something bad. His fear came from her. He remembered, as a boy, her telling friends that she would never be an old lady. What a thing for her kid to hear! Though she'd always said it like a joke, he knew she was serious, as if she had no true attachment to this world.

"Well," she said the next morning as the shuttle driver pulled up, "time to go see what's trying to get me."

He was tired of hearing this stuff. "For god sakes, Mom, you're going to be fine." She was not a morbid person, but it sometimes seemed like death was what she wanted. That's what he told her, and when he did his eyes filled with tears.

"Oh, Ben."

"Can you stop with the stupid jokes?"

She laughed. "Look," she said, holding him close, "I don't want to die. Truth be told, I kind of like it here. What I want is a vacation. All right? You're in charge while I'm gone."

"Which means?"

He knew it couldn't mean much. She lived on a steep three-acre piece, with terraces of vegetables and medicinal herbs. Sure, there was plenty to do, but Miguel, her *guardián,* took care of everything.

"Your job, son, is to enjoy this land. Enjoy the lake. Enjoy your life, okay? Please, sweetheart, will you please stop your worrying."

Yeah, okay, he promised.

But a few days later, trying hard not to be the worrier he'd become, Ben again faced the fact that most things in life were beyond his control.

He'd gone to the lake for his morning swim. As usual, he stripped to his underwear and sat on the beach in the warming sunlight. He smiled at the three towering volcanoes, at their reflection across the wide glassy sheen. He softened his vision and took all of it in at once. Lake Atitlán was his therapy. It gave him a sense of trust, a feeling of inner confidence, a belief that he was able to accept whatever might happen. That was how he must learn to live, and this daily ritual always helped.

He rose, took a deep breath, and dove in, loving the water's icy jolt, the way his warmed skin tingled at its touch.

Then he opened his eyes. And stared. The once crystal-clear water showed countless translucent threads of cyanobacteria. He'd heard of the infestation but never before had seen it, or understood the immediacy of its threat. It looked like an alien invasion, like a demonic force, and he felt overwhelmed, his body going limp. Though the bacteria had nothing to do with his mother's illness, his mind went to that same awful place. He saw intention in its fluid, slithery movement, as if the tiny squiggles of slime were watching him, pursuing him, looking for ways to get inside.

Freaked by that thought, he raced to shore. He lay panting on his back, his mind focused on the lake, on the fact that after fifty years of human abuse this bluish-green pollutant had taken hold and begun to multiply.

Though there were many causes, he knew the main culprit was chemical fertilizer. Farmers had come to depend on it to maximize their harvests. And the rains carried its potent residue away, down from the numerous watersheds and into the lake, feeding the bacteria and making it grow.

For Ben, who each year came to visit, who swam in the lake every day, the contamination was frightening. It made him feel hopeless. Staring into the endless sky, he lay exposed, spread-eagled beneath the sun. His body needed its searing heat. After a few minutes, though, as if by instinct, he crawled to the shade of nearby reeds.

He curled up and fell asleep. He dreamt of a *cayuco* fisherman reeling in his net. As the man pulled and pulled, the water level dropped beneath him, at first by inches, then feet, then yards, falling and falling like a drain had been opened up, sucking him down until the little wooden boat sat stuck, marooned on a heaping mound of human junk—plastic chairs and broken toilets, aluminum cans and rusty cars—everything covered with that same bacterial scum.

Ben woke up feeling desperate. He had to do something. He didn't know what, but something.

He thought of his mom. He had to think like her. She'd done wonderful things since years ago leaving his father and moving to Guatemala. While his father lived in a gated community with a young pretty wife, his mom had come here, using her part of their fortune to start a women's weaving cooperative. She employed a lot of indigenous people. She paid everyone well. So well, in fact, that every year she lost money. Financial advisors warned that her savings would not last, but she continued to do what moved her, what fed her soul. Besides providing work, she sent children to school—at present almost a hundred—and made certain that the families' medical needs were met. Known as *Seño Fran*, she could not walk down a street in any Atitlán village

54

without Indian women coming to greet her, thankful for whatever she'd done to help. She would beam at their approach and quickly deflect their gratitude, gently touching their shoulders and steering the conversation around to them.

"How are things going?" she would say.

Some would touch her face and whisper a Mayan blessing. Some would bow, kiss her hand, and cry.

Still, after all these years, Ben was surprised whenever this happened, surprised at her sudden glow, surprised at her being transformed from a frumpy middle-aged foreigner into a graceful ageless spirit. He knew it was not from the women's display of devotion. It was because of what she would call "a meeting of hearts."

How odd to see his mother treated like a saint. Though impressed, and proud, it made him feel incomplete, a hanger-on, a failure. Now twenty-six, he worked part-time as a carpenter, time-off as a surfer, and spent his in-between-time looking for pretty women.

True, he had a degree in Botany from UC Santa Cruz.

A degree he'd never used.

True, in spite of that, what Frances called his "undeveloped talents," he'd always felt her unconditional love.

Okay, yeah, he was thankful for his mother's adoration, but for him there was something missing. More than anything else, he wanted her respect.

Ben rose and threw on his clothes.

This was his chance.

He walked the twenty minutes into Panajachel and went to the main market, where Indian farmers come every day to sell their produce. He needed to know what happened to the market waste. It had dawned on him, while at the lake, that maybe he could use it. He'd begun a small pile of compost on his mother's land, using kitchen scraps and garden trimmings.

She'd said, "What a great idea!"

Yeah, it was. So why not make it greater!

Ben looked around for the middle-aged man who he thought of as *the cleanup guy*.

Within a few minutes he found him, shuffling along, the toes of his deformed left foot twisted inward and back toward his right heel. The guy hobbled past the outside vendors. He stopped to stuff a mound of carrot tops into a burlap sack, then dragged it to a big tin shed.

Ben walked up and held out his hand. The Indian smiled apologetically. He lifted his palm, showing how dirty it was.

The young gringo shook it anyway. Dirt was no problem for him. *"Me llamo* Ben."

"Hola," the man said. *"Me llamo* Alberto.*"*

Ben glanced into the shed at the discarded vegetation. Though his Spanish was fairly good, he did not know the proper word. He pointed. "I would like to take the garbage that comes from plants."

"I don't understand."

"La basura vegetal," Ben said, and pointed again at the green stuff against the far wall. "That is what I want."

"That? Really?" When Ben nodded, Alberto lit up. "Yes, of course. Less work for me." The gringo smiled at the Indian's honesty. "Yes, Señor, you can come at five o'clock. I'll help get what you want."

Ben checked his watch. It was a few minutes after one. "Thanks," he said, and hurried off before Alberto could change his mind. He walked home and climbed to the top of the property. He was thinking of the project in Bali that he'd studied in college. Local farmers had taken the market's green waste, composted it, and used the natural fertilizer to increase their harvest. Why not do the same in Panajachel? He looked past the pile he'd started. He imagined the undeveloped terraces rich with mounds of homemade humus. He imagined farmers coming to see what he'd done, and realizing they could do it too. He would spread the word to different villages. Maybe do workshops. People could use a lot less chemical fertilizer, which would help to heal the lake.

Ben staked out eight new piles. Tired and sweating, he went to the house, ate a sandwich, took a shower, and lay down for a nap.

He woke with the four-thirty alarm. After changing into work clothes he went down the hill for his mother's old Volvo station wagon. On the way to the market he stopped at a hardware store to buy three large plastic bins, then parked the Volvo by the garbage shed. Taking one of the bins, he went inside. Alberto wasn't there.

What Ben found, mixed with the greens he'd seen four hours ago, was a scattering of plastic bags, Coca-Cola bottles, and several well-used Pampers. The place reeked. His eyes burned. To the side was a slab of meat covered with maggots. He gagged. Hurrying for the exit he tripped on a big gray rat, its head dismembered and its body half eaten.

A policeman was watching from the door. The officer looked confused and not the least bit friendly. "What are you doing?"

Ben put down the bin. He tried to explain.

"Please," said the policeman, "come with me."

Ben followed. The remaining vendors watched and talked among themselves. He was led down a ramp into the main market, past the various food stalls, the air thick with scents of steaming black beans and frying corn tortillas. They went to the back of the lower level, toward the public toilets and their stench of stale urine.

The policeman turned into an open doorway. He gestured for Ben to come inside.

A mustached man in a clean white shirt looked up at them from behind a cluttered desk. The policeman apologized in Spanish for the interruption, then launched into their indigenous language, *Caqchikel*. He must have assumed that the Spanish-speaking gringo would not understand.

57

He was right.

The man behind the desk looked at Ben and laughed. "The officer thinks you are a problem," he said in slow, well-articulated Spanish. "He thinks you want our garbage."

"Well, um, yes," Ben said. "And no."

The policeman glared at the gringo, then went to stand by the door.

The mustached man rose from behind his desk. "Please, sit down," he said. Along with his clean white shirt were ironed black slacks. "My name is Chalo, I am the manager here. What exactly do you want?"

Ben began by saying that Alberto had given him permission to sort through the garbage.

"And why?" said Chalo.

"That's harder to explain."

"Try."

As best he could, Ben outlined the threat of cyanobacteria to the lake, how chemical fertilizers were a big part of the problem. "And no one seems to care."

"I care," Chalo said. His face was changed, as if Ben had pushed some button...as if some long-lingering complaint needed to be spoken. "The real problem here is that my fellow Indians do not think it is a problem. They know nothing about science."

He did not say it in a disrespectful way, simply as a fact. And to make clear that he no longer thought like an Indian. He was not, in other words, a part of the problem.

Ben did not think it fair to blame the Indians, who were only in part responsible for the pollution. In truth, everyone was at fault. Increasing tourism made it worse and local governments did nothing. Expats like Frances built houses around the lake despite its lack of sewage treatment. He and Chalo, too, whenever they washed their hands in a sink, or flushed a toilet, increased the contamination.

Poor Indians could not be blamed for any of that.

But this was no time for an argument, not with the policeman looking ready to pounce. Ben stayed focused on his desire to help the lake. He said he wanted "*la basura vegetal*" from the market. He explained his idea of a compost project.

Chalo said, "You want to make *abono*."

Abono is the generic word for fertilizer, purchased from a local chicken farmer: chicken manure that's been mixed with dirt. The problem is, it's not too useful, or plentiful, and people keep buying chemicals.

"Yes," Ben said, "but *abono* that anyone can make, for free, from what usually gets thrown away."

Chalo smiled. "Ah, I see." His face looked suddenly innocent, like a child's. "I love good dirt," he said. "My father was a farmer. I worked with him, growing beans and onions. We threw our weeds and old plants into a big hole. We never thought of it as making fertilizer, but that's what we were doing. Soon as that hole was filled we planted something on top of it."

"Smart," Ben said. "Do farmers still do that?"

"Yes. But times have changed. Sad to say, the holes are now used for other things as well. Things that should not be there, same as in our shed. Too much trouble for most people to separate it. Whatever they can't burn gets buried."

"It might be good for them to see me take away, and use, what is *not really garbage*."

"Maybe," said Chalo. "I don't see how it can hurt." The market manager looked off to the side, and nodded, as if conferring with an invisible adviser. He turned back to Ben. "I have an idea. If you pay for burlap sacks, I'll have the farmers fill them with their vegetable waste. Most of it will come Sunday, on market day, but during the week too. There should be plenty. My helpers will put the sacks on the upper balcony by the road. You can come get them every Monday morning."

Ben could barely believe this was happening. For the first time in months he felt relaxed. Sure, his mother's illness was on his mind, but this tiny victory made him happy, which was exactly what she'd want. He wondered if Chalo knew he was Seño Fran's son? Did that explain the man's kindness? Ben doubted it, but didn't care. This was something he would do, and he would accept whatever help came his way.

"You can start next week," said Chalo. Though the man did not say it, he seemed excited by the plan. "I am thinking that twenty sacks would be a good start."

Ben agreed, paid, and shook Chalo's hand.

That night he called his mom. It was early evening in New York. Helen, her friend, answered the phone, said hello, then handed it to Frances. His mom sounded tired, and like she was trying, very hard, not to sound tired.

"Hey," she said, "how do they know Jesus wasn't born in New York City?"

"Ya got me."

"Because there were only a couple of wise guys and not a single virgin."

"Funny," said Ben in his driest voice, his playful way of dissing her joke.

"Yeah," she said, laughing. "Speaking of which, what have you been up to?"

He wasn't ready to tell her what had happened. For now it could stay a secret. "As ordered, boss, I'm enjoying the hell out of myself."

"I bet."

"And you?" he said. "What's going on?"

"Good question. These things take time, one test leading to another."

"They must have some idea."

"Nope," she said, "not yet. Soon as I know something, Sherlock, I promise to spill the beans."

"C'mon, Mom, I need to know what—"

"Listen, Ben, I have to say good-bye. Helen and I are going to the opera."

"Opera? Since when do you like opera?"

"Don't know that I do. Thought I'd try it out. Really, Hon, I gotta go."

"Figaro!" he sang. *"Figaro! Figaro! Figaro!"*

"I love you, *Benjamin.*

"I love you too, *Francis.*"

All that week he prepared for Monday's haul, heaping up mounds of dirt and dry leaves. Strange how quickly perceptions can shift. In San Diego, Ben noticed things like roof designs, glassy swells, pretty faces and shapely bodies—but here, each and every day, he thought of decomposing waste, great piles of it, and the good loamy soil it would create. He looked at weeds and saw nitrogen; he shoveled dirt and imagined billions of hungry microbes; he went to bed and dreamt of worms.

He told the guardián what he planned to do on the upper terraces, and said he'd need his help. "This project has to be well on its way before my mother returns."

Miguel, who had always been friendly to Ben, looked at him like he was a stranger. The man's job, as guardián, was to do whatever Seño Fran wanted, but he seemed uncomfortable taking orders from her son. Perhaps believing there was no other choice, he gave an unconvincing nod.

Ben covered the Volvo's bed with an old blue tarp, then drove them down the bumpy road, across the tainted San Francisco river, into Panajachel. At the market he found a place to park close to the entrance. He led Miguel up the stairway to the terrace. Both of them stopped. Ahead, like a vision from hell, was a jumble of bulging burlap sacks enveloped by a cloud of flies.

The stuff had not been put in the shade. After a week of long hot days and marinating nights, it smelled like putrid soup.

"Ugly," said Miguel.

Ben sighed and turned his back to the mess.

A bleary-eyed man came wobbling up the stairs toward him. Ben knew the look. This guy was no stranger to *Quetzalteca*—the cheapest of cheap street alcohols, a favorite of drunks throughout Guatemala. It appeared that little time had passed since his last bottle. The guy smiled, showing dark decaying teeth, and waved like an old friend. *"Hola amigo! Me llamo Diego!"*

Ben stepped aside. Though the guy looked friendly, Ben ignored him. He was in no mood to humor a drunk. Then Diego went over, lifted up a sack, and smiled at Miguel. Miguel smiled back, hefted a bigger sack, and headed off in front of Diego. *Aha, a game!* Ben grabbed one too and trailed them down the steps, past the women selling fruits and vegetables. Some giggled as they passed, some stared, some held their noses. The sacks leaked a sticky pungent juice, a dark and milky vinegar.

To avoid problems later, Ben handed Diego ten *quetzales*. A buck and a quarter. "That's all I can pay."

The man smiled, patted Ben on the shoulder, and climbed the stairs for another load.

"Is ten enough?" Ben asked Miguel.

"Yes, Señor, for him that is good. Any more and he will just get drunk faster."

They carried down all twenty sacks and filled the back of the station wagon. The last five were tied onto the tailgate. Diego, who could have left at any time, stayed till the end. It was clear that he'd not helped them just for money. Maybe it was because no one else in town ever wanted his help.

Ben shook the man's hand, said he'd be back next Monday, got into the Volvo and drove away.

It took five hours for him and Miguel to haul the sacks up Frances's one hundred and thirty-two steps, past her house, and toss them onto the highest, most distant terrace. The heavier sacks weighed about 100 pounds.

100 pounds of malodorous drooling slop. They emptied them, cleaned them inside and out, and hung them on a line to dry. By the time their work was finished the men had taken on the disgusting stench. They hosed each other off and went for their private baths.

The next few days were spent starting new piles. While Miguel was busy doing his regular work, Ben dug a couple of four by six foot pads, each six inches deep, then covered them with a dense crisscrossing of twigs. After that came a few inches of the decayed vegetation, topped by an equal layer of dirt, another of dry leaves, and again the market waste.

His mom called Friday morning. They couldn't talk long because she had a full day of doctor's appointments.

"Sorry, son, but I'll be here a wee bit longer. They're running another series of tests, blah blah blah, and I have to wait around."

"What do they think it is?"

"Could be lots of things. Something weird, I guess, but they tell me not to worry. So that's what I'm telling you, all right?"

Ben didn't know what to say. His throat tightened up. His hands were trembling.

"All right?" she repeated like an order.

"Yeah, all right."

"You promised to take it easy, son, remember? I'll call you next week."

On Monday a new stash of rot was waiting. And Diego. The sky glowed blue; the rooftops were alive with chirping birds; the air was scented with freshly cut flowers.

As Ben descended the stairs with his first stinking sack he knew what the Indians were thinking:

Here comes Mister Garbage.

That was okay. The whole point here was to get their attention, make them wonder what he was up to. Well, he'd certainly done that, though their suspicious glances bothered him. Maybe they knew his mother was Seño Fran and were embarrassed on her behalf. Perhaps they thought him a problem child, *un problema,* or as some would say, "a pain in his mother's heart."

He turned to one giggling woman. "I'm using it to make *abono,*" he said. "I'm trying to help the lake."

Though Ben wanted to explain, he could see she wasn't listening. The woman nodded, as if she fully understood, but what he sensed beneath her wandering eyes was more than mere confusion. Perhaps, because of respect for Seño Fran, this woman would not laugh out loud. But inside, yes. *Oh yes.*

To her he must look like another crazy gringo. That was probably what all the Indians thought. They must have seen many over the years, people with bizarre styles and colors of hair, with random tattoos and piercings—mere personal adornments—who dressed and acted in ways that native people could not comprehend.

And now, to top it off, some fool was hauling away their trash!

As Ben hefted the last of it into the station wagon, a woman came from across the street.

"Señor," she said, "I think I have something you want."

He followed the woman past a corrugated sheet-metal gate. There, beyond her concrete hovel, inside a rickety enclosure full of fowl, were twelve large sacks of chicken shit, strewn around like decomposing bodies.

Ben, who was holding his breath, tried to see them as piles of gold.

"Five quetzales for each," she said.

It seemed she'd been waiting years for this crazy gringo to show up. Ben was thrilled to pay her price.

64

He and Miguel hurried their market load to Jucanyá, dumped it at the base of Frances's land, then returned for the manure. Much of it was wet and moldy and mixed with feathers. The cured weight would be less than 300 pounds, but for them it was easily half a ton.

It took until Friday to haul all of the sacks up the mountain. The neighbors weren't happy. A few went out of their way to say so.

"Don't mind them," Miguel said. "Seño Fran will be impressed."

She'd left a message that morning while he was out working: "Hi boy! Sorry I didn't call earlier. Some results came in yesterday—something haywire with my immune system. Weird, huh? I'd have thought, having brought you up, I'm immune to everything."

To him she sounded far too happy.

"Anyhow," she said, "you guessed it...another round of tests! They'll know what's up by Monday. Which means, for now, my job is to have fun! Helen and I are taking off for the weekend. Turning off the phones. Talk to you next week, okay, and oh, please do me a favor. Go jump in the lake!" Then came an unnatural pause, her voice now thin and soft. "I miss you, Ben. I miss you dearly."

He called back and got Helen's answering machine. "Dang," he said, trying to sound calm, "you're already gone. Listen, if you get this, please give me a call."

On Sunday night, not hearing from her, he left another message: "Hi there, welcome back! I hope you're still having fun! By the way, Figaro, I've started a project on your land. How's that for a tease? I miss you too, Mom."

Chalo was waiting Monday morning when Ben and Miguel arrived. "We need to talk," he said, and headed for his office. As they passed the vendors Ben sensed a difference, an open friendliness that made him feel good. Their smiles looked genuine. A couple of them patted him on the back.

He thought to himself, *Oh my God, it's working!*

Once inside the office, Chalo closed the door, went behind the desk and offered them a seat. "I am sorry," he said, "there is a problem."

"What?" said Ben. He asked if it was about Diego, who had not been waiting for them out front.

Chalo shook his head. No, he said, it was *codicia*, a word Ben didn't know.

"Ah," said Miguel, a look of recognition on his face.

"I don't understand," said Ben.

Chalo defined the word by pulling out his wallet, shaking it in the air and saying, "Indians believe that to survive they must take advantage of any opportunity. In this case, Señor Ben, that means you."

He explained that when the farmers saw a gringo carrying away their *basura vegetal*, they assumed it must be worth something, that he was somehow making money.

"They do not understand how you foreigners get rich," said Chalo. "And they don't care. They just want their part."

"Did you explain to them why I—"

"I tried. But do not be discouraged, my friend. In a week or two, when no one buys it, they'll again be throwing it away." He looked off to the side, as if conferring with his invisible advisor. Apparently upset by what he was hearing, Chalo sighed, gave a short derisive laugh, and blew out air. "Until you come to get it. Then they'll probably go back to wanting money."

The market manager looked embarrassed, perhaps shamed, by the ignorance of his people.

Ben could not leave it like that. "Actually," he said, "this is good. Let them sell their *basura vegetal* if they can. Or maybe they'll keep it and start their own compost piles. That's the whole idea, right?"

"Yes, yes, right," said Chalo, who seemed relieved by Ben's positive words. "You know, young man, this is an important lesson for everyone." He crossed himself and looked toward the heavens. "We must listen to what The Good Lord tells us."

"What's that?"

"That one person's garbage is another person's treasure."

Though Chalo acted serious, he was clearly trying to keep things light, to lessen their disappointment.

Disappointment?

No, get real, that wasn't why he'd made the joke. He thought it funny that poor Indians wanted money for their trash. Ben glanced at Miguel, who was grinning.

Well, yeah, they were right, it was funny.

Fucking hilarious.

But for Ben the humor was dark, like his mother saying to plant her in the garden when she died, under a cactus, and "be sure not to water it." He hadn't laughed then either. Why would she joke about that? Why would Chalo joke about this? Why was everyone so full of cheer, so goddamn easygoing?

This meant that the lake would keep suffering. Or maybe die. Shouldn't they feel sad? Hell, you know, someone has to worry!

Ben shook his head and looked into his lap. Funny, he thought, that if "The Good Lord" made us better, we wouldn't be so great at dodging sadness. Wouldn't be so afraid to feel it, really feel it.

That was the real problem. Normal human beings know how to keep their emotions in check. They avoid feelings that disrupt the minimal order in their lives. How else to deal with daily challenges? How else to keep on going? He could hear it playing in his head, as if The Good Lord Himself, full of love and mercy, were singing from up on high: *Don't worry, you little people down there. Don't worry...Be happy.*

67

Though not a man of God, Ben had always believed in goodness...that good people and good intentions might someday heal this sad, sick planet.

What a laugh.

The two Indian men were watching him. They knew, like Ben, like anyone forced to be realistic, it would take more than heaps of compost, more than acknowledged feelings—more than big talk or strong beliefs or the noblest of intentions—to change what people do. Maybe nothing could save the lake. Maybe things had gone too far. It would be much better for him to accept that, to swallow that bitter pill and move on.

"You understand?" said Chalo, as if this gringo might have missed the joke.

Ben thought of his mom. She'd be sad too, but that could never stop her goodness, her doing what she knows is right even as things get worse and worse.

"Oh yes," he said, smiling, patting Chalo's back. "God is a very funny guy."

TEMPLE OF MONKEYS

Hampi, founded in the 1300's, is a temple town that sits along the Tungabhadra River in an otherwise arid valley of massive boulders.

In 2001 it became a World Heritage Site, yet most tourists continued to pass it by. Susan was baffled to hear that, though not displeased. She loved her long quiet strolls through the ancient Hindu ruins. She was grateful, as well, for the variety of quaint guesthouses and restaurants and shops. But none of that explained why she and Ty were there. They'd come to get away from India's terrorizing traffic. In remote Hampi there were no loud busy streets blocking their way, no speeding buses or mechanized rickshaws. Or, worst of all, motorcycles—at last they'd escaped the motorcycles—which was why she stared with disbelief when Ty suggested that they rent one.

"Seriously?"

Ty had freed his long blond hair from its ponytail. He looked younger than his thirty-five years. The boy in him was alive and well, and hard to resist.

"For a few hours," he said, his blue eyes shining. "I want us to see the Hanuman Temple."

"There are plenty of temples here that we can walk to."

"This one's special," he said. "A guy told me we have to go. It's not just a temple, it's a monkey sanctuary. Only thirty miles away."

"We can take a taxi," said Susan.

"Cheaper to rent a motorcycle for the entire day. Gas included. I checked it out."

"Come on, Ty, you don't know how to drive a motorcycle."

"No, but…it's not a *real* motorcycle, the guy told me, more like a motorbike. Smaller and simpler. The guy says they're easy to drive, says they're perfect for these country roads."

"Who is this guy?"

"I met him this morning. He rents them. We talked for a long time, and I resisted, I did, but he convinced me that this is a great place to learn how to drive one." Ty's excitement gave way to a blush of what looked like shame. "I'm tired of hating the damn things, Suze, I really am."

Having been married for nine years, Susan could see he'd made up his mind. And she knew why. It was something Ty would not dare admit: how envious he was of men who drove motorcycles. *Real motorcycles,* that is, like The Royal Enfield, the cycle of choice for adventurers in India. She'd seen him watch those men and their mighty machines, with their shiny helmets and thick dark visors, their black leather pants and jackets and boots. He pined for the hutzpah to be like them, and she had to keep her knowledge of that secret.

"I understand," she said.

"Yeah," Ty said. "And the guy was real friendly. Charged me half-price. I already paid."

"What? For when?"

"Tomorrow. He'll have it ready by noon. That gives us plenty of time, he says, to see the monkey temple and be back by dark."

"Bummer," she said. "Guess I'll have to cancel lunch with the Dalai Lama."

Ty took her head in his hands and kissed her on the nose.

They stayed up late that night, drank a bit too much, and the next morning slept in, finishing breakfast at noon. Then Ty led them to the guy's shop—what amounted to a flimsy

70

metal shed. Susan was not impressed. Tools lay in the dirt among a few dusty motorcycles.

Out of a squeaky door came an old man. He had huge brown liquid eyes. Thin white hair shot up from his balding brown scalp, reminding Susan of a halo. The poor man looked exhausted, and scattered, as disheveled as the shed, like an overworked angel who'd lost track of his wings.

"Hello," he said, shaking her hand, "I am Amir."

"Nice to meet you," Susan said. She held his friendly gaze as long as she could stand it, then looked around. Next to a blue Royal Enfield motorcycle were two motorbikes, one black and one white. "Are we renting one of these?"

"No," said Amir.

"No?" said Ty. He pointed at the black one. "I thought you said—"

"No," said Amir. "Do you not remember? We discussed what a beautiful machine it is, and more powerful than the white one."

"Yes," said Ty, "I remember us saying that. That was why, when you offered it for half the price, I agreed to pay you in advance."

"No, my friend," said Amir, smiling and shaking his head. "You forget me saying that these are both reserved this week. And, I know also, they are too difficult for you to drive. I have another one, a very special one. Perfect for you and your wife."

"You never showed me another motorcycle."

"Because it was being used. But, lucky for you, now it is here."

Susan looked around the shed at gallon bottles of gasoline, quarts of oil, old tires, old helmets, and a few old bicycles.

Ty was looking too. "Where?" he said.

"Wait," said Amir, and hurried off behind the shed. A minute later he wheeled the thing out. It was slightly smaller than the black and white ones. It was pink.

Ty started laughing. "You're kidding, right?"

71

"Kidding?" said Amir.

"Joking," said Ty. "This has to be a joke."

"No joke, my friend, no, this is a very special motorbike, given to me by my late beloved father, may he rest in peace. I do not rent it often."

Yeah, thought Susan, *I wonder why?*

"Listen," Ty said, "I'm sorry for the misunderstanding, Amir, but this is not what I had in mind. May I please have my money back?"

"I too am sorry, but no."

"Why?"

"Because, my friend—*because of you*—I said *no* to someone else."

"Well," said Ty, "now you can say *yes.*"

"Now it is too late."

Ty chewed on his lower lip, which meant he was frustrated and didn't know what to do. Perhaps he thought Amir was trying to cheat him. He looked at Susan.

She smiled and turned away, believing the old man. She knew her husband well; knew that because of his chronic optimism he sometimes missed unwanted details.

"Do not worry," Amir said, patting her shoulder. "I promise you will be happy. Like my father, I am most loving of this motorbike. I call it 'Dear Beloved.' I swear, it is as precious to me as my own mother." He reached into his pocket and felt around. "Wait, I forgot the key," he said, and went inside the shed.

"It was incredibly cheap," said Ty. "I guess I should have known better."

"Oh well," said Susan. She smiled and kissed his cheek.

Amir came hurrying back, his angel hair flying. He inserted the key, turned it, and pushed the starter button. The little engine whirred. "You see what a beautiful sound?" He turned it off and demonstrated how the gears worked. Even Susan understood. "It grew up on these hills," said Amir, fondly patting the dented gas tank. "It knows them well and will have no problem taking you to the temple." Then his eyes got glossy. "I am happy, *so so* happy, for you to learn on my Dear Beloved."

"Seems there's no other option," said Ty.

"No," Amir agreed, apparently missing the sarcasm. He went to the far corner of the shed and came back with two old helmets. "You will need these, but nothing else. The tank has plenty of gas for your trip today. You go that way out of town, then left at the next small road. It will take you across the Tungabhadra River. In twenty minutes, nice and easy, you go through a village. After that, not far, the Hanuman Temple is on your right."

"We'll figure it out," said Ty. He put on his helmet and climbed aboard the pink motorbike.

Susan whispered, "My hero."

"Fuck you," he whispered back.

At least that got them laughing.

She donned her helmet and climbed on behind him. Because she had no choice. Because this was happening and she had to make the best of it. Because marriage sometimes means being a fool to support the one you love.

Ty turned the key, pushed the starter, and revved the engine.

Susan closed her eyes and prayed for luck.

"Oh," said Amir, "something else. The speedometer, it is not working so good right now. That is why I charged you half the price."

Ty glared at Amir, then pulled out onto the empty road.

They lurched a bit at first, as Ty practiced shifting gears, but by the time they reached the river he was getting the hang of it. He drove across the bridge and down by the water, parked behind some bushes and turned off the engine. Ty looked proud to have conquered the pink motorbike.

They took off their helmets and sat on the sandy shore.

Susan felt happy. "I must admit, it's fun."

"Yeah," Ty said, letting loose a grin. "Who needs a speedometer, right? After a day of this, I'm thinking, I'll be ready to try that black one."

Susan imagined Ty's short paunchy frame decked out in black leather. Tempted to joke, she decided against it. His Hell's Angels days would soon be over. In a week they'd be on a train to Mumbai, then a plane back to New York, where his mind would again be consumed with selling real estate. He would sublimate his lack of excitement, as usual, with an endless stream of hero flicks: undaunted do-gooders and daring underdogs. Was it believable that those innocent little hobbits could keep overcoming evil wizards and horrendous monsters and impossible odds? *No.* But he loved that they did, and their incredible victories lifted his spirits. Hey, he was a happy guy, why should she complain?

"I love you," Ty said, "for being such a sport."

He kissed her, a long passionate kiss, and brought her down with him to the warm, soft sand.

His hands were moving fast.

"Not here," Susan said, gently pushing him off. She stood, pulled up her skirt and buttoned her shirt.

Golly gee, this motorcycle thing could be good!

She mounted their trusty steed and hugged up close to Ty. He gunned the engine and they zigzagged up the sandy little hill, back onto the road.

A few minutes later came a village without a name. Or, rather, no name she could see. It looked like the Wild West, but instead of cowboys and cowgirls there were men dressed all in white and women in colorful saris.

Ty pulled up to a restaurant and turned off the engine. "Hey," he said, real casual, "how 'bout some chai?"

"Sure," said Susan.

He went to the lavatory while a waiter led her to an outside garden area, to a table facing a large fragrant lemon tree. To one side was a small pond. Through the dark murky water she spotted some lumbering, sad-looking koi. She ordered the chai, then said to the waiter, "You should clean the pond."

He looked puzzled, as if the thought had never once occurred to him. "Pond?"

She pointed.

"Oh, yes," he said, smiling, walking away, "pond."

Never mind, she told herself, and leaned back in her chair. The spicy mix was waiting when Ty arrived.

He hugged her from behind, then sat close, held her hand and said, "I wonder where we should travel next?" He told her he'd always wanted to see Indonesia, go to the most reclusive islands. "There are some," he said, "that can't be reached except by a private boat."

Yeah, thought Susan, *and some of those have cannibals.* She'd read that in a National Geographic and knew not to mention it now. She smiled at his romantic nature, his innocent dreams, his constant and unflappable hope. That's what mattered. "Well, honey," she joked, "maybe first we should get to that monkey temple."

"Ah," said Ty, "what's the hurry?" He checked his watch. "It's almost two. You hungry?"

She was, so they decided to have lunch.

The food was a long time coming, but worth the wait: a lovely pumpkin soup along with an entree of korma, with mango chutney and garlic chapatti on the side. After that they ordered another pot of chai. They moved away from the murky pond and lounged in comfy chairs under the lemon tree. Susan breathed it in, closed her eyes, and let her mind go blank.

She dreamt of walking barefoot through a huge cavernous ruin. The air was warm and fragrant. She was happy to be there, happy to be alone, like a spiritual devotee at the end of a long hard pilgrimage. Sunshine lit up the soft orange dirt. The ceiling was bright blue sky. The ancient walls were translucent, and beyond them were more translucent walls. She saw something on the ground and knelt to pick it up. It was a shiny black stone, round and flat, and in her open palm it transformed into a pure white lotus flower. Maybe that's what she was smelling? She lifted it to her nose, woke up, and saw that Ty was fast asleep.

Susan checked her watch. *Ten to four?*

She gently shook him awake and showed him the time.

He yawned. "Guess we should go," he said, but without any hint of feeling hurried. She could see that he felt in total control and was pleased with their carefree pace.

Next door was a shop selling jewelry.

Ty walked inside. Susan followed. He insisted on buying her a bracelet. She insisted she didn't want one. They looked anyway, and in the end, as a compromise, each bought a jade ring. The saleswoman, though clearly disappointed with the lesser sale, smiled and said, "Jade, you know, gives lasting peace."

We'll see, thought Susan, but on their way out of town, as if to squelch her hopes, a huge truck abruptly cut them off. Ty slammed on his brakes, swerving to avoid a crash.

"For christsakes!" Susan yelled. She felt shocked to be back in the real world, suddenly exposed and vulnerable on their tiny pink motorbike. "Those trucks are friggin' crazy!"

"Yeah!" Ty said, turning his head sideways and widening his eyes. "Not to mention, big!"

She laughed at his silly joke, but could tell that he was also shaken. "I guess you'll have to be extra careful."

"Always am," he said.

As soon as he said it she felt his disappointment. His sadness would not have been noticed by anyone but her. He was usually proud of the cautious, ethical way he lived. He tried never to be careless, and had no respect for people who took unnecessary chances. Still, because he was a thinking man, a man who acknowledged and considered the realities of life, he knew that sometimes, under extraordinary circumstances, risks must be taken. At times there was no other choice. Maybe Ty doubted that he could rise to such an occasion—could be like those celluloid heroes he admired—could ever, for whatever reason, put his body on the line.

She hugged him tight and kissed his shoulder. While road noise made it necessary to raise her voice, she kept it as soft as possible. "Thank you, honey."

"For what?"

"For being a good man."

They reached the Hanuman temple at twenty to five. It took every bit of the motorbike's minimal gusto to climb that final hill. "The gas gauge reads full," said Ty. "This thing gets fantastic mileage."

"Either that," said Susan, "or the gauge doesn't work."

Ty sighed but said nothing, a sign of annoyance with her, or Amir, or both.

He took Susan's hand and they walked up the path, beyond the arching gateway, into a courtyard crowded with begging monkeys. Avoiding the piles of excrement, they found the tiny temple at the base of a massive boulder. Outside was a man in a flowing white robe. He smelled like monkeys mixed with mint. "You are blessed," he said. "Hanuman is a mighty god. He is not afraid of trouble, is devoted, no matter what, to keep you safe."

"Cool," said Ty.

"Yes," said the caretaker, "cool." He seemed familiar with the American word. "He is very cool, this god. And brave. Hanuman will take away your fear."

Keep moving, Susan told herself, and entered the temple.

"If you like," said the caretaker, calling after her, "there is a bowl to make your offering."

"Sure," said Ty as he followed her in.

The room had many Hanuman statues. Ty parked himself in front of the largest, most serious-looking simian, whose scowl felt to Susan ominously judgmental. She cringed. The god's wrinkled brows, deep sockets and dark eyes, brought to mind *Planet of the Apes*, a movie that had creeped her out. Beneath the scary monkey was a big brass bowl.

Ty said, "Namaste," and dropped in two rupee coins. He hesitated, then dug into his wallet for a twenty-rupee note.

Susan just smiled.

They left the temple, climbed the boulders above it, and

joined other tourists, most of whom were taking pictures of the monkeys. The animals were playful. They would run up, touch someone, and run away, like in a game of tag.

A middle-aged woman came over to them and said, "Be careful." She pointed at a skinny white monkey with a cute little face. "That brat stole my camera."

"How?" said Susan.

"He knocked it loose and tossed it into a crevice between the boulders. I swear, it seemed like he'd been trained. Another way, I bet, for that *priest* to get his offerings."

Right then, a different monkey came from behind and tugged at Ty's leg, close to the pocket where he kept his wallet.

Ty spun around. The monkey backed off.

"Careful," repeated the woman, and walked away.

"Maybe we should go," said Susan.

"Yeah," said Ty.

They went back to the pink motorbike. Ty started the engine, looked up at the fading blue sky and said, "What do you say we keep going?"

"Where?"

"I don't know, but we have ol' *Dear Beloved* till tomorrow at noon. That's the deal. There's a couple more hours of daylight left, so why not check out what's up ahead? I looked at a map in the restaurant. This road loops around to the main highway, close to Hampi."

Susan could not bear to squelch his excitement.

"Okay," she said. And was glad she did. The road, not too curvy, coursed through a valley of scattered brown boulders like a slender gray thread through thick raw wool. The air was warm against her cheek. It smelled like hay. In gaps large and small between the ubiquitous stone were flocks of goats and sheep. It felt as if she and Ty were leaving the modern world behind. She forgot about time. The sun eventually reminded her, now hovering above the distant hills. Her watch said five-thirty. She tapped on Ty's shoulder. "Think we're close to the highway?"

He said, "I hope! I can't believe it's taking this long! First, if I remember right, we need to cross the river."

If he remembers right? If?

"How's the gas?" she said.

"Don't know. I think you were right about the gauge. It still shows mostly full."

"Lucky," yelled Susan, "we're not his precious mother!"

"Yeah!" he yelled, "but these motorbikes do get great mileage. I'm sure we're fine."

That was when—because she knew he wasn't anywhere close to *sure*, knew he was being optimistic in order to keep her calm—she felt a rush of genuine worry.

Another twenty minutes passed. There were plenty of goats and sheep, but no sign of the river.

At last they came to what might be a village.

Certainly, Susan hoped, they could find gas here, and someone would know the quickest way to Hampi. The sun had dipped beyond the hills. It was getting dark.

"Maybe you should turn on your lights," she said.

"Yeah," said Ty, "good call." But nothing happened. Susan waited, was about to say it again when he yelled, "No, I don't believe it!"

"What?"

"The lights don't work!"

"You must've pushed the wrong button!"

"It's not a button, okay, it's a switch, it's labeled *Lights*...and there fucking aren't any!"

"Shit! Shit! Shit!" she said, and thought of Amir. *You will be happy,* he'd told her. *Yeah, right.* Why did he give them such a piece of junk? How could she have read him so wrong? In fairness to the man, he'd assumed they'd be back by dark, but what kind of excuse was that?

Thankfully, this was a village. Another village with no apparent name. They pulled up to what looked like a store. Three new wheelbarrows were leaned against the outside wall. Inside was a man with a big black beard and a dark red turban. "Yes," he said, "can I help you?"

"We're lost," said Susan.

"I am sorry."

"Not exactly lost," said Ty with a dismissive tone, like she was making too much of the situation...like she was getting all worried over nothing.

Though his petty arrogance pissed her off she knew not to react. She took a breath, she let it go.

Ty said, "We're looking for the highway to Hampi."

"Ah," said the man, "that is Highway 67. Nine kilometers down the road."

"Thanks," said Ty. "Do you sell gas?"

"You mean petrol." The man's calm and cool expression seemed immutable. "Yes, I do."

Susan said, "How many minutes to drive to Hampi?"

"Twenty."

"We can make that," said Ty.

"Wait," said the man. "I forgot about traffic this time of day. Sometimes, who knows, it can be quite bad. To Hampi now might take an hour."

Susan said, "We also need a flashlight."

"Torch. In India we call it a torch."

"Fine," she said. "Then that's what we need. The biggest torch you've got."

The man sold them batteries, too, and filled their tank.

"You had enough petrol to make it," he said. "These tires, however, are not good."

Ty said, "Lucky we're not going far."

"Yes," the man said, "*lucky* for that. Also *lucky* there are not many cars on this road."

"Geez," said Susan, "*lucky* us."

The man tugged on his big black beard. "The highway will be a different story. It is farther to go back the way you came, but—"

"From the highway," said Ty, "it's close to the Hampi turnoff, right?"

"Right," said the man. "Four kilometers."

Ty smiled at Susan. "Just two and a half miles!"

"Yes," said the man. "However, as I said, the traffic—"

"No problem," Ty said, like this guy was wasting their precious time. "We'll be fine."

"Fine," said the man, who surprised Susan with a smile. In fact, he looked about to laugh. It seemed that as his patience diminished his sense of humor increased. "Will there be anything else?"

"Nope," said Ty.

"Good," the man said. He took their money and bowed his head. "Farewell to you."

While the bow made Susan feel vaguely honored, the words came like a warning. They sounded prophetic, as if he'd glanced into their future and saw a bad ending. But hey, what could she expect from a bearded guy in a turban? Indian men, and especially the devout religious ones, seemed cocksure of their intimate connection with the gods, convinced that meaningful visions and insightful decisions were privy to them and lost on common tourists like her and Ty. Did this guy actually see into their future? *No, hell no.* But he was good at looking like he could. Susan held his stony gaze, intent on letting him know she was not impressed. She smiled and returned his bow.

"Farewell to you, too."

Now after six, it was already quite dark. Ty stayed close to the shoulder. He drove slow. Then came a swarm of flying insects, buzzing and splashing against their visors, forcing Ty to go slower. Susan held the torch above his head. It did not supply much light, but at least others could see them coming. They found and crossed over the river.

On the other side they pulled up to the highway.

Ty stopped and looked to his left. Susan looked to her right. Both saw, for as far as they could see, an endless row of truck-and-trailer combos, bumper to bumper, heading in the direction of Hampi. Though the traffic, in the British way, was on their side of the road, it would be impossible to squeeze a tiny motorbike into that line. Nor would Susan

81

want to. Trying to stay positive, she said, "Thank God the bugs are gone."

Ty said nothing, just kept looking to his left. Maybe he was chewing his lip. She couldn't tell. Anyway, he seemed stuck, and that was it for Susan. It occurred to her...could not help but to occur to her...that Ty's *motorcycle envy* had brought them to this awful place. Now what were they going to do? *What?* Well, first off, he needed to get unstuck, perhaps by hearing the obvious.

"The shopkeeper," she said, "was right about the traffic."

"Yep."

"I guess we should have listened."

"Yep."

"Well, Ty, now what?"

"Now?" he said. "Now, I guess, you tell me." It was the sound of impetuous anger that comes from feeling shamed.

Okay, Susan thought, *no sense making things any worse.* Wanting to forgive him, and give both of them some hope, she hugged Ty from behind. "Maybe," she said, "we should turn around and go talk to Mr. Turban. Maybe he knows someone with a pickup and we can get a ride to Hampi back the way we came."

"Nope," Ty said, and turned onto the narrow dirt shoulder that paralleled the line of trucks. Down to their left was a rocky slope pitching toward the river, twenty feet below.

"What the hell are you doing!"

"It's less than three miles. I'll go slow."

"No!" she yelled, "this is too dangerous!"

"I'll be careful!" he yelled back. "I'm always careful!"

Susan squeezed his shirt with her left hand, the torch with her right. They could not have been going more than ten miles per hour, but it felt fast on that hard, dusty, uneven surface. Fumes from the idling trucks made her feel nauseous. They hit a bump and she slipped to the left. Struggling to regain balance, she hugged his waist with her right forearm and almost dropped the light. A terrifying thought. Then, a moment later, it dawned on her she didn't need it. The shoulder was well lit by the trucks crawling along beside them. She turned off the torch, slid it between her and Ty, and held on to him tight.

A few minutes passed. Then, around a corner, came a bridge, their dirt shoulder suddenly interrupted by a high concrete curb. Susan gasped.

Ty swerved from the obstruction, up and onto the road. They missed the side of a trailer by a couple of feet. At the far end of the bridge he bounced back down to the path. Dust rose into Susan's face. She pushed her nose against Ty's shirt, closed her eyes, and gave in to her numbing fear. She felt paralyzed by it. Their movement, slow as it was, seemed unnatural to her frozen mind. It felt like she was being erased. Susan tucked her shrinking self deep into the fabric of his shirt. She remembered her mom holding her close like this, squeezing her from behind, and tried to feel those loving, warming arms around her…tried to remember how safe, always safe, she'd felt as a child.

Then Susan noticed, by the lack of noise, that the highway was behind them. They were off the dirt path. She opened her eyes to what looked like an asphalt road.

Ty yelled, "Where's the light?"

"Oh, shit," she said, "okay, okay," and pulled the torch out from between them. She flicked it on. Aided, as well, by the rising full moon, she saw they were alone. Not another car in sight.

Ty increased his speed to maybe thirty miles an hour.

"Yee-haw!" he screamed.

"Yee-haw!" she mimicked, rubbing his belly with her free left hand.

"Was that crazy or what!"

"Or what!" she yelled back, laughing.

For several minutes, both were quiet with their private thoughts. Susan gave thanks that she'd returned to this world, that they had not been killed, that the ordeal was over and they'd soon be back in their cozy room. The empty road was silent except for their whirring little engine. She began thinking of what restaurant they might find open. She imagined the taste of curry on her tongue. And whiskey! She looked forward to her nice firm bed, and being naked next to Ty, the two of them snuggled together.

"Hospet!" he yelled back to her.

"What?"

"Do you remember a town called Hospet?"

"No," she said. "Why?"

"Because the sign says it's coming up, ahead of Hampi."

"That can't be right. Maybe you were supposed to take another road!"

"Yep!" he said. "MAY BE!"

Though Susan would have expected his confusion, or angry frustration, that's not what she heard. It sounded like a conclusion, and the fevered way he said it gave her chills.

Or was she worrying for no reason? Except for that loony stunt back there he was always a responsible, compassionate guy, and must understand how hard his little *adventure* had been for her. There was no sense in overstating it. Ty would not like that. He prided himself on being reasonable, and the reasonable thing now would be to pull over, turn off the engine, and let them decide, together, what to do.

But that's not what was happening. He wasn't slowing down. It seemed like he was in some sort of trance, like fear had blocked his ability to think.

Maybe he needed to hear her voice. "Honey?"

"No!" he yelled like a battle cry. "Not now!"

That came as a jolt to her entire being. For a moment she felt disconnected from him, flying alone through endless space without any idea who or where she was.

Then came Hospet. It was like entering a nightmare circus tent. Trucks and cars, motorcycles and rickshaws—honking horns and glaring lights—were crowded all around. A cow stood in the middle of the road. There were dogs running, kids riding bicycles, drunken men wobbling across in front of them, and Ty, wow, he just weaved through the whole disjointed mess, dodging whatever showed up and not slowing down. It was as if he'd sworn off brakes. Or maybe they'd stopped working too.

Susan did not know what to say, and knew he had no time to listen. His continuous flow of evasive swerves muddled her mind and made her feel tipsy. Her head felt light. It felt open to the sky. She wondered what was coming next.

Oh my god, she thought, giggling, astounded by her genuine curiosity. *What is going on?* It wasn't fear she felt, it was excitement. Her fear was gone. *Huh, when did that happen? Why?*

But those kinds of questions did not help. Though it made no sense, no sense at all, she felt strangely invulnerable, even blessed, and knew better than to doubt it.

They came to a red light and Ty proved he could stop if he needed to. Neither of them spoke. Not a word. Engines revved all around. There was a motorcycle on their right. A young woman sat on the back, sideways. Beautiful and elegant, like a fairy princess. There was a red dot on her forehead. She wore a blue sari, very fancy, and had a flowing pink scarf that dangled down just above the wheel, as if that were perfectly safe. The woman smiled at her and waved. Susan smiled and waved back. She saw an old man staring at her from inside a rickshaw. He gave her a toothless smile, then laughed.

The light turned green. Off they all went.

At one busy intersection Ty charged in front of a bus, forcing *it* to brake for *him.* Susan's heart raced. She tightened her grip around his belly. She was loving this, that she felt part of this. They shot down an empty road. She had no idea why. They rounded one corner, and another, suddenly faced with a camel standing sideways, blocking their way. *Yes, a fucking camel!*

They bounced onto the sidewalk, squirted past the baffled beast and back down to the road, as if nothing could be easier, as if nothing could ever make them stop.

GYPSY

It is late afternoon. Warm and breezy. Andrew sits alone on a wrought iron bench in the central plaza of Antofagasta, Chile, thinking about his life.

Yesterday he turned forty, and he suspects that no one gave him a moment's thought. That was what consumed him throughout the eighteen-hour bus ride from Puerto Montt. It was an overnight bus but he didn't sleep, wondering then, as now, *why have things gone so wrong?*

On the west side of the plaza, beyond the fountain and far benches, is a row of huge palm trees. Their long-fingered fronds twist in the wind like angry knives. Andrew stares at them, unable to calm his mind. Angry knives? Why is *that* what he sees? Why not the skirts of exotic dancers fanning the humid plaza? He looks away, down at his feet. He's unable to get a full breath of air. The salty breeze wafts over him, stifling, like a thick wet blanket.

There he goes again!

Why does everything seem such a threat?

He needs to lighten up, needs to relax.

On a bench to his left, across the path, sits an old man, someone Andrew would consider the very image of dignity—his dark brown skin a perfect complement to his silvering gray hair and silky white herringbone suit—except kneeling at his feet is a voluptuous young gypsy woman.

To Andrew, who would rather see it otherwise, this looks anything but innocent. She cups the old man's palm in her slender fingers. Her earnest face is bent toward its lines. The old man's eyebrows crinkle and twitch, perhaps at what she is seeing in his future. Or perhaps, more likely, at the breasts bulging above her blouse.

Andrew saw the gypsy tents that morning on the edge of town. A capricious wind was swirling. Though the thick fog of dawn had surrendered to the first rays of sun, the tents stood shivering on the desert plain. Most everyone on the bus was awake and eyeing the encampment.

A small girl in her daddy's lap hoped out loud, *"Tal vez es un circo!"*

What innocence, thought Andrew, to believe it might be a circus.

"No," said the woman sitting behind them. *"Gitanos."*

The woman next to her said, *"Un circo de monos."*

Then the gossiping began.

From what Andrew could gather, given his shaky grasp of Spanish, the women had nothing good to say about gypsies. To call them "a circus of monkeys" was bad enough, but the words "shameless" and "whores" were repeated often.

The men kept to themselves, or nodded in agreement, while ogling the camp with obvious interest.

Later, from his hotel's cafe, Andrew saw some gypsy women passing by, dressed in their layered veils, a fluttering sensuality he could almost feel.

"Gitanas," said a voice behind him.

Andrew turned to see the cook leaning over the counter. Since the man never shifted his gaze from the passing women, it could be assumed he'd been talking to himself. When Andrew looked back to the street they were gone.

"Cheap-seas," said the cook.

"What?"

"Chew needs berry berry caredfool meestair."

"I speak Spanish," Andrew said in Spanish, with what he believed was a perfect accent.

The cook looked doubtful. An old crust of a fellow, his dark eyes seemed to perch within their swollen sockets like a pair of owls. He smiled and wiped at his face with a big beefy hand. Then, in the slowest of Spanish, he said, "Pretty women, you like to look at them."

"Whenever I can," said Andrew.

But for the cook it was plainly no joking matter. "Well, friend," he said with a scowl, "don't look too close at those."

"You know them?" said Andrew.

"No, I have never seen them before."

"Never? Then how can you—?"

"Hah!" laughed the cook. "Good try, friend, but you can't fool me. Or them. And it's lucky for us that they don't fool the police. Why do you think gypsies travel? It is not because they like to, *no no no,* it's because they must."

Not sure he understood, and, if he did, unimpressed by the logic, Andrew decided to focus on what interested him most: "Why are there only women?"

"What?"

"I mean, where are the men?"

"Oh, the men, yes, the men. They stay at camp. Stay in their tents and drink, make their silly baubles, you know, bangles and trinkets, while the women are in town making money."

Unfamiliar with the Spanish words for bauble, bangle, and trinket, Andrew ignored what struck him as irrelevant details. He did, however, get what he wanted to know: that the men were not around. "The women are probably out looking for us tourists, right?"

"For any man who looks like he has *pesos.*"

88

"What is it they sell?"

The cook cracked up at that. "Your trouble, friend, is having all these questions!"

Andrew did not appreciate the man's sarcastic look or tone. What was wrong with having questions?

The cook laughed again and pointed. "You are like a bird with your back to the cat." He then slowed his speech to a stalking sort of crawl. "I am warning you, mister, to be careful. Yes, you may speak our language, but you do not speak theirs. You have no idea what can happen."

The clear condescension was like a slap to Andrew's face. It reminded him of his father, another know-it-all type, and triggered in him, as it had when he was a boy, the compulsion to ignore everything being said. His mind shut down while the cook kept talking, the man's emphatic words and gestures flying past in a meaningless blur.

Then it got quiet again, and there was the cook's red face, his intense dark eyes. The tourist in Andrew regretted having blanked. What if he'd missed something valuable? "I am sorry," he said, "I do not understand."

"That is what I am telling you! That is the problem!"

The cook's jowls were quivering. He was not finished, not by a long shot, and would have kept talking had the waitress not waved an order in his face.

Andrew paid his bill. After leaving the cafe he walked the streets for hours. But the cook stayed in his head and needed to be dealt with. The man had made him feel like an idiot, as if there were something wrong with being curious. Andrew disagreed. He was proud of his willingness to ask questions, to admit his uncertainty. He was not, like most men, afraid of looking vulnerable.

Eventually he found the central plaza, and this empty bench, and now, because of the old man and the young gypsy woman, he has a whole new set of questions. *Onward!*

Suddenly feeling better, he looks up into the cloudless sky. He is thankful for a place to sit and gather himself;

thankful for the warm sunny day; and, yes, thankful for the swaying palms and thick salty air.

He must never give in to cynics like the cook. The way he sees it, the verb *to question* is derived from the root *to quest*. And that's what life is, isn't it? A quest? A journey? A journey, to be sure, with its share of risks, but how else does a person get where he needs to go?

Would he have left an unhappy marriage had he not questioned his feelings for other women?

To take risks, of course, can sometimes be quite risky. *Hah!* Like his love affair with Ishana. He'd like to laugh it off, but can't. He thinks of her last letter, of the sentence: *I do not want a relationship that insists on definition.*

Could that mean she no longer wants to be with him?

It seems that no matter how hard he tries to understand, some things remain a mystery. How, for instance, can Ishana say he is *meant to be hers,* that she can *see him beside her in dreams and visions,* while demanding the freedom to have sex with others? How can she have it both ways? What makes her think that he will blindly swallow whatever the hell she says?

"We are part of each other's destiny," she once said, as if such new-age spiritual claptrap should be taken seriously!

As if angels were real!

As if the Age of Reason never happened!

Andrew shakes his head. Since life is full of actual mysteries, why compound the confusion with wishful fictions? Why not ponder things that matter, like how to wean oneself from insatiable self-serving fantasies? Simple truth is what counts, that much is clear, but one must be willing to seek it out, must not be afraid of the quest.

It is not the right answer you seek, he tells himself, *it is the right question.*

With that in mind, he ponders the beautiful young gypsy woman. What might she be saying to the old man? She seems innocent enough to Andrew. Or is she, as the women on the bus would believe, a whore? Is she being intentionally seductive, her forearms stretched across the old man's thighs, her eyes holding his as she whispers, softly, like a child wanting candy?

Andrew wonders if she is aware of him watching from his bench; watching as her henna-tattooed feet meld into the cobblestones; watching as her pert young breasts graze the old man's knees. Curious about the body beneath those diaphanous layers, he imagines what a joy it would be to remove them.

To his credit, Andrew looks away, disgusted by how easily he's aroused. He remembers the cook's warning. And agrees. There are better things to contemplate than the breasts of young women! That geezer in the suit could be him one day if he doesn't watch out!

He swings his attention back to the palms, back to the slicing knives. But why be so hard on himself? To be fair, what normal man would not get excited by those breasts? How can such feelings be avoided? Why should they be? Yes, granted, he has his share of inappropriate thoughts, but for the most part Andrew keeps them private, as any civilized person would, and tries to be respectful.

He looks back to the bench.

The old man and the young gypsy woman are gone.

What happened?

Oh, who cares? Whatever it was, Andrew congratulates himself for missing it: *a victory for serious self-contemplation.* He closes his eyes and calms his breath, hoping for greater insights, when suddenly distracted by a whiff of lavender, a hand on his knee, and the dark-haired beauty crouched in front of him.

"Speaka English?" she says.

She is younger than he thought, perhaps in her late teens.

"Why, yes," says Andrew. "But I am surprised you do."

"I speaka leetle."

She glances behind her, as if aware of being watched. And he sees it's true. Three adolescent girls now occupy the bench where the old man sat. They turn to each other and giggle. On a bench to his right sits a middle-aged man with a white fedora and thick round spectacles. The lenses shimmer like two little mirrors as he stares at Andrew, purses his lips, and gives his head a barely perceptible shake.

Andrew looks back at the girl. "What is your name?"

"Oh no," she says, blushing. "You say again?"

"Como te llamas?" he says, purposefully using the familiar tense.

The girl's face relaxes as she leans forward. Her eyes grow bigger, brighter than before, and reach out for his.

"Me llamo Flor."

Flower. What a beautiful and fitting name.

"Tu nombre," he says, *"es muy bonita."*

"Gracias Señor. Esta es para ti."

Her breasts graze his knees as she opens her hand and holds, severed from its stem, a single white rose. Their fingers touch as she lays it in his palm.

A haggard old woman drops down beside them. Andrew flinches, unable not to stare at the frazzled gray hair, the long arching nose, the brownish mole protruding from her chin. "Hello sir," she says in English, with no trace of an accent.

"Oh. Hello."

She takes the rose out of his hand and whispers in Flor's ear. The girl listens and watches Andrew, her lips trembling.

"Adiós," Flor says to him.

She jumps to her feet and runs away.

"What's wrong?" he says to the old woman.

"I told her she must leave."

"Why?"

"Because it is not safe. Because you are in danger, terrible danger, and I do not want my grand-daughter dragged into it."

"What do you mean?"

"You know what I mean," she scolds, getting to her feet. "You know exactly what I mean!"

Andrew says, "Wait a minute. You must have me confused with someone else."

Now it's the old woman who flinches. She hesitates, then drops back to her knees. A look of wonder covers her face and her eyes soften.

"No," she says, "is it possible you are not aware?"

"I don't know. Of what?"

"There is a woman, yes?"

"A woman?"

"A young blond woman. She pursues your soul, I see it...like a hawk after a mouse to feed her hungry chicks."

Andrew shivers as she speaks, a vision of Ishana popping into his mind. He sees her curly blond hair and keen blue eyes. He remembers her conscious affinity to hawks, and how she once danced naked on the bed, hovering above him, pretending to be one. "Tell me more," he says.

The old woman reaches out. She takes his right hand, opens it, and places Flor's rose back into his palm. "All will be told," she says, "when you are ready to be told."

"I am ready."

The old woman cups Andrew's hand in hers, gently squeezing his fingers together around the rose, and intones, like the holiest of vows, "I bless you with the innocence of my Flor." Her dark eyes feel unpleasantly large and close. "You understand, young man, that this is a serious thing?"

He nods.

"You are certain?"

"Yes."

"If you truly understand," she says, "you will give an offering."

"Oh." *What was I thinking? I should have known this would not be free.* "How much?"

"You can decide what Flor's blessing is worth."

He feels a wave of distress. Again the cook is in his mind. "I am warning you, mister, to be careful." Though Andrew hates to admit it, maybe the guy was right, maybe this is a big mistake. What should he do?

As he hesitates, the old gypsy's eyes bore into his. "It is not a question of *money,* sir, it is a question of *sacrifice.*

You must offer something of personal worth. The spirit needs to know what you are willing to give."

"I'm sorry, Señora, I am not feeling comfortable with—"

"Well, what do you expect? Do you think a sacrifice can be easy?"

"The truth is," he says, lying, "I can't spend much right now because—"

"Forget the money. My Flor cannot give her blessings unless you open up, open up completely and—"

The old woman stops talking. She squints, looking worried, then stands and crosses herself. Slowly, she begins to back up. Andrew hears the sound of a distant whistle, wondering if that's the problem. He watches as she turns and hurries across the courtyard. She settles beneath those palms at the far edge of the plaza.

Examining the flower in his hand, he feels flushed with the odd sensation that there is something missing. Though he has grown tired of this little drama, and is hungry, maybe it's not quite time to leave. Maybe, with the grandmother gone, Flor will return for her rose.

The thought of it frightens him. Why? It's doubtful she'll come back, but if she does it's no big deal. He can afford to spend a few bucks for a make-believe blessing from a sexy young woman. What could be wrong with that?

He sits on the bench for another ten minutes, basking in his strong desire to see her again. He imagines Flor holding his hand and rubbing up against him, wanting to believe it is all somehow meant to be. He waits, flower in his open palm, and with each passing moment his excitement builds.

But Andrew can't fool himself for long. What an idiot, to think this might be simple! He sees the old lady under the palm trees. She sees him too, is aware of him waiting, as she talks with other gypsy women.

Flor is nowhere in sight. They've made sure of that.

He is not surprised when one of the women starts walking his way. *Oh, dear, here it comes.* Andrew knows he should get up and leave, but doesn't.

94

The woman smiles, says hello, adjusts her many skirts and sits next to him on the bench. Her tangled auburn hair is streaked with gray. She looks burdened by the many strands of stone around her neck.

She says, "My mother is worried about you."

It's in his interest, Andrew decides, to show he's thought things through. "Or perhaps," he says, "she's worried about police...being harassed by the police."

"You do not understand."

"That's what I keep getting told."

"It has nothing to do with police. We are trying to help. This hawkwoman, she has powers, she can hurt you."

"How?"

"She already has. You let her inside and now can't get her out. And it will get worse, believe me, much much worse. You need my Flor's blessing."

"Yes, all right, I want her blessing, but you need to tell me what it will cost."

"It is not a question of money, sir, it is—"

"I know, I know, a question of *sacrifice*, okay, and I—"

"This is about your soul!" the gypsy says, her voice low but sharp, her eyes electric. "The hawkwoman, she possesses it. Possesses you! She has you in her grasp the same as you have my Flor's rose. Mother sees these things...sees that my daughter can free you from this evil. You will never again need to fear such creatures. Your life can begin like new. Who knows what wondrous things might happen?"

Andrew is impressed by the truth within her lies. Yes, Ishana does, in a way, possess him. Unfortunately, even if he could be freed, he's not convinced he wants her to let go. The truth is, he would probably do anything to keep her holding on.

Anything? Oh, Christ, how pitiful is that!

How did he get so tangled up?

He thinks of Flor, of her gentle eyes. Maybe this will be more than spending time with a beautiful woman. Maybe a gypsy reading his palm will, indeed, help, will untie his knotted mind, will give him back his needed self-control.

"You can go to a private place and receive my daughter's blessing," says the gypsy. "But first you must give something of personal worth, to show you are sincere. Something small, some valued possession. Do you have an icon of your patron saint?"

"I don't have a patron saint."

"A picture of your mother?"

"No."

"A crucifix?"

He shakes his head.

"Please, sir, there must be something."

"I'm traveling light," he says.

"Too bad," the woman says. She sighs, and looks like she's thinking it over. "I suppose, though it's not worth a great deal in matters of the spirit, you could give money."

Andrew nods. No surprise there. Even if he had the icon of a patron saint, he's certain this would have come down to money. That is what these gypsies want, and they won't stop until they get it. But he's not worried. He remembers the old woman saying that he can decide what to spend.

Yes, well, good luck with that!

Having been in the country only a few days, Andrew is still struggling to understand the currency. As with Argentina before, Chile has an outlandish exchange rate, rising and falling in leaps and bounds on a daily basis. At the bank that morning he cashed three hundred dollars. His wallet is full to bursting with twenty-thousand peso notes. He used one to pay for breakfast and was shocked to get eighteen thousand in return.

Calculating fast, deciding on what he believes to be ten dollars, he says, "From here I'm going to Peru and Ecuador. I can afford five thousand."

The gypsy takes a breath. She holds a hand over her heart, as if injured by his words. "That is what my beautiful Flor is worth?"

96

"Wait," he says, re-calculating, "let me think."

"I see the creature in your mind, this very moment, saying you should not take my daughter's blessing!"

Yeah, right. She must know that there is nothing in his mind *this very moment* except for lovely Flor. After five weeks of traveling, sorely missing sex with Ishana and afraid it will never happen again, he cannot help lusting for the young gypsy woman.

The sad truth is, at *this very moment,* he's hoping, almost praying, that Flor will give him more than just a common blessing. This gypsy pretending to be her mother knows that's what he's thinking. She's playing dumb, stringing him along, but they both know that if he wants Flor to hold something other than his hand it will cost extra, a negotiation to happen later. What's happening now is the opening gambit, when he shows interest. The lower he can keep the initial offer, he figures, the less he'll end up paying.

These and other tactical concerns churn through his mind; also waves of self-disgust for giving in to the seduction.

And yes, it must be said, Andrew regrets his undeniable depravity. But the chance of having Flor to himself is like an ocean liner at full steam, slicing through his guilt without a splash.

"Please, sir," says the gypsy woman, "do not let yourself be tricked again!"

Her words send a sudden chill swirling through his chest.

"Sir?"

He registers her voice but does not respond. The chill has reached his mind and stiffened, taken form, surfaced like an iceberg: a freezing cold and sobering thought: a thought he would rather not have, but, thank God, cannot avoid:

You're not fooling anyone, you fool!

"Sir, are you all right?"

As if the heavens opened up, swallowing the darkness, he looks past his starved libido, past his self-delusion, past the gypsy's searching gaze, and sees the waiting trap!

Oh yes, this woman knows he'll pay plenty to be with Flor. Knows he'll do whatever it takes to make that happen. He imagines the cheap hotel room on the edge of town. After being alone with her for less than a minute, a group of men will barge in, harangue him for taking advantage of their sister, or cousin, or wife—*whoever*—then beat and rob him, tie him to the bed frame, stick a dirty rag in his mouth and leave him there, bloody, alone, and penniless.

The stark vision shakes Andrew back to common sense. As if by design, this has happened in order that he learn what must be learned.

Truth comes as a question he shudders to ask.

Is suffering always the cost of desire?

"You see!" cries the gypsy. "She is there, inside you, spreading her lies!"

"I need to go."

"If you go without an offering, sir, I am afraid Flor's rose will rot inside your soul."

"Take it then."

He offers the flower, but the gypsy leans back on her haunches, out of reach. "No," she says. "Now it is yours. If you are not wise enough to give something for its blessing, the creature will take hold of it, will use it as a curse."

Clever, he thinks...*a game that cannot be lost!*

He doesn't know what to do. Though he could, right now, get up and walk away, that would leave this thing unfinished. He must admit that her threatening tone has shaken him. His mind is buzzing, his heart is beating fast. Sweat drips from his armpits.

You screwed up again, Andrew, and now you have to pay! Don't try worming out of it, don't go making things any worse!

"Okay," he says, setting the rose in his lap and pulling out his wallet, "I will give you the five thousand."

"Sorry, sir, but five is not enough."

"Well, too bad, that's what I'm going to give."

He fingers open the wallet to its thick pack of currency, trying to remember where he put the smaller notes. But before he can find them she is there, in and out, a fistful of money in her hand.

He grabs her wrist and glares into her eyes. *"Let go!"*

"Please," she pleads, "you do not know what it takes. This demon is not easy to get rid of. You may not have another chance."

He squeezes hard, then harder, until she cries out and lets go of the bills.

She pulls her hand loose and gets to her feet.

Andrew gathers the money from his lap, then looks up. Her eyes are wet, full of outrage, and also, it seems, resolve, as if their little skirmish were nothing compared to what is coming.

"Too bad," she says. "You have sealed your fate."

With that she turns and goes, joining the old gypsy beneath the far palms. He sees Flor too. They listen as the woman tells her story, shaking their heads and crossing their hearts.

Andrew feels their eyes as he gets up from the bench.

He leaves behind the mangled white rose.

When the gypsies hurry off in the other direction, Andrew sighs relief. He praises himself for escaping their claws.

For over an hour he walks, happy and carefree, street after street, thinking he's in search of a good restaurant before realizing, to his surprise, he has lost his appetite. In fact, feels slightly ill. As night begins to fall his head begins to pound. With no idea where he is, he asks a policeman for directions and learns that his hotel is around the next corner.

He hurries to his room, locks the door, makes it to the bed and buries himself under the covers.

Though not his original plan, Andrew leaves Antofagasta early the next morning on a bus bound for Arica. He tries to sleep, but the road is bumpy and the wind is blowing hard. His eyes flash open. Sand fills the air, beats at the windows,

99

envelops the bus in a dark howling whorl. The driver pulls over, announcing he will wait for the storm to pass.

A few minutes later a huge dump truck crashes into them from behind. No one dies, but many of the passengers have scrapes or bruises, and there are some serious injuries. Andrew has what feels like whiplash. He's unable to move his neck from side to side.

He returns to Antofagasta in an ambulance.

The hospital is clean, codeine takes away the pain, the nurses are kind and the doctors concerned. Still, he does not feel safe. He hears the gypsy woman in his head.

"You have sealed your fate!" she keeps saying.

What the hell does that mean?

After two days, still in pain, he moves to a hotel by the airport. He double-bolts his door. The following night he catches a flight to Houston, then another to San Francisco.

For a week Andrew lies at home in bed, doped up and despondent. The assurance by three separate doctors that there is "no apparent damage" does not make him feel better.

What do they know about curses?

And he doesn't want to believe in curses either. There must be some more reasonable explanation.

Be patient, he tells himself. *Patient.*

Though tempted, Andrew resists contacting Ishana. He's not supposed to be back for another two weeks. She might interpret his early return as a sign of weakness. He knows it would be best to put her out of his mind, once and for all, but he's not quite ready for that. No, not yet.

When his vacation ends he agrees to a neck brace and resumes his duties as a docent at the de Young Museum. He expects that Ishana will call him. Day after day she doesn't. He grows weary of his museum tours, weary of the people and their silly questions, weary of the paintings he's seen too often. After a month, Andrew insists he cannot handle the pain and goes on extended sick leave.

100

At last he breaks down and calls Ishana. He leaves a message but she does not call back.

From then on, every day, he calls. Her message of "Leave me a message" is all he ever gets.

He chews his nails like he did as a teenager. At night he wakes up scratching his scalp. He looks for ants in his hair, or maybe fleas, but finds nothing. Sleeping pills don't work. Wine seems to makes things worse.

This goes on for weeks, when at last he dials the number, bursts into tears, and screams into her answering machine, "Where? Where are you? Where?"

The next afternoon Ishana is at his door, saying she is sorry, saying she arrived late last night from a long trip, saying she has missed him too.

He wants to know where she's been, but will not ask.

She does his pile of dishes and cooks him dinner.

He apologizes for his outburst on the phone.

She smiles, rubs his neck, and says not to worry. She is sweet. Irresistibly sweet. He's already feeling better. Maybe this was what he needed all along?

She helps him off with his shirt and massages his shoulders and back. She tells him to relax, to "let things go."

When he invites her to spend the night, she agrees.

He wants to make love.

Carefully, they do.

In the morning, before leaving, she promises to come by when she gets back from yet another trip, refusing to tell him where she's going, or for how long, or if she's going alone.

"You have to trust me," Ishana says.

He closes the door and goes back to bed.

Days go by, uncounted. When unable to sleep, Andrew bides his time with a precarious juggling of whiskey, pot, and pain pills. That usually knocks him out. He often dreams of birds, streams of them, flying from bottomless nests, and long lizard tails disappearing down slick dark holes. "You're losing ground," he tells his reflection in the mirror. That makes him laugh. His condition has become so pitiful that even he can't miss the humor.

And he knows it's not Ishana's fault. How wrong to think that she could make him whole.

It is a question of sacrifice.

That's what the old gypsy woman said.

He walks to the florist shop on Divisadero and buys a single white rose. He returns home, removes its stem, and places the flower in the center of his kitchen table, in full sight of the south-facing window. With great discomfort, but greater resolve, he drags his rocker from the living room. He finds the perfect spot, at the north end of the table, not caring that the oversized chair blocks access to the bedroom.

Drinking only water, eating only apples and almonds, Andrew watches the rose wilt. Occasionally he dozes off, or uses the bathroom, but mostly he sits and watches.

Two weeks pass by as he waits with what seems to him must be faith.

The pedals have long since dropped off.

Delicate as angel wings, they slowly turn to dust.

INDIO

They'd started south, many hours ago, from Mexico City. After a long breakdown in the hot mid-day sun, the bus was fixed and rattling down the road.

"Ah," said Molly, who'd been complaining she had a headache, was hungry, and needed a toilet, "the pleasures of cross-country travel." Lance felt the intended jab. Usually they flew to Guatemala, but this year, because he'd wanted to "shake things up," they were on an old rickety bus. "A mistake," Molly told him, "we'll never make again."

The driver pulled off for gas. While the bus was still rolling, Molly charged down the aisle and hovered near the exit, her face pinched with suppressed panic, desperate for a stop that could not happen fast enough.

Soon as the door opened she was off and running.

Lance waited outside the bus.

It was at times like this he envied smokers.

A man walked up and stood in front of him. He was short, lean, and had a noticeable odor, as if he'd just finished a hard day's work. The man smiled and said, "Hello."

"Hello," said Lance, returning the smile, though he never felt comfortable around strangers, especially ones so eager to be friendly. Such unwarranted niceness made him nervous. Suspicious. And the look of this guy didn't help. It wasn't that his left arm was gone from the elbow down. It wasn't that his clothes were dirty.

What worried Lance, along with the guy's big bright smile, was the Bible clutched in his right hand.

"You are American," the stranger said with a strong Spanish accent. "From where?"

That question gave Lance hope. He'd heard it often in Mexico and Guatemala, and guessed, based on those experiences, that this guy wanted to talk about where he'd worked in the states.

Sure, Lance thought, *we can talk about that.*

"We live in Northern California."

"Los Angeles?"

"Well, no. But close enough."

"Is pleasing to meet you," the guy said. "I am Gerardo."

Lance widened his smile. What else could he do? It felt odd that because of the missing arm, and Bible, they could not shake hands. "Nice to meet you, too," he said, and introduced himself.

"I am working in your country," said Gerardo. "I have two years in Houston."

"That's great. Where?"

"Houston. I am working in a place that is calling Houston," he said. "Is in Texas."

Limited as Lance's Spanish was, it had to be better than Gerardo's English. "Yes," he said, "I know where Houston is. What did you do there? I mean, where did you work?"

"Oh, you speak good Spanish," Gerardo said, seamlessly switching languages. "At first I washed cars and houses. Then I washed dishes at Hooters."

Gerardo said it as if confident that all Americans were familiar with Hooters. It would be like assuming that all Mexicans were familiar with bullfights. Well, yeah. But few had ever been to one. Lance now expected, perhaps as prelude to a Christian rant, some big-titty jokes. A week in macho Mexico had twisted his sensibilities, made him cynical, because Gerardo said nothing of his job—or its voluminous perks—only that he'd done it, was tired, and was returning to his home in Guatemala.

Lance was wrong to prejudge this guy. He appreciated Gerardo's soft voice, his gentle eyes, his indigenous simplicity.

Molly returned and handed Lance a bag of jalapeno cheese puffs. She was smiling, was clearly over her bad mood. He hugged her close and introduced Gerardo.

The driver coaxed them back into the bus.

Gerardo shifted places to sit across from Lance and Molly. That was not good news for the woman he sat next to, who had previously managed a seat to herself. When a casual hand gesture failed to evict the intruder, then an icy stare, she winced, snorted, and scooted past him.

"Pinche Indio," she said, moving to the rear of the bus.

Gerardo seemed familiar with the racist snub. Lance also knew her kind of prejudice. Many Mexicans, like this woman, acted as if they were allergic to Indians. Lance had a Mexico City friend named Joaquin. He loved the guy except for his Indian slurs. Joaquin would taunt some pal by calling him "Indio," as if there could be nothing worse.

One day, fed up, Lance asked why Mexicans hate Indians.

"No," Joaquin said, "of course we do not hate them. We only joke."

"Why?"

"You want me to be honest. Fine. It is because of their smell and the way they act. For us they are like animals."

"No, man, they're just poor."

"I am also poor," Joaquin said, "but I am different. I do not sit around like them with pitiful dirty faces. Like dogs or

105

pigs. You do not live here. It is easy to think whatever you want. A dangerous mistake. Watch out, friend, because you never know how an Indio thinks. Never."

Gerardo continued to clutch his Bible, but the sermon Lance expected never came.

Oh yes, there was the inevitable *"Gracias a Dios"* when referring to the good parts of his difficult life. Other than that, not a single allusion to God. Nor did Gerardo mention any problems he'd had as an illegal in the United States. It would have been easy to play the victim, to tug on Lance's and Molly's sympathy. Instead, he talked of his village, Escuipulas, on the outskirts of San Marcos: of the tiny piece of land he owns, *Gracias a Dios;* of the tomatoes and beans he grows there, *Gracias a Dios;* of how good it will be, *Gracias a Dios,* to see his family again.

He told them about María, his wife, "who can talk with chickens," and how she saved the money he'd sent until she could buy some special pig. His five-year-old daughter, Maricela, has a harelip. "She also has the eyes of an angel," he said. "I have not seen my boy, Pablo, since he was a baby, but he knows who I am. María says he points at the picture of me standing in front of Hooters and says *Papa.*"

Of Hooters, Gerardo said merely that they liked him, were upset he decided to leave, and promised he could have his job back the following year.

"I told them no. If God permits, I will stay home. I want to be done with America."

"Good for you," said Molly.

Lance knew, because she'd said it often, how upset Molly was by Guatemalan men leaving their homes, ruining their families, chasing the dream of a better life in *El Norte.* Clearly heartened by Gerardo's decision, she asked more questions. Given enough time, she could get the most intimate information out of the shyest stranger. Lance likes to joke that within five minutes she knows how many times a woman has been married, the date of her last period, and the kinkiest details of her sex life.

Good thing that Gerardo loved talking about his family. His stories were wonderful—a great distraction from the road and his strong pervading odor. *But hey, who wouldn't smell after three continuous days and nights on a bus?*

Tapachula came like a shock. Close to the Guatemalan border, a known hub of drug smugglers and thieving gangs, Lance had been warned it was a frightening town, even in the daytime, and it was now nearly two in the morning. Gerardo whispered to him, "I was here two years ago, Señor, on my way to Texas. This is a bad place. We should stay together."

The man looked defenseless with his missing arm, his death-grip on the Bible.

"Yes," Lance assured him, "we will."

While he and Molly collected their duffels from the bus, Gerardo waved down a taxi.

Lance looked in his *Lonely Planet* at the few hotels he'd circled. To each of the names the taxi driver shook his head.

"Ya no existe." No longer here.

Their five-year-old guidebook again turned Molly's mood dark and sour. Lance's fault, because it was he who'd decided not to buy a new one. He'd argued that they didn't need it, that Mexico hadn't changed much since their trip in 1994. Well, yes, in general that was true, but generalities didn't matter when specific needs—like finding a safe hotel in a town like Tapachula—could not be met.

Lance had always been opposed to guidebooks. One of his over-used jokes was that anything recommended in the *Lonely Planet* is something to be avoided. He'd tried his best to ignore *the gringo trail*. But because of Molly's recent inheritance, and increased desire for comfort, it was a trail they were growing accustomed to. His constant complaint was that a guarantee of comfort negates the chance of a true experience. Molly would jab back that, no matter what he said, Lance was thankful they no longer traveled like a couple of hippies. They had money now. They could afford to eat at good restaurants and sleep in nice hotels. And yeah, she was right, he did feel thankful.

Still, he missed the days of pure adventure, the risks they'd sometimes taken, when they never knew what might happen next.

Molly said, "Take us to the best hotel in this town."

"There is one," said the taxi driver. *"La Posada.* But it is full. The rest are all the same."

Gerardo looked nervous, perhaps worried he could not afford the kind of place that Molly wanted. Lance said to him, "Where did you stay before?"

Gerardo said, "I know of a good place. Very safe. It is called *La Penguina.*"

Molly took the guidebook and looked it up. "Not listed." She stared at Lance and slowly shook her head.

The taxi driver did the same. "Well?" he said.

Well, okay, with no opportunity at two in the morning to shop around, Lance decided to take their new friend's advice. They piled into the taxi and took off.

"It's not much farther," Gerardo told the driver after what seemed too long a time. They passed by squat, filthy, paint-starved buildings, down bumpy pot-holed streets getting narrower with every turn.

Suddenly they saw it, a tiny whitish hotel crouched in the looming darkness like a homeless ghost. On its drooping sign was a faded pink penguin. Had they been alone, Lance would have gotten them out of there fast.

Molly looked frightened. "What should we do?"

He didn't know.

Gerardo said, "It is a good hotel, Señora Molly. The owner, Manuel, is a very nice man, and the rooms have locks."

"At least he knows the owner," said Lance.

It sounded so lame coming out of his mouth.

Molly leaned back in the seat and closed her eyes.

Lance and Gerardo climbed the steps. They took turns pounding on the door.

A slot opened up. "It's late," a man said. He did sound reasonably nice considering they'd woken him in the middle of the night. "You want a room?"

In the old days, Lance would have asked to look inside, check the beds and get a sense of the place, but he knew there was no chance of that. "Yes," he said. "Thank you."

Decisions get easy when there aren't any options.

A couple of drunks meandered up the street, arms around each other, singing. Dogs howled in the distance.

The taxi driver helped the Americans lug their two big duffel bags up the stairs and into the front hallway. There was little room to stand, but the place looked clean enough. The manager's name, however, was Rafael, not Manuel, and he had no memory of Gerardo.

By then Lance didn't care. Raphael was smiling, perhaps because his lost sleep was paying off. He pointed at the heavy, oversized bags. "Lots of clothes," he said.

Molly said, "No, old shoes." And to Rafael's expected confusion she said, "I have a way for people to donate the ones they don't want. Shoes for children. I bring them down to schools in Guatemala."

"She's been doing it a long time," said Lance.

"Ten years," she said. "It's not usually this difficult."

"Usually we go by plane," Lance said, hoping that might suffice to acknowledge and clearly justify her frustration. Apparently, it did.

Rafael put the Americans in his *very best room,* the five-dollar special. Its private bathroom had a sulfur-stained toilet, a dripping sink, and a waterless shower. Lance closed the door to diminish the stench of urine and chlorine-treated mildew. "Ah," he sighed, "good to know that some things never change."

He could see that Molly was not amused.

Gerardo had taken the cheapest room. It cost five *pesos*—fifty cents—and was out by a stinking chicken coop, far from the communal bathroom. Lance went to say goodnight. The Guatemalan peeked past a thin rusty chain. He stared at Lance, making sure it was him, then dragged a chair away from the door and opened it as far as the chain would allow. The American handed him a few pieces of toilet paper, knowing none would be provided.

Gerardo thanked him, then said, "Did you hear what Rafael told me about the shuttles?"

"No."

"They leave for the border at six in the morning."

"Oh. Yeah, okay. My watch has an alarm. I'll set it."

"Good," Gerardo said.

The guy looked exhausted.

"Well," said Lance, "see you in a few hours."

Gerardo nodded, closed the door, and Lance could hear him dragging the chair back. *What the hell?* He hurried to their room, latched the door, and pushed one of the chairs against it.

"What are you doing?" said Molly.

"I don't know," he said. "Stupid," he said, pushing it aside.

"No," she said, "smart," and re-blocked the door.

Christ, he should have known not to kick her paranoia into gear! She helped him stack their bags behind the chair.

Then, warm though it was, she kept her clothes on and got under the covers.

Lance set the alarm for five-thirty and lay down on the bed. It was hard as a granite slab. He reached under Molly's shirt and began rubbing her belly. He wanted to make love, if for no other reason than to release his nervous tension.

She pushed away his hand. "You've got to be kidding."

Lance wished he was. He turned away and tried to fall asleep. Not an easy thing with dogs howling from every corner of the night. Thinking it might help, he imagined they were having a sing-along, a kind of mongrel hootenanny. It went on and on, in harmonies too primitive for humans to appreciate, with sadness too base for humans

110

to comprehend, a sorrowful dirge lamenting their life on the street, their daily hunger, their constant fear. Joaquin looked down from the dense dark sky, like a god. He whispered, "Careful, my friend, Indios are full of fleas." Lance felt a large hairy beast lying next to him, could smell its thick, wet, unwashed fur. He didn't want to look, didn't want to know what it was. He tried to get away but could not budge. Something grabbed his shoulder and his head began to spin.

"Wake up," Molly whispered.

His eyes shot open. "What?" Then he heard a knocking on the door. Was he still dreaming? He tried to get up but Molly held on tight, would not let him go.

"I couldn't sleep," she whispered. "I kept wondering about *him*."

"Him?" he whispered back. "Him who?"

"Gerardo."

"Why? I don't understand what—"

"Because it seems like, like he's hiding something, like he's, I don't know, I—"

Lance threw up his hands, suddenly awake and certain what was happening. "Geez, Moll, where do you get this shit?" Pushing past her, he removed the bags, shoved the chair aside, cracked open the door and stared out at Gerardo. The American felt exactly like the Guatemalan looked last night, protected by a thin rusty chain.

"Señor Lance, Rafael says the vans are leaving soon."

Lance remembered, and looked at his watch. A quarter to six! "My alarm," he said, "it didn't go off, I guess, or—"

"Please, Señor, we have to go!"

"Yeah, okay. We'll be right out."

He closed the door and went for his pants.

"Well?" Molly whispered.

"We have to hurry."

"Something's wrong, *Lance*."

"Wrong?"

"He doesn't have anything. Tell me why he doesn't have anything."

"Well, *Moll,* how should I know? What do you expect him to—"

"He's got a Bible."

"Yeah."

"A Bible, yeah, perfect. That's perfect."

Her whispering was at a fevered pitch. A glaze of sweat covered her face and her perfume had gone flat, could not disguise her musky scent. He felt alarmed by the look and sound of her. He tried to stay calm. "Is everything packed?"

"How can he have nothing after two years in the States? Two years, Lance, and now he's leaving. He's going home for good, see what I mean, and he doesn't—"

"Please, honey, we have to—"

"They always bring stuff for the wife, the kids. To have nothing is weird!"

Okay, there was some truth to that. They knew other Guatemalans who bought lots of stuff to prove they'd been in The United States. *But it's not like there's a law!*

Lance could see that Molly was freaking out. She used to do this years ago, before the inheritance, when they had no choice but to travel on the cheap. Sometimes they ended up in grungy dives like this. And she would worry, as if evil forces were aligning against them. She never needed proof, just her acute sense of the darkening gloom. The freak-outs hadn't happened often, but often enough, and he no longer had patience for her irrational fear—especially now, in a place like Tapachula, that was, in fact, frightening. They needed to stay positive. Lance believed that, if focused on fear, his mind could transform into a kind of malevolent magnet, could pull scary things toward them. He needed to stop her from creating problems that did not exist! Was Gerardo planning to rob them? Was such a thing possible? Yes, there was that one in a million chance. But he refused to believe it. So the guy carried a Bible? Big deal! Couldn't they view that as a positive thing?

I mean really, why be threatened by a Bible and a missing arm and—

112

"And the one arm thing," she said.

"Gimme a break!"

"What?"

"You think he's faking that?"

"No. But I do think it gets our sympathy. Our trust. I do think it keeps us off-guard. It does do that, right?"

"Oh my god."

"Look," she said, "I'm not accusing him of...I don't know...I'm just thinking this through, saying it out loud, okay, and yes, it does feel like maybe he's setting us up."

"Setting us up?"

"Yes," she said. "Maybe. How can we know? It's a feeling, that's all. Like this place."

"Yeah? Yeah?"

"This place was his idea. A place we don't know."

"Well," Lance said, *"what happened?"*

"What?"

"We stayed here, right, and we had no problem. Except you didn't sleep because you worried that something bad was going to happen. But nothing did. *Nothing.* And now we're leaving, right?"

"I guess," Molly said, though she did not seem convinced. "We're not gone yet."

Lance took her in his arms and held her close. "Please, Moll, you're tired, you're (he didn't dare say paranoid) *anxious*. Anxious, yeah, I get that. Me too. That's natural in a place like this. But do you honestly believe Gerardo can't be trusted?"

"I don't know," she sobbed. "I don't know."

"Okay," Lance said. He was always confident, once she arrived at her "I don't know" phase, of what had to be done. "Listen, honey, we'll do whatever you want. If you don't trust him, that's fine. We'll tell him to go on without us."

Lance knew she did not want to think bad things about Gerardo. After many trips to Guatemala, Molly had lots of indigenous friends. She loved and trusted the people—if anything too much—and would feel horrible to shun this poor Indian man without any concrete evidence.

"I can't do that," she said, as he knew she would.

He kissed her forehead, she dried her eyes, and as they hurried from their room it occurred to him that traveling with Gerardo could be lucky. Lance hated third-world border crossings. He hoped that being with a native made them look more worldly, and perhaps, therefore, less vulnerable.

The Americans dragged their duffels to the street. Though it was a beautiful clear morning, with no danger in sight, Molly again seemed close to tears. They needed to find the shuttle vans, needed to get out of this hellhole fast!

Then, like magic, one of the vans came pulling up, grinding to a halt.

A young guy jumped out of the passenger seat, grabbed their bags, and stored them on the rack up top. The Americans and Gerardo climbed aboard. Soon as the helper was back in his seat, off the driver bolted. Lance could not have planned it any better.

He looked around the van and noticed there were no other tourists. That made him feel good, even brave, to have ventured on a *road less traveled.* The other passengers must be locals. Every few hundred yards the driver stopped to pick up another.

Lance knew they were going southwest by the sun rising behind his left shoulder. A sign said they were headed toward Ciudad Hidalgo. He asked Gerardo if that was right.

"Yes," Gerardo said, "that was where I crossed."

Molly got out the guidebook. She silently read its recommendation, and nodded, thus confirming, *Gracias a Dios,* that what Gerardo said was true.

To top things off, the day was full of light and color. An emerald mountain loomed to their left; a shiny black raven flapped through the cerulean sky; a sheen of dew steamed from an ochre hillside as white-clad farmers picked or shoveled or hoed its umber dirt.

Lance felt drugged by his sudden peace of mind. Last night in Tapachula seemed far behind them, and the bus ride like another lifetime. He yawned. His eyes glossed over. His need for sleep turned the world soft and blurry. He smiled at one of the women in the van. She smiled back. *Oh yes, life is good.* His body sank down into the seat, his tired eyes began to close, and he might have dozed off except that something changed, something felt suddenly wrong, his feet now vibrating on the floor of the van, his stomach beginning to jitter. What was going on?

He looked out at the landscape flying by.

Huh? Why, Lance wondered, with Tapachula behind them, were they racing down the road?

What's the damn hurry?

Lance looked at the back of the driver's head, at his thick stiff neck. Though he could see this guy was not to be trusted, his mind refused to believe it. After last night he couldn't take another scary thought. He tried to ignore it. His eyes were trying to close, but couldn't. They watched as trees and cows and farmers went careening by.

Then, like being slapped in the face, it hit him. Their driver was either hyped on speed or mentally deranged.

Or both.

The guy's rear-view mirror showed a bit of his whiskered sneer as he swerved to the shoulder for another stop.

Waiting was an old Mexican man with a cane. He limped to the van and the young assistant helped him to a seat. That took less than a minute. The driver watched, his eyes slumped within their sockets, a look suggesting both exhaustion and disgust. Lance saw him as one of those rare angry Mexican men, akin to some jerk New York *taxista*, who felt no need to be nice—in fact hated to be nice—who daily resented his endless toil of hauling people's asses from one place to another.

He returned to the road, was soon at full throttle, and in less than a mile squealed to another stop, showing that same glower of impatience as a woman was stuffed into the last bit of remaining space.

"Ya no mas!" the driver said to his assistant. *No more!*

And Lance knew what that meant. Now there was nothing to slow this numbskull down. The way his hands gripped the steering wheel made Lance sweat. He wanted to strangle the guy, he wished he could, but knew it was best to *chill*, to *center*, to *calm* his rage, his nausea, his boiling fear.

They roared ahead like a wobbly, misguided rocket, now intent on passing a small white pickup truck.

The other driver increased his speed.

Their guy (Lance decided to call him *Pepe*) seemed to like that challenge, and the vehicles sped side by side down the narrow two-lane road.

Lance leaned forward to get a look at the pickup driver. All he could see was a woman in the passenger seat, hands over her eyes. Panicked, he glared at Molly, sitting behind him, who was lost in conversation with Gerardo. Oblivious.

Where's her paranoia when we need it?

Lance turned to face the road ahead. He spotted something red in the distance, coming their way.

"I think we're going to die," he said in Spanish, hoping that by saying it they might somehow avoid it.

But the pickup driver was not giving in. Or Pepe.

The oncoming vehicle was now in clear sight. It was another pickup, probably another macho asshole.

Hope was fast running out.

A woman up front said something to Pepe, who shook his head, grumbled a few words back at her, then inched closer to the white truck…and closer. Its driver had two apparent choices: either surrender or be bumped off the road.

To Lance's stunned amazement, in the teensiest nick of time, the white truck slowed and let their van cut in front as the red truck went zooming by.

A few of the passengers let out sighs. Others clapped.

Pepe grinned at Lance from his rear-view mirror.

"What's going on?" said Molly.

116

Pepe yelled back at him, "Gringo, you want to get off up here, by the bridge?"

Bridge? Here? They were in the open countryside, nowhere near a town. Lance looked back at Gerardo and the Guatemalan shrugged. *What does that mean?* Feeling Pepe's eyes in the mirror, Lance took the guidebook from Molly and opened it to the "Getting Away" section on Tapachula. He skimmed it fast and saw the reference to a bridge in Ciudad Hidalgo. But it wasn't clear. Maybe they were close to the town and this was it. Or maybe not.

How had this vague description settled Molly's nerves?

Pepe, no doubt certain he knew best, abused his brakes to a screeching halt.

The white pickup shot by with a long angry honk.

The helper hustled out of the van to retrieve their luggage.

"I don't understand," Lance said to him from inside. "Where is the bridge?"

The boy pointed. "There."

Lance looked across the street, where the boy was pointing, at what seemed an empty field. Then he saw a long dirt road that disappeared into a grove of trees. There was no sign of a bridge.

"Wait," he said to the boy, "I'm not sure."

Pepe twisted his head around to look him in the eye.

"This doesn't feel right," said Molly.

Lance considered that long dirt road. Even if there was a bridge, it meant quite a walk with their heavy bags. They'd be sitting ducks for anyone wanting to rob them.

One of the other passengers, a fat Mexican woman with a double chin and a serious frown, said, "Yes, there is a bridge. You should go."

Lance turned to Gerardo. "Is she right?"

"I don't know," he said. "Maybe here is best for you." He would continue on to Ciudad Hidalgo, Gerardo said, because "That's the way I crossed before."

The Mexican woman smiled and shook her head.

117

Molly looked scared. Lance could tell that she now trusted their friend, believed what he said, and wanted them to stay together. Others in the van also seemed scared, probably worried that Pepe was about to blow.

Perhaps to confirm that fear, he rubbed his whiskered face, sighed and said, *"I'm waiting."*

Lance interpreted that as: *Either stay or go, Gringo, but DO IT FUCKING PRONTO!*

"We'll go to Ciudad Hidalgo," Gerardo said.

Molly nodded and looked at Lance.

Lance said, "Yes. Okay."

Pepe growled and spit out the window. His assistant jumped in the van and down the road they charged, speeding off like gangsters from a crime.

Lance might have felt relieved, but he was bothered by troublesome thoughts. Why had Gerardo first agreed with the woman that they should walk off on their own? Was he so afraid to contradict a *Ladina*? Yeah, well, what about them? Would he have left them alone in the middle of nowhere just to please her?

As if reading his mind, Gerardo said, "Don't worry, Señor Lance, there is a good crossing in Ciudad Hidalgo."

"Oh," Lance said. "Good."

"Oh, yes, very good," said the same fat serious woman, "if your tires don't explode."

A few of the passengers laughed, and Lance's confusion returned in force. He was often thrown by colloquial phrases, where words with agreed-upon definitions (like *tires*, for instance, or *explode*) suddenly meant something different. Though familiar with the Spanish language, he had no idea what the woman was saying. Was she making a joke because they had listened to an ignorant *Indio* instead of taking her dependable *Ladina* advice? Lance refused to ask, assuming her intention was to insult their indigenous friend.

Never mind, he told himself. *Forget it.* More important was his stomach, now churning from the stressful, curvy ride. Those jalapeño cheese puffs were trying to come up.

He had to focus his energy on not getting sick. He could not bear the idea of puking in Pepe's van.

Ten minutes later they entered the small town of Ciudad Hidalgo, named after one of Mexico's revolutionary heroes. Had circumstances been different, Lance might have been interested. Today he could not have cared less. He was tired and hungry, but wanted most to be free of Pepe.

They stopped at a sign that read: TO TAPACHULA.

Passengers got out and paid their fare. The assistant handed Lance their duffel bags.

A new set of people piled into Pepe's van and the demon roared off, back to the hell he'd come from.

Within seconds a bicycle rickshaw pulled up.

The driver said, "I can take you to the border."

Lance laughed. The absence of Pepe made him giddy. Maybe it was rude to laugh, but it felt good. "Look," he said, "with three people and these heavy bags *(Are you blind or what?)* we're going to need a taxi."

The guy said, "Yes, I am the taxi."

Lance smiled. "No, I mean a real taxi. A car taxi."

"There are no car taxis."

Lance stopped smiling.

"Don't worry," said the guy on the bike, and gave a couple of big whistles.

In a few seconds another bicycle was rolling up.

Molly said, "How far to the border?"

"Ten minutes," the first guy told her.

Oh, why not, Lance thought, deciding it could be done. One bicycle for him and Molly, another for Gerardo and the duffels.

"Ten pesos each," said the driver.

Two measly dollars. *For godsakes, it's time we started having fun!* "Okay," Lance said, "let's go." He felt like a seasoned traveler, a master of the road.

Gerardo said he was running out of money, he would meet them at the river, but they insisted on covering his fare.

119

He shook his head and took them aside. "Please," Gerardo said, "I feel shamed by you paying my way."

"No," said Molly, "it's the least we can do for the help you've given us."

Lance put his hand on the small man's shoulder and said, "We're not going without you. We would be shamed if you didn't join us."

Molly smiled at Gerardo. He smiled back, nodded his head, and slid in next to their bags.

"Bueno," said the rickshaw driver, and off they went, jostling along the cobblestone streets like clowns in a lost parade. A great lesson for Lance. Oh yes, this was what traveling meant for him. *Unbelievable, the things that happen when one accepts whatever comes.*

Villagers stared and giggled. Some pointed, as if they'd never seen a tourist before.

Lance loved every second of the crazy ride.

Then, out of nowhere, there it was: a wide, brown, nearly stagnant river, its bank littered with plastic bottles and bags and other assorted garbage. Lance got a whiff of long-lingering decay, a disgusting smell that he knew to ignore.

They slid to a stop. Two big kids ran up, got the driver's nod, and each pulled a duffel from Gerardo's rickshaw.

"So," Lance said, glancing around, "where is the bridge?"

"What bridge?" said their driver. He stepped up to Lance, looking all business. "Señor, you had two bags, right? Ten pesos for each."

"You're going to charge us for bags?"

The kids were dragging the duffels down toward the river.

"Wait!" yelled Molly. "Where are you going?"

The kids didn't wait. "To the boat!" one of them yelled.

That was when Lance had his first true suspicion about Gerardo, his first visceral sense of dread. He looked at the man, at his missing arm, his Bible. Gerardo gave him a furtive glance, then turned and ran after the kids.

Oh shit, oh no, was Molly right?

"You go!" she said to Lance. "I'll deal with these guys!"

He hurried after Gerardo, who hurried after the kids, who hurried to one of the several tiny docks below and dragged the bags to its end.

Seeing that, Gerardo stopped. He turned to Lance and said, "Don't worry, it's all right."

What? thought Lance. *What's all right?* He ran past Gerardo to the end of the dock. The bags had been tossed onto a large raft made of plywood, its four delaminating sheets laid atop three huge truck-tire tubes. The kids held out their hands and the biggest one said, "Ten pesos, please."

Lance looked out at the river, where several rafts were floating toward docks on the other side. Or were on their way back. He knew that must be Guatemala and suddenly understood. *This is illegal.*

Two young guys on the raft, each wearing swimming trunks, pushed the tourists' bags to the center. One of them looked at Lance and said, "A hundred pesos for each person. The bags are free."

The big kid on the dock touched the American's elbow and again held out his hand. Lance paid each boy ten pesos, which made them smile.

Molly came running down the dock to join him.

"What's going on?" she said.

Three other men climbed onto the raft, followed by Gerardo. He gestured for Lance and Molly to climb aboard, but the tourists stood still, as if unable to move, as if waiting for someone to come save them.

One of the young boatmen dropped himself off the raft, down into the river. The water barely reached his knees. "We're going," he said, and untied a rope from the dock.

Molly grabbed Lance's arm, gestured with her chin, and the Americans jumped onto the plywood deck.

The boatman pushed it out into the river, then climbed aboard. He collected money while his partner began paddling.

Molly turned to Lance. He expected fear, or anger, and was surprised by her squinty, good-natured grin. "Ah yes," she said, giving his shoulder a chummy slap, "adventure!"

The guy collecting money smiled at her.

She smiled back.

Lance paid and smiled too. *Adventure, yep, that's what this is, and no damn way to stop it.*

Gerardo said, "Don't worry, Señor, I promise the tires won't explode."

Molly laughed, kissed Lance on the cheek, and was soon yacking with Gerardo.

Lance felt distracted. Did not want to talk, or listen, to anyone. He went to the front edge of the raft and sat down. He looked down at the muddy water.

Things had to be considered, like what this little adventure was going to cost. Entering Guatemala illegally meant they could not leave in any sort of normal way. That would be a problem. They'd already bought one-way tickets home from Guatemala City, which meant their passports must be stamped. To get that done they'd have to find a legal crossing and explain what happened.

Could they be put in jail? Doubtful. They were tourists, he'd say, they'd made a dumb mistake, it was not their fault. An embarrassment, for sure, but there must be others who had gone through this. There must be some procedure. There would be forms to fill out on both sides of the border. Yeah, right, and probably corrupt officials to bribe.

Shit! Who knew how long this would take, or how dearly they'd have to pay. Some adventures, Lance had to admit, were not worth having. Like falling off a cliff, or being eaten by sharks. Or this. This was also not a choice they would have made.

Against his will he began to resent Gerardo. Though the man could not be blamed, not really, they were in trouble because he'd given them bad advice.

Lance thought of Joaquin, who had tried to warn him. "Watch out, friend, because you never know how an Indio thinks."

Maybe that was true. Maybe they shouldn't have gotten so attached. Lance realized that in an odd, unintended way, Molly had been right not to trust this stranger. He glanced over at the two of them. They were talking and laughing like old pals, as if going *mojado* into Guatemala were perfectly normal.

Molly looked at Lance, her alert and pointed gaze signaling she understood. Her eyes were clear. Oh yes, she knew that trouble was coming. She smiled, a long calm smile, then turned back to Gerardo.

Amazing.

Yeah, okay, sometimes she got paranoid and went a little crazy, but he admired how open and loving she could be. Molly would not let a future problem destroy the good that was happening now.

Gerardo pointed at one of the other rafts, perhaps telling her something he'd learned on his first trip across the river. They were in his world now. This was his way of getting across a border. He had no clue how to do it legally because for him that was never an option. His days came with few good choices, with little comfort, and not a single guarantee. All he had were dreams, faith, and the hope of mercy, *Gracias a Dios.*

KLEPTOMANIA

Lynn is in Portofino, Italy, saying goodbye to her girlfriend and blind to what might happen next. Without Eva the whole world will look foreign. She feels lost at the thought of being without her, of maybe never seeing her again.

Lynn sits at the table, sipping from a mug of coffee. She's traveled a lot in the last ten years, has been lost before, and knows that the way she needs to go is usually close by, usually within sight.

Or could she already have passed it by?

Is it behind me? Is that what's going on?

She stares out the rear glass doors at the Gulf of Genoa. Plenty of space between her and California.

Or is there? *Oh no, is that where this all came from?*

Lynn thinks of her dad. Not a thought she wants to have. Usually there's no problem pushing him away, but today is different. Today she hears his voice and knows she has to listen.

She remembers back fifteen years, to the Arcata Marsh, where blindness first raised its head, first looked her in the eyes. She remembers her gangly teenage body, her pimples, her budding breasts...remembers wishing every bit of her would fly away, dissolve into the sky like sandpipers, hundreds of them wing to wing, spinning through the air like a visible wind. The scent of fennel filled her nostrils. Sun burned through the wispy fog. She wished there were nothing but sweet-smelling herbs and soaring birds and warming light.

Her dad said, "Make you a deal, Lynny. I'll tell you a secret. Something I've never told anybody else. The deal is, you tell me one too."

Hello? That was Lynny's first thought. That had become her automatic response to anything she did not understand. What it meant was, *You can't be frigging serious!* That summarized how far her dad had slipped in credibility.

Now, looking back, she feels certain he could think of no other way to get them talking. At the time, they were halfway finished with their walk. They moved steadily along, the dirt path rimmed by reeds and thistles. They passed a mossy green pond full of cattails and ducks. She had nothing to say, did not want to be there. The trail's only comfort was that it led, step-by-step, closer to the end.

"Well," her dad said, "what do you say?"

Lynny felt like she had to be careful, had to keep up her guard. Even the marsh, one of her favorite places, seemed unfriendly. She knew exactly where they were, they'd gone on this walk lots of times, but today, because of him, it looked dangerous.

She was thankful for the birds, thankful for the pond's cool calm surface, thankful for the fennel and the sun.

Her dad glanced down, trying to read her thoughts. She tried not to let him. She kept her eyes focused on the path.

"Contact," he said, pulling to a stop. "Contact, contact, earth to—"

"Okay," she said, but continued walking. It took him several seconds to catch up.

She hears the bathroom door close, which means Eva is awake. Lynn isn't ready. She carries her coffee to the veranda and looks out at the open sea. There are boats on the water and clouds in the sky. All of it fades as she remembers.

Her dad hadn't expected that "Okay." She'd agreed to his "deal" because she could not stand the strangeness between them.

"Okay," she said again, like a vague complaint. "You first." She hated that there seemed no other choice. She needed her anger to show, could not let him think she'd softened.

"You sure, Lynny? It has to be a real secret."

"You...first."

"Okay," her dad said, "me first."

She watched his jaw start to twitch, a sign that he was nervous. It looked like he had no clue what to say. Maybe the whole "Let's Make A Deal" thing was spontaneous, a frantic attempt at connection, and now he had to think up something fast.

It reminded her of "Story Time" when she was a kid of five or six. He wasn't like her mom, who would read stories from real books—books right there on the shelf by Lynny's bed—books with brightly colored pictures and boldly printed words.

"You first," he used to say. "Who is it about?"

126

Lynny had known it was best to say whatever popped into her head. A horse, she might say. Or a lion. Or, often, a little girl. Or all those things at once. It didn't matter. With whoever Lynny decided the story was about, her dad would make things happen. Fantastic things. At least they seemed fantastic to her as a kid. Some nights he went on and on, like magic, taking them to unknown planets in far distant worlds. Better than any storybook could ever be. Other nights, when he was tired, he might get stuck and ask her to help remember. Both Lynny and her dad pretended it was real...a real story being told. Things happened, she'd believed, in a definite order (were meant to happen) *and there had to be a happy ending!* It was their job to remember how that happiness came to be.

"I forget, Lynny, what happens next?"

"You know, silly!"

"I'm sorry," he'd say, "my head's getting fuzzy."

He might yawn, might act like he was falling asleep. She'd pinch his nose or pull his hair.

"What?" he'd say. "What?"

Then she would tell him in her loudest, most parental voice, that the little girl turns into a bird. Or a fish. Or whatever she decided.

"Oh, oh yeah," he would say, and off he'd go again, remembering that the rainbow-colored bird flew beyond the farthest star, or the silver-scaled fish swam across the ocean to a hidden, unknown island. And the story would keep going until Lynny's eyelids began to droop. That's when he'd head for the happy ending.

But there were times he couldn't get there, and she could tell he wasn't playing, that he was genuinely exhausted. Maybe he'd been working long hours, or didn't sleep the night before because he and her mom had one of their fights. Maybe he was drinking too much, like her mom said. Was that why he asked for help more than once? He would stare into space, would tell her to wait, would say he was trying to remember what came next.

127

Lynny had the feeling that his head was full of something else, something that stopped him from being there with her. She'd learned, when he looked like that, to say she was tired and could not remember either. She'd felt afraid to ask what was wrong. She'd give him a hug, a kiss, then pull the blanket over her head.

Lynn tries not to think of those nights. Or what happened that day in the marsh. Strange, though, how some things stick...won't let go...can never be forgotten.

"Okay," she said, "come on, Dad, what's your secret?"

Lynny hoped he hadn't made up the "secret" thing just to get her talking.

"Wait a minute," he said. "I'm thinking of the right way to say it."

"It has to be true. That's the deal, right?"

"Right."

She peeked up at him, at his face tilted toward the path. It looked like he was thinking hard.

Lynn remembers how she suddenly felt frightened. *Oh no,* she thought, *this isn't some game we're playing, he's going to tell me a real secret! That's why he's stalling, because this thing he's going to tell me actually happened, and he seriously thinks it matters, and I might not want to hear it! Oh shit, okay...whatever...but whatever it is, it better not have anything to do with my mom!*

It would not be beyond him to give intimate details of their failed marriage. Her mother used to get fuming mad at him for sharing "private things" at some bar or stoner party they'd been at. His answer, his constant defense, was that he believed in honesty—"honesty, no matter what"—which was rich coming from a guy who would one day confess he'd been cheating on her for months. There he was, at the "family meeting," sharing stuff about him and this other woman—even her name, *Sarah,* which from then on stuck in Lynny's head like a curse.

Lynn looks up at a seagull squawking overhead. Her mind then rushes back to the marsh. She gave her dad another glance, and remembered how sad her mother had been after hearing all his *honesty*. She thought, *Yeah, well, forget that. This better not have anything to do with that!*

"So," he said, "there was a time…"

Then he paused (one of those damn dramatic pauses of his) and again Lynny thought of his made-up bedtime stories. *Is that what this is going to be? Hello?* Weird, because a few seconds ago she had not wanted to hear his truth. Now she was afraid he might keep it from her.

Please, don't treat me like some silly little kid.

"A time," he continued, "when I took things."

"Huh?"

"I used to steal, Lynny. From stores."

"Steal?"

"Yes."

"You?"

"Yes. Me."

"Like what? What did you steal?"

"I don't remember. It depended on what I was looking at when I got the feeling."

"What feeling?"

"It's hard to explain," he told her. His jaw stiffened and a troubled look crossed his face. Maybe he was re-considering what he'd said, thinking maybe this *secret talk* was a huge mistake. But he must have known it had gone too far. There was no stopping now. "I'd be inside a store," he said. "I might be looking at—"

"Wait, wait. Were you with Mom?"

"No, I was always by myself."

"I mean, were you two married when you—"

"Oh. Yes. This happened when you were a baby."

"Did she know you were stealing?"

"No," he said, "I never told her." Then he kept on talking, saying how shameful he'd felt, that it was something he'd not been able to admit, not even to himself.

129

"I don't believe it," Lynny said, which she knew sounded weird. Sure, she was mad at what a liar he'd been, but hey, he was being truthful now about something bad, something he should know not to say, especially to his fourteen-year-old daughter, so how could she not believe him?

"I understand," he said. "It took years before I could believe it either."

"You walked into stores and stole things?"

He laughed and shook his head, but not like this was funny. He clearly knew this wasn't funny. "It was just in hardware stores, okay. I'd be looking around, maybe checking out the cost of chisels. That's the kind of thing I was needing back then to work on the house. Usually I'd see the price and leave. Sometimes, though, this feeling came over me. Like I was alone."

"Alone?"

"Not alone, not really, but it felt that way, that's what I mean. Like being apart from other people. Separate. Like whoever was around was not in the same place as me."

"I don't get it."

"Yeah, I know, it was strange, it was like….like being in a place that no one else could see. There might be people in the next aisle, or at the counter a few aisles over, but I knew they were in their own world, too, thinking their own thoughts, doing their own things. They had no idea I was there. Like I was invisible."

That was the feeling, he said. Like being invisible. He called what he did *kleptomania*, which meant a kind of stealing he was unable to control. He called it a sickness.

That's what he said, but Lynny wasn't stupid. She could tell that there were things not being told. "Why?"

He looked confused. "What?"

"Why did you do it?"

"Why?" he said. "I don't know."

"You don't know or you're not saying?"

"I didn't think about it, honey. I did it, that's all. That's the sick part. I couldn't stop myself. I wanted those things, of course I did, but it wasn't *that*, it was…I don't know…I guess it felt unfair that I had to always consider what things cost. It's not like we didn't have the money, but your mother and I decided, because we had a child, we had to be careful. I guess I resented that. It felt like the world was cheating us. We both worked hard and deserved the things we needed. I wasn't thinking any of this at the time, okay, but I guess that's what I was feeling. And the rest would happen automatically. I'd put that chisel in my coat pocket and walk around the store, pretending it wasn't there. I'd buy something cheap, a drill bit or a pack of pencils, believing, I guess, that made up for what I took."

"Wow."

"Yeah," he said. "Wow."

"Did you ever get caught?"

"No."

"Never?"

"No, never."

Amazing.

"Okay, Dad, but what would you have done?"

"Done?"

"If you ever got caught, I mean."

"That's not something I thought about."

"You weren't afraid of getting caught?"

"Honey, you don't understand. The stealing wasn't anything I planned. It just happened, see, that's what I'm saying. That's why I never worried about getting caught, or thought about what would happen. That's why I don't know. Does that make sense?"

Lynny said it did. She turned away and both of them were quiet for a while. They stood together, as they'd done many times before, watching bands of sandpipers rise and fall, flowing over Klopp Lake, changing shape, twisting out toward the bay.

Once, a couple of years before, a woman had come by and stood close to them as they watched. She'd said the birds fly that way to camouflage themselves. "They do it whenever a hawk is near. It's their instincts kicking in, their way of evading predators."

Lynny had said, "That's awesome."

Her dad had kept quiet. Smiled but didn't say a thing.

After the woman left, he'd laughed.

"What?"

"People are not birds. We have no idea why birds fly the way they do. And that's okay. Not everything needs to be known."

Well, yeah, Lynny supposed that was true, but why not know things if you could?

She'd felt separate from him that day—sad to see how different they were—and she felt that way again. Alone. Invisible. To her it seemed important to think things through. The hard stuff anyway...the stuff that matters. There were things Lynny wished he could help her with, things she was confused about, urges really hard to control, but she doubted he would understand. Although she'd never stolen, she worried every day about getting caught.

"Okay," he said, "your turn."

My turn? Hello?

Since he hadn't told his whole secret yet, not even close, how could it be her turn? How could he still not know why he stole? That was the big one for her. If he didn't know why, why would he ever stop?

No wonder he'd never worried about getting caught.

No wonder he'd cheated on her mom.

My turn? Okay, if that's what you want. Maybe I should tell you I smoke cigarettes down by the river. Maybe I should tell you I smoked dope a few times, too, and sometimes spit into your bottle of Jim Beam. Or maybe I should tell you that my best friend, Gil, had sex with me. Maybe I should confess how much I didn't like it, how it made me sick to my stomach. First, I guess, I should say it was me who got Gil to do it...how I'd been letting Gil know for a long time that I wanted him to.

132

Up until he did, she'd hoped Gil might be *the one*. She was afraid of what might happen if he wasn't.

"Your turn, Lynny. What's your secret?"

Though it's painful to remember this, she's doing it for Eva. Because she doesn't want to lose her. Eva's complicated, and sometimes difficult, but with the others it was way too easy. Same as Lynn, none of them wanted anything to be hard. That was the unspoken deal. Eva though, she's not like that. She wants whatever there is. "I don't understand," she said last night. "Why do you keep holding back, Lynn? What is it you're afraid of?"

Maybe, Lynn fears, Eva wants too much.

She wipes away a spurt of tears and remembers her father's face, that expectant look, the hope that his little girl might be willing to open up. Lynny could have told him why she'd tried to make Gil the one. Could have told him what she truly wanted, wanted bad and didn't know why, was to lay down naked with her physical education teacher, Claudia. Yeah, maybe she should have told him that. That was a good secret, huh?

"Come on," her dad said, "you promised."

Promised.

As if promises mattered anymore. As if they ever did.

"Lynny?"

"Yeah."

"What is it, honey? What?"

"I don't know."

Holy shit, this was getting bad. The fog had thickened, had swallowed the sky and erased the birds. She could have told him lots of things, but didn't want to. Those were her secrets, hers, and it felt like he was trying to steal them.

"It's okay," he said. "You can say anything, anything at all. Whatever you're feeling is okay."

"I'm sorry, Dad."

She started to shiver. Not from the cold, it came from inside. Then tears started spilling out.

Lynny could not believe this was happening. She never thought it possible to feel this far away.

He pulled her close and held on tight.

She held him too. Held on fiercely.

"Please, sweetheart, don't worry. Tell me what it is."

It seemed wrong to feel how they used to be. She pushed away and looked into his blank unseeing eyes. He was as blind to her as he was to himself.

"I don't trust you," she said.

He looked shocked, but said nothing. Not a word. He didn't try to hold her again, either, or make her explain a single thing. They sat together on the ground. He held her hand and let her cry. She was grateful for that. She could tell from his silence, from his tender yet tentative grip, he did not expect a happy ending.

Eva comes out to the veranda. She is naked, rubbing her long brown hair with a towel, smelling like a lemon. This girl is fresh, and not the least bit shy. She kisses Lynn on the forehead, then gives her a peck on the lips. "Decided where you're going?"

"No," says Lynn, "not yet."

"Maybe meet me later in Rome?"

"Yeah, maybe."

Eva's eyes gloss over. "Well," she says, turning away, "I guess I'll get some breakfast at the station. My train leaves at ten."

"Wait," says Lynn. She reaches out and pulls Eva close. "I need to tell you a secret."

THE BLUE BUDDHA

Daniel and Kat came out of the Ratchanatda Wat, a small Buddhist temple in Bangkok. A man walking by looked at them and stopped. "You Americans, yes?"

He was small, rather dainty, and immaculately attractive as many Thais are. He smelled of myrrh. His smile seemed almost doll-like. Daniel gave an amiable nod, then turned to the business of waving down a *tuk tuk*, leaving the politeness part to Kat. The man probably wanted to sell them something, or maybe practice English. Daniel knew it wouldn't matter to her. She loved meeting new people.

Kat said to the man, "How did you know?"

"Oh," he said, "I can see from face."

"Amazing," she said, and seemed to mean it. "Yes, we are from—"

"No no no," the man said, throwing up his hands, shaking his head, not letting her answer. "I hear, I can hear it. Chicago, yes?"

"Yes!" she said. "Can you believe that, Daniel?"

"Amazing," he said, removing his Cubs hat to wipe his sweaty brow.

"Yes," the man said, "I know. Al Capone. Michael Jordan. Barack Obama."

Daniel put on his cap and looked back to the street. It was jammed with rush-hour traffic, a dense weave of barely controlled chaos. Several tuk tuks saw him waving but could not safely get over to where he was.

Kat said, "My name is Kat, and this is my husband, Daniel."

The man gave their hands a vigorous shake. "Very nice, very nice. I am Aroon. I am schoolteacher. How long you in Bangkok?"

"We leave tomorrow," said Kat.

"What? One day in Thailand?"

"No," said Daniel, "we've been here a week. Tomorrow we'll take a train to Chiang Mai."

"Ah," Aroon said, "Chiang Mai beautiful part of Thailand! You lucky people. Lucky too for this day in Bangkok. Only day, this day, Blue Buddha open to public."

Oh no, please. Daniel guessed what was coming and regretted the truth, that he couldn't care less about the countless Bangkok Buddhas, blue or otherwise. He knew it was strange to feel that way, but he was too tired, too hot, too preoccupied with his own thoughts. He was writing a new story and could not seem to focus on anything else.

That morning Kat had suggested he take a break. At the time it seemed a good idea. Unaware of what he was getting into, he'd traipsed beside her for hours in the soaking heat, through a jabbering, ill-mannered Chinatown, in and out of tiny crowded stores. Bargains, bargains everywhere. Most of it junk. Eventually, thankfully, they'd found the kind of place she was looking for, a wholesale shop that specialized in sterling silver jewelry. Daniel waited next to the fan while she rummaged through rows of plastic bins.

An hour later, pleased with her purchases, she'd agreed to go back to their hotel. "Of course," she said with a big fake smile, "back to your lonely laptop."

Around the next corner she spotted a store full of bronze statuettes.

Daniel kept walking, pretending not to notice.

Kat touched his arm. "Give me a minute, honey."

Hoping for another fan, he followed her in. Though there wasn't one, he sensed they wouldn't be staying long. Kat sells to students at universities in the Midwest. Things have to be small and inexpensive. These statues were neither, which for him was great. But Kat got to talking with the owner, quite a talker, who went on and on about his business, his family, the beloved old King of Thailand *("May he be blessed with a long and healthy life")* and, finally, where she could go to find miniature bronze statues.

That's how they'd ended up at this "holy" temple—for the past two hours sweating in the shade of breathless stalls, sifting through buckets of tiny icons.

Yeah, okay, he had to admit it was worth the trouble: they cost a fraction of what she could sell them for. Thank you Laughing Buddha! Thank you dear Ganesh! Sixty-three of one and fifty of the other. Then, a great surprise, he found a crazed-looking Kali lunging from her throne, gripping in her many hands a Rama-sized penis. Kat's eighty-year-old dad would get a kick out of that, and that had made Daniel happy, for about ten seconds, but he yearned to get back inside their air-conditioned room and lock the door.

"Blue Buddha very special," said Aroon.

"Wow," Kat said. "A Blue Buddha? Really?"

"Wow," Daniel said to her. "Really?"

"Yes, yes," said Aroon, "happen once in year, this most auspicious day!"

His childlike smile was irresistible. Kat's too. Her need for a distraction could not be denied. She'd been working hard every day, out in the boiling streets, alone, while Daniel sat around luxuriating, imagining, moving words around.

Aroon had lots to say about *this most auspicious day*, and Daniel spaced out.

He thought of his new story. It features a guy named Dirk, a graduate student from Chicago, who while traveling in Bali gets lost in the "Monkey Forest" of Ubud. An hour before, Dirk was sipping cappuccino at some hip cafe. Now the guy has no clue where he is. Trying to relocate the tourist path, he spots something watching him from a tree. The size of a cat, it has huge round curious eyes. Dirk doesn't know that what he's seeing is a Cuscus, a wooly-haired marsupial known for its relative tameness. What he thinks he knows, from his graduate studies in psychology, is that animals, even wild ones, pose no threat unless they feel threatened. He looks away from the creature and takes a calming breath.

Daniel wanted this story to reflect the mystery of life. He believed life to be, in the purest sense of the word, unknowable, and thought it slightly brilliant that in Ubud's famous "Monkey Forest" he'd chosen to put a Cuscus. *Totally unexpected.* And now he needed something like that for Dirk. Some hidden, complicating truth. He'd made his main character a smart and likeable guy. No problem there. Dirk always found that things went well when he had a positive attitude. An admirable trait. *Or was it?*

After that calming breath, Dirk looks back at the Cuscus, certain he hears it purring. The guy cannot imagine it might be growling. He glances around and sees, within the shadows of dark foliage, many other sets of eyes. There might be hundreds of them watching. But Dirk is not alarmed. He believes in the goodness of nature. *These animals,* he comforts himself, *have no antipathy toward me.* On the other hand, their steady stare is a bit unnerving. For Dirk this is a moment of truth. Maybe his discomfort is necessary, a primal fear he must overcome. Believing that, he stands his ground, stares back, and smiles.

Daniel knew this was the climax but could not decide what happens next. He'd tried various endings, all of which seemed reasonable and were therefore unacceptable. What he wanted was a complete surprise. What if, through some telepathic connection, the Cuscuses help Dirk find the path? *No, too damn romantic.* Maybe Dirk needs to learn that things don't always turn out as he would wish. Maybe Cuscuses are more unknowable than anyone would think.

Maybe Dirk gets mauled and eaten?

Whoa. That thought made Daniel nervous. Though the guy may need a lesson here, why would he deserve such a grisly fate? Just for being human? No, Daniel could not accept that. He had to reconsider the entire story. Again. There was something particular about Dirk's character, or the situation—or his own way of thinking—that Daniel had to figure out and deal with. *But what, damn it! What?*

That's what he'd been struggling to figure out. For weeks. He'd kept hoping for a breakthrough that never came, and each day by nightfall was exhausted.

To make matters worse, Kat always worried about him when he got stuck like this. Then her spirits dampened, she got depressed, and he would start worrying about her, which rattled his mind and made writing impossible.

"Come on," she now said, "maybe a Blue Buddha is exactly what you need."

"You like!" Aroon said. "This most sacred day. Many celebrations! Much much wisdom!"

Well, Daniel could only hope so. "Okay," he said, forcing a smile, "where is it?"

Kat held his hand and kissed his cheek.

"Yes, yes," said Aroon, "make you so so happy. Me as well. This morning I bring students to see Blue Buddha. You go, you see yourself."

Daniel said, "Yes, we want to go." His weary brain had hatched a plan. "First," he said to Kat, "we'll bring our stuff to the hotel, take a shower, rest up a bit and—"

"No no no," said Aroon, checking his watch. "You go now. One hour left to see. Blue Buddha this day is free ride in tuk tuk."

"Free?" said Kat.

Yeah, right, *free.* Though Daniel used to love that word, he'd learned not to trust it. This felt like a mistake and he regretted having given in. The heat made him say things he did not mean. There must be some way out. He just wanted to get back to their room, back to his story, but felt trapped by Aroon's cheery face. Then Kat squeezed his hand, looked into his eyes, and smiled. Case closed.

"You go in government tuk tuk," Aroon said. "Have blue color with yellow plate and—"

"Oh," said Kat, pointing at a blue tuk tuk with a yellow plate. "You mean like that one?"

The driver spotted her pointing from three lanes over. Like an arrow in the wind, he sliced a squiggly line toward them, between vehicles swerving this way and that, and pulled up to the curb, illegally parking in a temporarily vacant lane of traffic.

"You want go?" the driver yelled. "You come now!"

Equally abrupt, Aroon shook his head and waved the guy on. The two exchanged a spattering of harsh Thai words before a huge truck came honking from up the lane toward the idling tuk tuk, thus ending the argument and forcing the enraged driver to speed away.

"No," said Aroon. "Like that one for certain, but has blue flag on top. Flag tell you is government run, to celebrate Blue Buddha."

Daniel felt faint. Melting sunscreen burned into his eyes and sweat dripped from his armpits. Wet inside his baseball cap, wet inside his thin white shirt, wet inside his underwear, he was mad at the unrelenting heat and humidity, mad at the traffic, mad at himself for feeling so mad, so overwhelmed. Trying to stay calm he turned away, needing a break from Aroon's insistent smile.

But the break was far too short. Their new friend gently took hold of Daniel's arm and gave him a solemn look. The American saw he'd done something wrong, had in some way offended the Thai man, whose weakened smile betrayed a noticeable hint of irritation. It seemed that Aroon needed more than Kat's enthusiasm. Perhaps he was disappointed that this American tourist, with a wife needing to be pleased, did not appreciate the good fortune of his advice.

"Free ride," Aroon repeated, as if that essential fact might have been missed. The teacher took a notebook and pen

from his pants pocket. He wrote *GASOLINE TICKET*, and
gave Daniel a hopeful look. When the American did not
respond, Aroon scratched his head and blinked hard.
"Because of that," the teacher said, pointing at the words.
"You know, you know, driver gets for bonus, like ticket for
gasoline."

"A coupon!" said Kat.

"Yes!" Aroon shouted, "coupon, yes, coupon," and went
back to his notebook. *TICKET MEANS COUPON,* he wrote
in big bold letters, and underlined it twice. "Yes, yes, for
this one day. Government tuk tuk bring you to Blue Buddha,
then clothing shop for coupon. You not buy a thing.
Included he takes you home."

"Wait," said Daniel, "I'm still not sure what—"

"Here!" Aroon shouted, signaling to a tuk tuk with a
bright blue flag waving in the wind. The driver pulled up
and Aroon pointed at the tourists.

Daniel felt the urge to run.

Kat climbed aboard.

The driver, seeing Daniel's hesitation, said, "Free ride,
mister. Everything free!"

"He also takes you home," said Aroon. "You go now!"

"Ah shucks, honey," said Kat, grinning like a drunken
pirate, "*Wat* the hell!"

Daniel sat next to her and off they went, bolting away
from an overjoyed Aroon.

The driver wasted neither words nor time. He sped through
the crowded streets, then down a narrow alley. He rounded a
corner, parked behind another tuk tuk, and pointed to his
right. Behind an opened metal gate was an ancient wat. The
white plaster on its main building was cracked and chipping
away, but the arched roof tipped ever upward, adorned with
traditional gold trimmings.

"Blue Buddha *inside*," the driver said. "You go see."

Kat and Daniel walked toward the gate. Coming out were
two grinning tourists, a man and a woman.

The man, tall and blond, said something that sounded German, then flashed them the peace sign as he passed.

Straight ahead, in the shadow of a banyan tree, stood a monk in saffron robes. He led them beyond the main building. There, under a low canvas overhang, were two life-size statues in the lotus position. The first, Daniel presumed, was the Buddha as a young disciple, the second as a wizened master. Neither of them were any shade of blue. Both would be best described as greyish-black in color, with gold paint dribbled haphazardly over their bodies.

The monk sat against the building and closed his eyes. Perhaps they had not made themselves clear.

"Excuse me," Daniel said, "we are here to see *The Blue Buddha.*" The man did not respond. "Please, sir, we came because—"

The monk opened his eyes, smiled, and pointed at the statues, at one no more directly than the other.

"Blue Buddha there. *Inside.*"

"Ah," said Kat. *"Inside."*

Inside? thought Daniel. He looked for a hidden door, an entry into some secret vestibule, and started moving in the direction of that vaguely imagined place when Kat took hold of his arm.

"No," she said, kissing his cheek and laughing, as if he'd been paying no attention.

The monk was laughing too, now pointing at the two black statues. *"Inside!"* he said. "You see *inside!*"

"Oh," said Daniel, thinking maybe he understood. *"Inside of them? The blue is inside?"*

The smiling monk gave an emphatic nod. "All of Thai people, we see."

"No kidding," Daniel said. "Darn it anyway, I guess that leaves us Americans out."

"Incredible!" Kat said. She squeezed Daniel's hand.

"Inside Buddha is forgiveness," said the monk, yawning. "Total peace. Not want anything."

"Us either," said Daniel. "Well," he said, "maybe just the teensiest bit of blue."

Kat bowed to the bowing monk, then turned to Daniel.

"Let's go," she said.

Their driver was asleep in the back of his tuk tuk. They shook him awake. The man rubbed his eyes and let out a groan. "What," he said, "so soon?"

Daniel nodded and handed him the card from their hotel.

The guy looked at it. "Okay, okay, I take you there for sure. First I get coupon."

"Yes," said Kat, "I'm afraid that was the deal."

The driver smiled and got behind the wheel.

As the tourists were hurried out to the bustling street, then down another alley, Daniel was feeling nervous. He tried to relax. Tried to stay positive. From what he thought he understood, they would now go to some clothing store and pick up a "gas coupon" that this government driver had earned for taking them to see the Blue Buddha.

All right, fine, no big deal. The government program must be meant to promote monastic values. The beloved old King had himself once been a monk. He was probably concerned with the degradation of Thai youth—spiky-haired, tattoo-covered, body-pierced—kids who preferred heavy metal and wife-beater T-shirts to chanting and saffron robes.

They pulled up alongside four other tuk tuks, each facing a big window stocked with over-dressed manikins. The name of the store was Ten Thousand Threads. The driver turned to Daniel. "This is place. Please not say coupon. Not say gas. You look at suit."

"Suit?" Obviously Daniel had missed something. "But I'm not interested in any—"

"No, no, not say that. You not need to buy. You go happy now for looking. Easy. Five minutes to listen, then you go."

"And they give me the coupon when I—"

"No, not say that. Not give to you. Man see me here. I get at 5 o'clock, I come back myself."

"*Get it?*" said Kat, as if wondering how Daniel could possibly not *get it.*

Yeah, well, piss on that! He felt unfairly slighted. He was hot and sticky and tired and hungry and did not like being told what he didn't *get.* Hell, if it weren't for her, he wouldn't have to *get* a goddamn thing!

Kat whispered, "Sorry, honey, I should've known," making clear that until right now she didn't *get it* either. He could tell that she was surprised, and embarrassed, to have gotten them into this mess.

Daniel whispered to her, "It's all right. Let's run for it."

"I don't think we can," she said, eyeing the store window.

He saw that they were being watched. Then he glanced at the driver, who was humming and smiling while fidgeting with his keychain. If this guy didn't get the expected *Gas Ticket,* things could turn ugly fast.

Kat squeezed Daniel's hand. "We've gone this far, right? I don't think we can—"

"No, I guess not."

The driver turned and faced them, his eyes giving a gentle shove. "You go now. Please."

They nodded and walked to the door.

Waiting was a young, handsome, well-dressed Thai man. Daniel expected a show of fake smiles, followed by hard salesmanship. Surprising him, the young man bowed, shook their hands, and said, with a perfect English accent, "My name is Wirat. I am honored to help in any way I can." It was as if he were stating facts. "Please," he said, "come in."

The place was air-conditioned. Daniel appreciated that. It smelled of jasmine, and something else, something that made Daniel think of Elmer's glue. They followed the salesman to a couch. On the coffee table in front of them was a large black binder.

"Have a seat," Wirat said. "Would you care for tea?"

"No, thank you," said Kat.

"No," said Daniel, "I'm good."

"Yes, I see you are," said Wirat—an obvious joke, though not funny, that got all of them smiling. The young man leaned down and opened up the binder. "First," he said, "you look at styles. Take your time. When you find one you like, then you pick the fabric."

Wirat displayed a flawless mix of calm and confidence. *No way,* Daniel realized, *is this going to be easy.* Kat, he saw, was thinking hard, working her way through the binder, planning some reasonable exit strategy.

Daniel looked around the store. He counted four other tourist couples, each attended by a separate salesman. The tourists were bent over binders, focused and curious, flipping through the pages, nodding their heads, and silently, it would seem, ticking off their requisite five minutes. He recognized the German who had passed them at the wat. The guy had taken the process to its next logical step, standing before a mirror with swatches of colored fabric draped over his shoulder. He caught Daniel's eye and winked.

Daniel looked away. He did not want to play this silly game. He felt humiliated. Why the hell was he here? Because he was a coward, that's why. Because he'd given in to Kat's need for distraction. Because he'd not been willing to defend his selfishness—his need, whether she understood or not, to at times be indefensibly selfish. This was his punishment for not being honest. He should stand up and say that, loud and clear, and head out the door. But he couldn't. The world, as usual, made true honesty impossible. That's why he wrote fiction.

Hah! Sad, so sad, but true. He had no problem creating characters braver than himself. He could force them, like it or not, to face unpleasant truths.

The new story flashed into his head. What will Dirk discover in the presence of those Cuscuses? That's what Daniel needed to find out, and it was maddening to be stuck here in a suit shop. He sighed, he looked around.

A suit shop, that's where he was, with a guy trying to sell him something he did not want. Yes, okay, that was the truth, so maybe he should re-think this, consider it an opportunity. The best way to pass his time was to be honest about what he felt right now. A healthy dose of nonfiction! Yes, of course, that's what he needed!

The German tourists were on their way out the door.

Kat said to the salesman, "These are beautiful, but we can't afford to buy one."

"You might be surprised," Wirat said. The salesman pulled up a chair by Daniel's end of the couch.

"I think we should come back later," Kat said, "at the end of our trip. We're right at the beginning, just getting started, and—"

"This one is incredible," Daniel said, pointing at the photo of a dark gray three-piece suit, the likes of which he would never wear in a million years.

Kat wrinkled her eyebrows at him, perhaps thinking he still didn't *get it.*

But he did. He got every bit of it and now would make that clear. By "incredible," as Daniel was tempted to point out, he meant *absurd, preposterous, unthinkable.* He held up the picture and said, "I assume we can choose the color we want it lined with, right?"

"Any color you choose," said Wirat.

"Great," said Daniel. "How about *Buddha Blue?"*

He could feel Kat staring at him.

"Oh," said Wirat, apparently moved, his eyes like large crystalline pools, "are you a Buddhist?"

Daniel guessed he'd heard the joke before. "Actually no, I'm not. Are you?"

Wirat smiled. "Actually yes, I am."

"Interesting," said Daniel. "I'm wondering what that means to you, Wirat, to be a Buddhist?"

"Daniel," said Kat.

"Mean?" The salesman searched the tourist's face. It was a penetrating look, a quick yet thorough examination

146

that immediately unraveled Daniel's bravado, made him feel small and childish. "Buddhism means making ethical choices. Our path, you see, is focused on right action, when our mind is at peace with what we do."

Is this guy serious? How could Wirat believe it ethical to use a fabled Buddhist temple in order to sell a suit?

Daniel wanted to tell this salesman off, but was interrupted by a strong sense of self-doubt. Something about the young man's eyes, their calm observation, made him aware of how his own tourist mind worked—its incessant suspicion, its constant judgment. The thought occurred that maybe he was not being fair with this guy. Was there something he'd missed? He reached over, took the binder from Kat's hands and opened it up.

"Daniel," she said, a bit louder than before.

He ignored her. Staring at the photos, he saw that the young man's suits were, in fact, beautiful. *That is, for someone wanting a suit.* Beautiful, yes, and Daniel was certain they were far less expensive than in any "first-world" country. So how could Wirat be blamed for trying to sell one? This was no scam, the tourist realized, just business.

Just a guy doing business.

But wait, hold on now, wasn't that the point? Wasn't that what made him feel uncomfortable? He checked his watch. Their five minutes were up and a brand new minute was beginning. All that mattered was what happened next.

Daniel flicked the binder shut.

"The truth is," he said, "I don't like these fancy suits."

"Oh," said Wirat. "Why?"

"It's what business people wear. To truly *be a Buddhist,* I think, a person must follow a different path, must choose to be poor."

Kat nudged him with her knee.

The salesman laughed. "Being poor, my friend, is not a requirement." His smile seemed pure, and did not waver.

For Daniel this was a battle of wills, and he could feel himself losing. Frustrated, he steeled his nerve. He stared into Wirat's eyes. They were big and gentle, ageless and wise. There was no fight in them, not a trace, and nothing at all to fight with. Daniel looked deeper. It was like wading into a cool clear pond. It was a quiet place, a peaceful place, a place that felt safe, a place without fear.

Oh, he thought, *if only life could be so simple.*

"The Buddha does not look at what we wear," said Wirat. "Only what we do. That is what I've learned."

Kat squeezed Daniel's elbow. He could barely feel it.

He sat, solid as a bronze statue yet light as air, his skin warm and tingling, his anxiety gone, forgotten. He felt himself floating in Wirat's luminous gaze. If Daniel did not know better, he would swear that this young man knew and forgave his every sin. Their connection felt mystical, it truly did, and for a few long seconds, one eternal moment, Daniel became a true believer, convinced he was in the presence of a saint.

Were he to ever write this story, it would end right here.

Kat took hold of Daniel's arm. She glared at him with absolute resolve. "We need to go."

"What?"

"Now," she said. "Please."

She seemed so far away. Almost out of reach. Her eyes were angry, yes, and also pleading. She looked frightened, as if he'd left her behind, abandoned her, and might never be coming back.

That snapped him out of it. *Oh God,* he thought, *oh no. Did I just get half-baked dreamy over a guy selling suits?*

He turned to the young Thai man and gazed into his perfect eyes. "I'm sorry, Wirat, I made a mistake. I should have been honest with myself and never come in here."

Kat guided him to his feet. She grabbed the bag of silver, the other of icons, and headed for the door.

Wirat, still smiling, nodded his head as if he fully understood, as if he and Daniel were lifelong friends and would always be close. The salesman handed him a card.

"Here," he said, "in case you ever change your mind."

AMIGOS

After a bumpy five-hour flight from Santiago, Art didn't know what he was seeing. It looked like the shadow of a cloud floating on the water. The plane took another dip. His stomach lurched and he closed his eyes.

"Adelante vemos la Isla de Pasqua," the pilot said in Spanish. "What we're seeing, for you English-speaking folks, is Easter Island. Or as the natives call it, *Rapa Nui.*"

Art waited for wheels to hit the ground before he looked again. Though the ocean was visible to his right, he kept his focus down on the narrow runway, grateful that his nausea had begun to lift.

Danni touched his arm. "You okay, Dad?"

He turned from the window, gazed into her sweet, apprehensive eyes, leaned over and kissed her cheek. Though now eighteen, she was still his baby girl. "Thanks, honey," he said. "Don't worry, I'm fine."

Art resettled in his seat and again closed his eyes. He could not calm poor Danni's nerves unless he calmed his own. *Why do I feel anxious?*

He thought of Liz, his oldest. It was like thinking of a casual acquaintance, a person he barely knew—a person, it seemed, he might never understand. Was it wise to have committed five weeks on an island because of her?

He remembered that at the time it had been an easy decision. "I've got a great connection," she'd said. "A free place for you to stay." The year before, after dropping out of graduate school, Liz had traveled to Chile. Art was awed by how she'd pulled that off. Who knows where she got the money? She'd spent a month on Rapa Nui, had stayed in a hut with a native family. "You'll see," she said, "why I love that place."

Art glanced over at his youngest. Danni gave him a brave smile and held his hand. Such a tender child, thoughtful and bookish, and perhaps, like him, a bit too stuck in middle-class American culture.

That was why, for a high school graduation present, he'd followed Liz's advice and offered Danni this trip to South America. Liz had gone out of her way to arrange their time on Rapa Nui. She seemed bent on proving that her wayward years were over, that she could now be trusted. Art hoped it was true. Waiting at the airport, Liz had told him, would be a guy named Cacho, "*un buen amigo*" of hers who'd offered to let them stay at his house.

Well, thought Art, we'll see.

At the gate, people were brandishing signs. Danni spotted the one with their names on it and headed that direction. A man stepped forward and held out his hand.

Art blinked, smiled, and shook it.

Liz had mentioned that Cacho was a native islander.

Nothing else.

She must have known how shocked her dad would be. He tried not to stare at the broad chested, dark-skinned man, who was wearing just a loincloth. The guy's body was tattooed all over with arcane symbols. He looked like a model for Rapa Nui's renowned stone statues—his hair, like theirs, wound up in a topknot—his face wider, but equally invulnerable.

"*Bienvenidos,*" Cacho said. Even his voice was hard.

Though Art had never been interested in native cultures, his curiosity was now fired up. This could be a life changing

150

experience! He admonished himself for questioning Liz's judgment. He needed to give her credit. He should make more of an effort to be her friend, he really should.

Cacho drove them to his spacious bamboo hut. It was dark inside, lit by a single dangling bulb. Art's eyes needed several seconds to adjust. The floor was dirt, he could see that much, and there was one small window. Hanging from the walls were things he did not recognize—tools of some sort, or maybe weapons.

There were people, too, off in the shadows.

Cacho introduced his wife, who was fingering the crucifix hanging around her neck.

"And these are my sons," he said. Like a four-headed creature, they huddled together in one dim corner of the hut.

Art, pleased that he and Danni knew the language, said in Spanish, "Hello, nice to meet you."

Danni gave a shy wave and said, "Hey, how's it going?"

The wife, Victoria, said to her, "We're fine, thank you." But she did not seem to mean it. There was something going on, Art guessed, perhaps a domestic squabble, because she would not look at her husband. It reminded him of Bev, his ex, on the day he and Danni were leaving. Bev hadn't wanted this trip to happen. She feared that he would not take good care of their daughter.

He looked forward to proving her wrong.

The smallest boy began to cry. Victoria picked him up and held him close. Now she glared at Cacho. Art looked away and smiled at the older boys, who stared back without emotion. Then he remembered the letter Liz had given him. He dug into his satchel, retrieved it, and handed the envelope to Cacho. He assumed she'd written a greeting to the whole family. Maybe that would chill things out.

Actually, no. Things got even hotter. Cacho backed away a few feet and read the one page letter silently to himself. Victoria moved to the stove and stirred a huge black pot of something boiling. The oldest boy, Haéte, barely a teen, sharpened a stick with a butcher's knife, from

151

time to time glancing at his mother as if awaiting her order to skewer and throw them in the pot.

Cacho folded the letter with care. He tucked it below his proud round belly, down into his loincloth, and signaled his guests to follow, exiting the hut and leading them up the narrow rutted road. To their left, beyond a rocky knoll, was the ocean. Cacho pointed to a hill a few hundred yards ahead, to a small, bright, lime-colored building.

"The new house I'm building," he said. He did not say another word for the ten minutes it took to get there.

The house was made of concrete block. It had a metal corrugated roof. Inside, surrounding a cheap pink linoleum floor, stood haphazardly plastered walls that were painted, with visible brushstrokes, a watered-down blue. There were no interior doors. In the small living room, and smaller bedroom, was a mess of scattered junk and tools. Art got a whiff of something rotting. Perhaps dead mice.

The Americans smiled and nodded their approval. They expected, as Liz had assured, that a place would be given, free, for them to stay. And hey, they didn't mind roughing it, right, so why not smile and nod?

Art saw there were a couple of foam pads to sleep on. A couple of blankets, too, and pillows.

Cacho pointed to the bathroom.

A toilet and a sink. A mirror but no shower.

No big deal, Art thought, *real campers don't get showers!* There must be a hose outside. That would be good enough in this hot humid climate. He looked around for the kitchen. No wonder he'd missed it. There, by the front door, was a rusty one-burner stove on a filthy old card table. No sink or refrigerator. On the table next to the stove were a few dirty forks and spoons, two plastic plates, and one glass. Art took a breath. None of this was what he'd hoped for, true, but hey, it would be a challenge to do without! That's how he had to think. Yeah, this could be fun. They would wash dishes, and themselves, outdoors. What a treat that he and Danni could experience this together.

152

"You can stay here," Cacho said, "in exchange for working with me on the house."

He called them *amigos* several times while walking around the perimeter of the building and pointing at piles of trash to be burned. That would be part of their work.

Cacho handed Art a lighter, then walked off.

He and Danni went back into the house. She looked around at the dirt, the grime, the cobwebs. "Oh my god."

"Yeah," Art said, "ain't it great!"

She smiled and handed him a broom.

Art used a bandana to cover his nose and mouth, then swept the ceiling, the walls, the floor. Danni was outside. While waiting for the dust to settle, she shook out their pads, blankets, and pillows. She hosed off the table and washed the few dishes. Art put the obvious garbage, including three dead mice, a dead snake, and the skeleton of what looked like a bat, into a big black plastic bag. Then, together, they organized the tools, and usable materials, into one corner of the living room. In another corner, Art put his mat. He hung an extra blanket in place of the missing bedroom door. Danni, needing privacy, would sleep in there.

In the evening Cacho reappeared. He said nothing of the changes. He'd brought an extra glass, which meant that his guests would each have one of their own. A thoughtful gesture, it was, and Art was about to thank him when Cacho said, "We need to talk." He was holding up a cardboard liter of wine, was shaking it like a rattle. Then he filled the two glasses. He handed one to Art and kept the other for himself. Did not even look at Danni.

Art saw that she was angry. Trying to soften the blow, he offered her his glass. She shook her head, grabbed her book and the lamp, and disappeared into the bedroom.

Cacho went outside. After signaling Art to follow, he motioned him to sit on the stoop. Cacho sat too, and made a toast, "To your beautiful daughter, Liz!"

Art took a sip while Cacho drained his glass. He refilled it, saying they needed to have *un discurso de hombres*.

"Okay," said Art. *Man-talk, huh.* He knew what Danni, his avid feminist, would say to that. Oh yes, this guy was going to be difficult. They would need to be patient, would need to tolerate other ways of thinking.

"I call this Casa Liz," said Cacho. "Soon we'll be adding rooms on for our children."

What? He has to be joking, right? Or maybe not. Art wanted to believe he'd misunderstood, and was afraid he hadn't. "You don't mean with Liz?"

Cacho laughed. "Who else, amigo?"

Instantly the guy looked different, no longer the native mystic Art had hoped for. There was a prehistoric quality to his dull brown eyes. Like an animal's eyes. A predator's eyes. Cacho's tattoos reminded him of scales, his topknot of a furry horn.

Oh for Christsakes! thought Art, startled by his bizarre reaction, which at any other time he would regard as a kind of racism. But for crying-out-loud, it was his twenty-four-year-old daughter being discussed here, damn it, and this guy was freaking him out!

"Listen, Cacho, I—"

"She will be coming soon."

Her father felt the words like a spear through his brain.

"She wrote you that?"

"Not necessary," said Cacho. "I know."

Art cleared his throat, gathered himself, and told Cacho that he must have misunderstood the letter. "She has a full-time job in Denver," he said. "And a boyfriend."

The man laughed again. He shook his head, then downed his wine. He was acting as if Art had no idea of Liz's plans, was not important in her life, and therefore did not merit his respect. He grabbed his carton of wine. "Tomorrow we work," he said, got up and left.

Five weeks of this shit? No. No way.

How had Cacho gotten the idea that Liz would come make babies with him? Had they shared his wine and watched some awesome sunset, was that all it took?

154

Or had Liz hugged him when she left the island, maybe cried and kissed his cheek, wishing out loud that she could stay, promising to come back soon. Had she smiled her tender smile and blinked her big blue eyes and let him think he could believe it?

Liz might have done any of that, or more, and never known what Cacho was thinking. Because she didn't want to. It was not uncommon that some guy thought she was in love with him, later finding out he'd made the whole thing up. She refused to see how her beauty and overt friendliness affected men. According to Liz, she was always *just being herself.* How could anyone question that? Was it her fault they misunderstood? No. That was their problem, right?

Well yeah, sure, Art agreed, but wasn't it wise to be aware of their problem? She did not seem concerned with how men might willfully misread her intentions. That's what worried Art. Knowing how fucked-up men could be, he wished Liz weren't so certain, and self-righteous, about her innocence.

With Cacho, of course, she may have shown nothing but genuine friendship. It wouldn't take much for a macho man like him to believe whatever he wanted.

Art decided, for Danni's sake, they had to get out of "Casa Liz." But to stay anywhere else on this infamously expensive island (at least a hundred bucks a night) was out of the question. He couldn't afford it, not with another two months of traveling ahead. The only reasonable solution was to leave the island as soon as possible.

The next morning, while Danni slept, he hurried to the airport, a twenty-minute walk. He was told that their return tickets to Santiago could not be changed. And, because it was high season, even if they wanted to pay for new ones, flights were sold out for weeks. The attendant must have noticed his unease. "Sometimes," she said, "there are cancellations. Not often, but it is possible. Do you want to get on a waiting list? Can you be ready to leave any day?"

"No," he said. The thought of being on constant alert made him feel small and weak.

Art walked back home on the narrow trail along the bluff. He watched the relentless waves crashing against the cliffs. *I can't let that arrogant prick ruin our trip!* He had counted on these five inexpensive weeks and was not going to give them up! *So what if the guy is delusional about Liz? Let him have his crackpot ideas. Let him dream.* Art would show Cacho that he knew better, was not affected by his bluster, and could not be pushed around.

But Danni did not need to know this stuff concerning her sister. Art would give his girl a chance to enjoy the heralded Easter Island. He wanted that chance too.

After a breakfast of bananas and mangos they explored the little town of Hanga Roa, then climbed to the rim of the Rano Kau volcano. They'd both seen Kevin Costner's flopped film, *Rapa Nui*, which focused on "The Birdman Cult." With that in mind, they found the 400-foot cliff where the island's bravest warriors had begun their descent to the sea. In the movie this happened whenever a king died, a long and hallowed tradition. Danni pointed at the tiny islet half a mile away. According to Costner (and what he'd claimed to be historically accurate) the warriors swam there through shark-infested waters, found the egg of a Sooty Tern, brought the prize back in their loincloth, and climbed the daunting cliff. First to arrive up top with an un-cracked egg was declared the new king. Or so the story went.

"I liked the movie," Danni said.

"Even if it wasn't true?"

"Geez Dad, it's, you know, a movie."

She was right. *Lighten up.* What did it matter that Art doubted some Hollywood movie? Yeah, he had doubts, about lots of things.

Un-doubtable, however, were the island's many massive heads. Three of them stood at the edge of the cliff. The ancient statues were called *Moai*. Their average height was 35 feet, their average weight a whopping 80 tons. While half of them remained unfinished in the remote volcanic quarry of Rano Raraku (the largest being 60 feet long, weighing 270 tons), anthropologists continued to wonder how the other 887 had been moved around the perimeter of the island.

Art had heard of numerous theories, each with its own rationale, its supporters and its detractors.

Since he spoke Spanish he could ask about the theories. Avoiding Cacho, he questioned other islanders. Few of them wore loincloths, favoring khaki shorts and flowery shirts, but they seemed as guarded as Cacho. What Art interpreted from their politely controlled laughter was that Rapa Nui people did not care what "outsiders" thought. For native islanders, how the statues got moved was irrelevant. The giant heads were not historic icons but daily reminders of a still-living past. This was especially true for the men. He could see they took great pride in their culture. The Moai were their omnipresent relatives, heroes, mentors. Each year the sculptures were honored with the weeklong *Tapati* festival—dance and song and copious amounts of pot and alcohol—its focus, though probably somewhat bleary, on the ever-powerful visage and vision of the heads. But no one would say what spiritual guidance they received from the Moai. It was not a thing to be discussed with Art.

He learned, as well, to keep his own thoughts private. His opinions did not matter. Rapa Nui people knew what they knew, and that was that. Easter Island, as they loved to say, was the epicenter of creation, what they called "The Bellybutton of the Universe." It was the place where everything began—and, in time, would end.

Art and Danni spent four days backpacking around the perimeter of Rapa Nui. On day two, as they were admiring a long line of Moai, she noted that every one of them had topknots. In other words, were men. "From what I've read, there's not a single female."

"Surprise, surprise," Art said.

"Yeah, right? *Duh.*"

It was a great experience for them both, until, on the final morning of their hike, Danni brought up Liz. They'd been taking in a gorgeous ocean view, at that moment moving past several fallen Moai, when she stopped cold.

"I'm remembering some weird stuff Liz said."

"Yeah?" Art said. "Like what?"

"In *The Birdman Cult,* she told me, a virgin had to sit alone in a cave for three whole months, to purify herself for the new king."

"According to the movie."

"No," Danni said, "according to Cacho. In the movie it was six months. He told her it was three."

"No kidding," said Art, "I thought Costner made that up."

"Well, someone did. That's what I mean."

"Huh?"

"Liz is full of shit, okay? To her this stuff is real. I've been reading the article Mom gave me. From *National Geographic.* It says there were plenty of things in the movie, like the 'caved virgin', that never happened. Total myth. I mean, don't you think that's weird? Why would Liz believe, you know, whatever, without doing any research? She also thinks 'The Birdman Cult' was part of the Moai culture. Another lie. It came centuries later, when the society was disintegrating. When men started thinking they were gods."

That last bit sounded overblown, but what could Art say? He hadn't read the article, didn't know its sources, and when Danni was this sure of herself, which wasn't often, he knew better than to confront her.

She must have sensed his doubt. She reminded him that they'd seen many more fallen Moai than those still standing. "Because they'd stopped being honored." That was Danni's explanation. She said it was known as "The Great Collapse." She claimed that it had happened during the late sixteenth century, after the big trees were long gone. "Without any forest, the soil eroded and farmland washed away. With fewer animals to hunt or herd," she said, "the

158

strongest clan, thinking they were gods, killed and ate the weakest. That was *The Birdman Cult.* Just a bunch of cannibals."

On a roll, she remembered other details from the article, many of them outlandish, and, for the most part, gruesome.

Art could not resist pointing out that any historical view was to some extent subjective. He'd learned to question the "documented accounts" of self-acclaimed "experts"—experts who came a thousand years after the fact.

Perhaps angry at her father's skepticism, at her inability to win him over, the moment they returned to the lime green house Danni went to ask Cacho. He was outside, unloading bags of cement with Haéte. Art followed. He watched as Cacho pretended not to hear, as he kept his back to her.

Danni apologized for interrupting. "My main question," she said, "is why are so many Moai lying on the ground?"

He never looked her way. "Japanese," he grumbled. He spit, tossed off the last bag, and walked toward a neighbor's place, shadowed by his son.

"What a pig," she said. Art was glad he didn't have to say it. Then she surprised him. "No way Liz had sex with that pig, right?"

"Uh, well, I hope not."

"No, I can't believe she'd…ooh, *gawd,* please…not with him," she said, and marched off down the road.

A few hours passed. Art was standing on a stool in the bathroom, painting the plywood ceiling, when Danni wandered in, stood at the mirror, and stared. She had his same thin frame, his freckled nose, his bright blue eyes. Her hair, though long, was also brown and curly. They'd always looked alike, but for Art it went beyond that. At times, though he did not believe in reincarnation, it was easy to imagine them in another life as friends. Good and trusted friends.

"Hey girl, what's up?"

"Dad," she said, her voice full of urgency, "can we talk?"

"Sure."

He put down his brush. They went to the front porch, sat on the stoop, and gazed out over the nearby dunes at the endless windswept ocean. Its dull gray color matched the late afternoon sky, except was sparked by flashing whitecaps.

"We need to get off this island," she said.

"Well," he said. "that's not as easy as—"

"Please, Dad, I..." Then she stopped, leaned on his shoulder and started sobbing.

"What's the matter, honey? What is it?"

"It feels like no one wants us here."

He hugged her close, agreed, then told her he'd already tried to exchange their tickets.

"I'll use the money Mom gave me to buy new ones."

He explained why that wasn't possible either. "Anyway, never mind," he said. "Why let our trip be ruined by this Cacho jerk?"

She continued sobbing, which hurt his heart and emboldened his mind.

"Look," he said, thinking what he hoped might be true, "together we're stronger than him, right?"

"Yeah, okay, right," she said, laughing through her tears.

Like old friends, they promised to suck it up, be brave, make the best of a bad situation.

Less than an hour later, Haéte showed up. He gave them a big smile, as if to show how welcome they were. His hair was long and black, like Cacho's, though not tied up. He wore old torn blue jeans and a faded red tee shirt that read, SAVE THE DOLPHINS. The boy had a handsome face, sincere and friendly. Art assumed he'd come to apologize for his grouchy old man. Well, no, he was there to make them realize that they'd misunderstood. "My father gets mad sometimes. He's sensitive about the Moai."

Uh huh, Art thought, *not to mention everything else.* "Why is he mad at the Japanese?"

"They're the ones in charge," said Haéte. "They want to be rid of us."

Art was wondering what to make of that when Danni took over and put the kid in his place. She brought up the article from *National Geographic*. "Rapa Nui was named a World Heritage Site in 1995. That brought necessary funds, and experts from Japan, to protect the Moai. Isn't that a good thing?"

"No." Haéte's eyes locked with hers. "That's the problem. The money all goes to Chile. Chile thinks they own us, can order us around. Police boats patrol the shore to keep us from the Moai. It is a crime to touch the heads. No one but Japanese scientists are allowed. My father says it's wrong, because we are the Hitoranga Clan, the Moai Warriors, the ones who believe in ancient ways. It was our ancestors who sculpted and placed the heads. We should be the ones to take care of them. Why should foreigners tell Rapa Nui people what to do?"

Hearing Haéte defend his father with such pride made Art feel sympathetic. It was easier to be pleasant when Cacho showed up to work on the house. It also helped Danni cope with being stuck on the island for another three weeks. Because he was grateful to the boy, and could see Danni liked him, Art encouraged Haéte to hang around whenever he wasn't at school or helping out his dad.

Haéte taught her indigenous songs and dances.

He introduced her to his friends.

Heck, thought Art, *this trip might turn out okay.*

In his gut, though, he knew it wouldn't, and he awoke each day with a sense of dread. He tried to stay positive. That was best. He started buying the wine that Cacho liked to drink, the two of them sharing it while they worked. Art wanted to show how helpful he could be. But he felt, as usual, ignored and disrespected. Though they both spoke Spanish, Cacho preferred other forms of communication: a vast array of hand and body gestures, grunts and groans and long contemptuous sighs. *"Amigo,"* he would add from time to time, especially when the gringo had an idea of how to build something. It didn't matter that Art was once a carpenter. *"Amigo,"* the guy would say, shaking his head.

One day Art said, "You know, Cacho, my name is Art."

Cacho laughed and slapped him on the back. "Names do not matter, friend. Mine or yours."

Art could see the man's colossal contempt, like a mountain impossible to climb. Instead, he tried to get around it—Art's version of spiritual non-attachment. But by their final week the subtle abuse had worn him down.

Cacho also seemed to be suffering. Art saw him one day sitting in his pickup, reading and re-reading the letter from Liz. Perhaps he was beginning to realize the truth, that she was not coming back. Ever.

Each day the guy spent less time working on the lime green house. He stopped wanting any help. For the most part he sat outside, kept to himself, and did not do much except smoke joints and drink wine.

Art was drinking more too. Far worse than Cacho's disdain was Danni's near-giddy happiness. It made him miserable, her and Haéte going off each day to who knows where. The thirteen-year-old boy was noticeably well built—in this culture on the verge of manhood! How had Art missed that? He'd begun to notice the secretive looks between them, and their muffled laughter, as if telling jokes not to be shared with others, and he shuddered whenever they rode off bareback on Haéte's horse, Danni sitting up against the boy, arms around his hardened belly.

Twice she'd mentioned the possibility of getting a tattoo. She also wanted a piercing for her nose. She wouldn't admit it, but her father knew this had to do with Danni's jealousy of Liz, who had neither.

At last a chance to outdo her big sister.

"To be honest," he'd said when pushed, "I think you look best the way you are."

162

Danni had laughed and kissed him on the forehead. "Well then," she'd said, turning to leave, "good thing it's not up to you."

Her saying that vexed his already frazzled nerves.

Three days passed and they hardly spoke.

In one more week they'd be gone (Art knew it, counted on it) but he could not quite imagine it happening. Each day seemed endless, and every hour a threat.

Depressed and desperate, Art went to see Victoria. Her face had been popping into his head. Once he dreamt of her standing over him with a stake and a hammer. *Weird.* He'd learned from Danni that she was a devout Christian, maybe that explained it. Also weird, because Art was not at all religious, it felt like he needed her forgiveness, like that might make things better.

Ridiculous.

He knew it was ridiculous, but went anyway.

She opened the door. "Oh."

Her sad eyes changed to angry.

"Hello," he said. "I feel like we should talk."

"Because my husband wants your daughter?"

"Well, no. I mean I'm sorry if, if somehow Cacho got the idea that—"

"Who knows how Cacho gets his ideas? Many years ago, when I first came to this island from Santiago, he had ideas about me. Now it's your Liz. Do you know he used my father's money, my inheritance, to build her that house? Do you know he waits for her to come?"

"Please, Victoria, that's not going to happen, okay, she's got a steady job now, she's—"

"I don't know what's going to happen. Only what he thinks will happen. Only what he wants to happen. And he'll treat me like a slave until it does."

She looked trapped, imprisoned, forever absorbed by her dark dank hut.

"I swear," Art said, now with genuine concern for her obvious pain, "I wouldn't have come if—"

"You shouldn't be here. You people go where you go because you don't know where you belong. You're lost," she said, and slammed the door in his face.

A few days passed, but Art could see no difference between them. He spent hours sitting on the cliffs, staring at the ocean, at how it changed and changed and always stayed the same. There was no understanding it, no escaping it.

Again at dusk he went back to the house.

Danni was sitting on the stoop. She hadn't brushed her hair for weeks, its curls now twisted into matted rivulets. She wore short blue-jean cut-offs and a white tank top. Her body was brown. Her feet were bare. She smiled and held Art's hand when he sat next to her. The joy in her eyes looked like a warning.

She kissed him on the cheek and said, "I love this place."

"Glad you're having a good time, honey."

"It's not that," she said. "I've never felt this way before, Dad, like I'm changing, becoming my true self." Then came the thing he most feared. "I'm going to use the money Mom gave me to buy a new ticket. In a month, the lady told me, when the high season ends, there won't be any problem. We can meet in Santiago when you get back from Argentina."

Art's stomach turned, his mind raced. He imagined her stuck here on this island, pregnant, a baby at her breast and naked grimy twins fighting at her feet. He asked point blank if she and Haéte were having sex.

Ooh, that pissed her off. Not a good sign.

"This has nothing to do with sex," she said. But she couldn't tell him what it had to do with. "It's something I can't explain. Something I have to figure out."

Art looked out at the endless churning sea. A month apart and he would lose all influence, of that he was certain. He turned back, put his hand on hers, and started listing the great things they'd do in Argentina.

Danni kept telling him he didn't understand. She tried to say why, but could not explain that either.

164

Art thought, *Bev will kill me.* And that was the least of his concerns. "Look, sweetheart, I'm sorry, I really am, but I can't let you stay." He was thinking of married life with her mother, of how their starry-eyed romance had faded more every year. Faded and finally disappeared. He did not want Danni to make the same mistake. "The whole time I'd be worrying," he said. "It doesn't feel safe."

Danni laughed and said, "That's what I mean, Dad. That's why you can't understand."

"Why?"

"Because I do feel safe. Get it? Because this is my life. Mine, not yours."

"Well sure, I, I didn't mean to—"

"I have my own feelings, okay?"

"Okay, honey, but please, get serious, we both know what you're feeling isn't love."

Danni's look turned smug, reminding him of Liz, which pissed him off. "How do *you know* what *I'm feeling?*"

"For god sakes, he's a kid! Can't you see that?" Art's mind was now on fire and he couldn't put it out. "He doesn't know shit about life, damn it! Neither do you!"

Danni got to her feet and walked away.

"Wait," said Art. "We have to finish this!"

That turned her around fast. She marched back and stood in front of him. "You may not be finished, but I am. I'm staying, Dad, and there is nothing you can say to change my mind."

Art watched as she walked down the road toward Cacho's hut. Though this would not be easy, he knew what had to happen. Their flight was in two days and she had to be on that plane.

"Amiga!" Cacho hollered. *"Levántete amiga!"*

Art opened his eyes and checked his watch. Five in the morning. What could the asshole possibly want? He hauled himself up, put on his pants, and headed for the door.

Cacho threw it open.

165

Haéte stood behind him. "We're going fishing," the boy said. "Danni wants to come."

She hurried out of the bedroom, carrying a jacket while buttoning up her shirt.

It felt like one of those impossible moments where there was no chance of Art being a good parent. Whatever he did would be wrong. And there was no time to think things through...no time to think at all. Uninvited but determined, he stumbled behind his pert young daughter through the humid darkness to an idling pickup. Danni ignored him. She sat on the bench-seat in front. Before climbing in next to her, Haéte re-arranged the truck's bed. He moved tarps and nets and five-gallon buckets, making room for Art to sit. His back was against a can that reeked of gasoline. His legs were scrunched up against the tailgate.

The harbor amounted to a short dock that angled into a protective, if minimal, rock jetty. Danni asked how she could help. Art did what he was told. Haéte handed each of them a bucket. The little wooden skiff, tied along with others at the dock, was sealed by fiberglass, layers of it applied with excessive resin. Inside the wooden hull were two sun-bleached benches, one at either end. They loaded the buckets, as instructed, in behind each bench. That left plenty of space in the middle.

Cacho filled the tank with gas, then yanked the engine's cord. The rest of them piled in. Haéte sat next to his father, forcing Danni to sit next to hers.

Art was surprised by his sudden curiosity. He looked at the thick rock jetty that shielded the dock from large incoming swells. During his daily walks he'd seen those swells, and the pounding waves they created, and did not understand how a boat could get in or out of the harbor before motors were invented.

Then again, for the life of him, he did not understand how anyone could swim half a mile through shark-infested waters in search of some damn egg.

Cacho idled until the ocean took a breath. Seeing his chance, he gunned the motor. Their boat, like an animal running for its life, carved a furious path out of the sheltered waters, up over a rising swell, out into the frothy open sea.

For twenty minutes they paralleled the coastline.

Not far away, waves crashed against the cliffs.

At his father's nod, Haéte stripped down to a loincloth. He tied back his long hair, put on goggles, leaned over the edge of the boat and plunged his head into the water. His slick brown calves muscled up behind, thighs flexing hard across the sideboard. Danni, Art saw, was impressed. He was too. Head submerged, the boy pointed Cacho forward, or left...no, no, farther left, farther left. Haéte came up for air, then again went down and kept pointing left.

Cacho steered as directed until his son's fingers tightened into a fist. Seeing that, he cut the motor and grabbed his carton of wine.

The boy pulled himself out of the water. He sat on the boat's edge, caught his breath, looked up and smiled. Not at Danni, as Art would have expected, but at his father, as if they were out here by themselves. As if no one else existed.

The two of them prepared their fishing lines. Well, not exactly lines, they were thin nylon ropes. At the end of each was a rock secured with bailing wire.

"Our anchors," said Haéte. And every six feet back from the rock they wired on a chicken neck. Dangling from each neck were three or four hooks. "This is the old way," he said. "This is how we do it."

Cacho grumbled something, perhaps irritated by the chatter. "Now," he said.

Haéte threw the rocks overboard. The many necks swirled down behind. Then there was a prolonged silence as Cacho gauged, by some means he never explained, how far the rocks needed to drop. Satisfied, he signaled to Haéte. The boy secured the ropes to thick metal cleats.

Cacho laughed, drank his wine, and soon, as if he'd willed it, both lines were getting dragged around.

167

After several minutes, father and son pulled them up. The boat came alive with gleaming silver bodies. Cacho and Haéte unhooked the catch, tossed the rocks overboard, and before long the lines were again getting dragged around.

Within an hour the deck was thick with squirming fish.

Squawking gulls had gathered overhead, full of frenzy, eyeing the pile of potential food and trying to best position themselves, fighting amongst each other like a swarm of spoiled and hungry children.

Cacho was clearly pleased by their squabbling.

Though Art had shown obvious fascination with the native fishing technique, no one asked if he or Danni might want to try. Outsiders, it seemed, were not allowed. Cacho and Haéte kept ignoring them, babbling between themselves in their Rapa Nui language.

"Why did they bring us?" Art said in English.

Danni shot him a glance. It felt like a threat. Did she think that Cacho or Haéte might understand and feel insulted? Did she think it was her father being rude?

"Don't worry," he said, "they're off in their own world, honey, they're not—"

Danni turned and gazed out at the undulating sea. Art got the message. She meant that he should know his place, that it was unreasonable to expect, or want, any more than this.

Maybe she was right, but he now noticed something very wrong. They'd drifted in too far, were getting dangerously close to the breaking waves. He noticed Cacho notice his concern, and laugh, and light a pre-rolled joint.

The morning sun was heating up. The air was heavy. There was no breeze, not the slightest stir, and something began to stink, perhaps the residual slime of former fish.

Art's gut felt swollen. His eyes were sore. His tongue was dry and salty.

A seagull swooped down, squawking, close to his head, as the boat was rocked by another swell. Scared, and trying not to show it, he took long deep breaths. It didn't help. He worried that his stomach would revolt. He had to end this thing, had to get them back to shore.

Cacho flicked away the roach and drank some wine.

Art, his fear twisting into anger, decided to say what he knew was unacceptable. He pointed at some Moai on the near cliff's edge. "I think I know how they were moved."

Everyone looked at him. No one said a thing.

Cacho put down the wine and lit another joint.

"I mean that's the big question," Art said. "Right?" By then the others had looked away. He felt the tense silence, proof that he'd broken some sacred rule. "The most plausible theory," he said, "also explains the decimated forests. The big trees were chopped down and stripped clean, sacrificed as rollers for the Moai."

Cacho shook his head and said, "Amigo."

When said alone like that, Art had learned, the word signified extreme impatience.

Good!

Cacho handed Haéte the joint. His freed hands then spread toward the sky. "Your most plausible theory," he said, "is *pure shit. Pura caca*," he repeated, his beefy fingers dipping down, gripping the tails of two slick silvery fish and dangling them in front of Art.

Glossy black eyes bulged in their sockets.

"Our Moai," Cacho said, "were moved by pterodactyls." He tossed the dead fish at Art's feet. "It was easy as that, amigo. The giant birds were our pets. They carried our heads wherever we wanted."

Holy crap, was Art actually hearing this? It was so scary stupid that he did not dare laugh. *I mean c'mon, I've got no problem with creation stories or invented gods or mythic battles between good and evil. But gimme a break, man...domesticated dinosaurs?*

Danni smiled and handed Art the joint.

He took a big hit before passing it on. He blew out smoke, feeling superior and hopeful. His daughter, like him, must be stunned by Cacho's romantic delusions, his denial of reality. Then Art looked closely. He scrutinized her smiling face and realized the truth, that Cacho's cosmic bullshit had her glowing. She was excited by it, perhaps even honored—privileged to be out on the eternal sea with native fishermen and their ancient wisdom.

Not wanting to believe she was that naive, Art tried a joke. "Wow...yeah...sure wish I had a trained dinosaur right now."

Danni smirked. At him. Like a medieval priest might smirk at talk of a round planet. Art felt her condescension. He felt shamed and disregarded, tossed back like the puniest of fish as they floated closer to the crashing waves.

What's going on? They should be packing their bags, pleased to finally escape this awful place instead of bobbing toward oblivion in a skimpy wooden boat.

Art could feel himself beginning to panic. He shouldn't have gotten stoned.

Think, you idiot, think!

Okay, okay, as a last-ditch stab at reason he'd play the Grateful Tourist card. "I am thankful," he said to Cacho, "that you gave us this experience. I'd like to buy you dinner tonight. At the best restaurant. Something special," he said, "because tomorrow we'll need to pack and—"

Cacho put his hand up like a stop sign. He looked Art dead in the eyes and said, "Do you think, amigo, it can be explained?"

It? It what? He couldn't mean dinner, or packing. He must be referring to the Moai, to how they had been moved.

Explained? Yes, of course, why not!

But that would be the wrong thing to say. Art felt another big swell beneath them, and knew he should tell Cacho whatever he wanted to hear. Maybe then the guy would laugh, would slap him on the back, and please, *for godsakes please,* start the fucking motor!

"Some things," Art said, "are hard for us outsiders to understand."

170

"No," Cacho said. "The truth is, amigo, we are all outsiders. Human minds cannot be trusted. Our thinking, you see, wants to deceive us." He took a final gulp of wine and threw the carton overboard. "We are blind to what truly happens in this world. We are not supposed to understand."

Fine, Art thought. *Whatever you say.* He was willing to concede, admit the limits of his modern mind, but could see that Cacho didn't care, that he would continue to ignore him and the mounting swells.

To prove it, the guy pulled out another joint.

Should a freak wave come they'd be swamped.

Art tried to convince himself he was thinking too much. He wanted to believe, needed to believe, that Cacho, an experienced man of the sea, would never let them get sucked into the break. For assurance he looked at Haéte, who was watching his father.

The kid's forehead glistened with sweat. His eyelids were quivering. His fear was palpable, undeniable, but he wasn't going to say a thing. Or Danni either.

Neither of them dared to make a squeak.

And Cacho knew it. He had power out here in the vast mysterious sea, and would not give it up. That was why Art had been allowed to come along: to be taken away from the life he understood...to experience a world he could never know...to be awed and humbled by Cacho's fearlessness.

So yeah, okay, the guy had succeeded. Bravo! Here they were at the edge of death. Here they all were, under Cacho's spell. The native had scared the civilized man, scared him shitless, and was not about to budge until Art admitted it.

Under normal circumstances, Art would have no problem doing that. He knew the dangers of misguided pride. The problem was, he felt something else, something deeper going on. It felt like a test he must not fail. Of course he wanted to quit this silly macho game, but Art feared that by letting Cacho win he would lose his daughter forever.

Wait, that's crazy. Danni loves you. She'll always love you. Relax, man, don't let him hook you in! Give the fucker what he wants!

There was an entire chorus of similarly sensible voices in his head.

Everything will be okay, they said. *This is not worth dying for. Especially since you have no chance to win!*

They knew that he could never beat Cacho. They knew that he'd always envied guys like him—envied and hated them—big strong men who had no doubts, no inner voices, no vague regrets or unresolved remorse. Guys like Cacho did whatever the hell they pleased. They never stopped until they won, cliffs and sharks be damned!

Fine, Art thought, *time to surrender.* All he wanted was a way of handing over his useless weapons without losing the last of Danni's respect.

But how?

He peeked at her for some kind of hint. She looked away, would not acknowledge him, and suddenly, though he did not want to accept it, he knew. He'd already lost his little girl. There was nothing he could do to bring her back. He was at a loss. A total loss.

That's what he was feeling, his heart full of dread, right up until the instant he burst out laughing.

It was loud and careless laughter, like something had broken loose inside his mind, surprising him along with the others—his surrender so great, so complete, it felt like liberation.

Danni gave him a strange look, less embarrassed than worried. "Dad?"

Now it was Art who turned away. *Let her worry.* Same as him, she was on her own. He stayed focused on the fact, the incredible fact, that he had stopped caring, about her or anything else. It felt like he was bobbing up and down, alone, in a world of his own, a world without beginning or end. He had no fear whatsoever. It was a peace his mind had never known.

Is this what it's like for Cacho?

Art smiled at the big burly man. "Amigo!" he shouted, grabbing away the joint.

No, this guy could not stop him. Nothing could stop him. Art was free, finally free, and ready to transcend, be dragged down under by that pounding break, bashed into eternity against those jagged cliffs.

He took a toke and grinned from ear to ear. "Amigo!"

Cacho laughed, his eyes swimming with drunken joy.

Art laughed back, louder.

Haéte slammed his fists against the sideboard. He glanced at Danni, at her stunned expression, and went for the motor. With one great tug he whirred it into action.

As the boy steered them away from possible danger, Art was already gone. He felt far away. He felt reborn. Everything was changed. The sea and sky were open, wide open, all of it flowing, swirling, mixing together.

He had no idea what would happen next.

AFTER THE RUINS

Jake was traveling with Orph, a small and somewhat sickly black lab, in the '67 VW bus he'd converted to a camper. Or, rather, a sleeper: no stove; no fridge; a space to crash in by the side of the road. His life as a budding Deadhead had come to a screeching halt when the band decided to stop touring. Ready for a change himself, he took a leave from growing weed and drove from northern California to southern Mexico in search of Mayan ruins and magic mushrooms.

Jake had read in his guidebook about Palenque. The ancient city sat atop a high plateau. At its back were steep limestone cliffs above a tall and tangled jungle, impassable by all two-legged creatures with the notable exception of howler monkeys. Out front, it looked down over a wide flat plain. Potential enemies were visible for days in advance. So yes, like the guidebook said, Palenque was an important Mayan spiritual center. Also an impressive fortress.

Jake had spent the night at a run-down hotel in the town named after the famous ruins. Less than an hour from the archeological site, he arrived early the next morning and was the first one in. Alone, and liking it, he came upon "The Palace" and gazed at incomprehensible glyphs, limestone sculptures, and layered bas-reliefs. The day was overcast, and cooler than normal. Lucky, because Orph had to wait in the van. Jake didn't mind that his dog would not be tagging along. He appreciated such moments to himself and tried not to waste them.

174

To ground himself in this amazing place he went to his primary destination, "The Temple Of Inscriptions," tallest of the Palenque pyramids. The hotel's owner, an old alcoholic Texan named Len, had told Jake about things not mentioned in his guidebook: "Temple's got a secret passageway down inside its center. That's where they buried the head honcho. Yessirree, young fella, the whole damn deal's just one big grave!"

Jake started climbing.

And yessirree, just like Len said, there were eighty-eight steps to the top, and they were steep, which left him winded and a bit off balance. He decided, before looking for the secret passage, to get stoned. What better way to commune with gods? But as he reached for a pre-rolled joint he heard a familiar sound from behind the near wall—a loud voice with a strong mid-western accent. He thought of his high school biology teacher, who used to make fun of their non-Kansan neighbors. Mr. Garth could imitate them perfectly, and glowed when his students, most of them flunking, could mimic him. Jake was curious whether he'd learned anything in that class. He leaned against the ruin wall and listened. A Hoosier maybe? Cheese head?

Oh no, much worse: a Chicago Illinoiser! Somewhere in Jake's head, Mr. Garth and all the gods were cringing.

The guy suddenly emerged from around the corner, mid-monologue. He was a stout, aging lion, with a cropped silver mane and a matching majestic mustache. His muscular tanned arms were covered with thick white hair. He was busy explaining to a young blond woman how "spiritual power often becomes a weapon of oppression."

Yep, Jake thought, Chicago. South-side raised, north-side evolved. And, true to form, the guy kept right on talking, as if unaware of Jake's presence. Or perhaps he'd merely seen it as an irrelevant detail, accustomed to people gathering around, listening to him talk.

175

"Take these temples," the guy said. "They may, indeed, be a testament to the gods, but were built by the forced labor of indoctrinated peasants."

Ah, Jake guessed with justifiable confidence, *a professor.* No wonder he'd dropped out of college. "Indoctrinated?" he said. "Couldn't it be a matter of belief?"

The lion professor glanced at him sideways. "Belief by force. That is what indoctrinated means."

"I understand," Jake said, "I'm just saying it might be possible, since no one knows for certain, that the peasants trusted their priests' visions and actually wanted to build the temples."

Though not believing it himself, how could he resist hassling this chump?

"Well," the lion professor said, "call it what you want. The fact is, given what we do actually know of Maya society, the options for a common man were to either kill himself lifting and lugging all day or be ostracized for betraying religious duty."

The young woman nodded, seemed familiar with the lecture. Maybe she was his daughter. Or, more likely, a student he was having an affair with.

The lion professor continued in his low bristly roar to explain the "hierarchy of oppression" in "primitive societies"; the lack of any "real choice" among its "servant class"; the "stark injustice" of it all. Jake nodded for a couple of minutes, pretending to listen, choosing to be polite, and looked for the chance to offer an opinion.

Finally realizing it was not going to happen, he turned and left. This day at least, in such a beautiful place, he would avoid a fight. Jake was amazed by his self-control. Forgetting all about the secret passage, he headed back down the steep uneven steps.

At last hitting bottom he felt disillusioned—not with ruins but with their inevitable experts. He wandered off into the jungle and sat at the edge of a flowing creek. He lit the joint, took a draw and held it in. At his feet a line of leaves marched by. Beneath them, Jake saw, were ants. *Lots of weird bugs in Vietnam, but none of these little suckers.* He exhaled a stream of smoke. He watched it swirl up, dissipate, disappear, and for a few grueling seconds imagined himself *there.* Like an angry rattle, his head tried to shake away the thought. He took several deep breaths, then another toke. Strange, in spite of the horror he'd experienced (things he'd hoped to never think of again) he let himself wander into a jungle...*idiot*...and get stoned!

A caramel-colored frog jumped onto his knee, its luminous green eyes half the size of its body. Jake looked up, looked all around. There were vines and roots everywhere, thick and strong, some twisting upward, grabbing anything they could get ahold of. Others hung from hundreds of feet above. In Nam they'd called them "Ladders From Heaven."

Oh, Christ, never mind for fucksake! Never mind!

Jake looked around for something less likely to freak him out. He tried to calm his breathing and focus on the beauty. It had rained hard last night. Big black spiders worked to repair their glistening webs.

Something to his right, probably a lizard, disappeared into the shadows. Much of what was here could not be seen. He remembered reading that fifty percent of the original city lies hidden, covered by roots and vines. The Maya had carved a place for themselves out of a jungle that would not stop growing. Ever. As a soldier he'd run through jungles just like this...run as fast and as far as he could...run until his breath had given out.

Sunlight broke through the dense overhanging canopy. Insects went ballistic, whether in complaint or celebration Jake didn't know.

The air had gotten warm and wet.

He wanted to go, go now, get out of there fast.

Instead, he stripped naked and lay his clothes on a rock.

Time, he decided, to stop running.

He stepped into the brown waist-high water and moved up creek, against the current. He was shivering but kept on going. Around one corner he saw a ten-foot totem of bright crimson flowers, like prehistoric birds, their beaks gaping open, their long sleek bodies diving out of spiky purple stems. Razor slim silver fish darted around his legs. White boulders hugged the shore, backed by heart-shaped leaves the size of small children. In Nam he'd be holding an M16, on the lookout for any movement.

A large bird squawked and took off overhead. Jake looked up. Blinded by the sun, he saw only a silhouette of flapping wings. A monkey howled in the distance.

Nothing to be afraid of.

After a few minutes he came to a wide pool beneath a short slender waterfall. An orange butterfly flexed its wings on a lime green leaf. Jake knelt in the creek, in front of a boulder. Water cascaded over its face. There, in the dappled sunlight, eyes watched him through the rusty moss. Beneath their gaze was a high arching nose, and a mouth that did not need to speak.

Jake saw—in that face, those eyes—the spirit that guided shamanic vision. Here was where the Mayan Gods lived, in the depths of a jungle that every day swallowed itself alive.

Then, from the back of his mind, rushing to consciousness came a vision of Orph, and the sound of him whining. *Oh shit, oh no, how long have I been gone?*

He gave a quick bow to the jungle deity and splashed back downstream to his clothes.

Sweating, barefoot and shirtless, he sprinted through the ruins to his van. Jake felt like a negligent father, but Orph greeted him with a slobbery kiss. He held the dog close, and saw that the bowl of water was still half full.

Yes, all right, he should have known, there really was nothing to be afraid of.

That's how he needed to think.

Good thoughts. Only good.

As Jake left the parking lot, the first tour bus pulled in. Soon the place would be crawling with experts. Good time to be gone.

Coming down the mountain, now somewhat sober, he saw the Palenque creek cascading to his right. For Jake it was a sign to stay by the water.

In the flatlands below he found the Otulúm River. Jake crossed over the bridge and saw a narrow dirt road that entered a grove of large-leafed trees. He took it, thinking there might be a place to camp. Other travelers had thought the same. Vans and mini-buses and trucks with camper shells were tucked into their own secluded spots along the water.

A guy walked over. He had long brown curly hair and a thick brown beard. Looked like a misplaced lumberjack.

"Welcome," the guy said. "I'm Ben, your camp counselor."

"Cool," said Jake, and shook his hand.

Then Ben explained the deal. Once farmland, this would someday be a big resort. A former worker had told him that now—because the new owners from Mexico City did not yet have the funds to build it—no one was around. Ben and his wife had been camping for days without a problem.

"Park anywhere you want," he said.

"Thanks," Jake said. He smiled and drove away, for ten minutes puttering along the scant dirt track. At the end of it he found a bald, gray-bearded, bony old man in a saffron-colored loincloth. He was spread-eagled under a bamboo *palapa*. Jake waved, turned around and headed back, settling at a spot approximately equidistant between *palapa man* and the next visible neighbor, fifty or so yards away from each.

He undid his ponytail, took off his clothes, and walked down to the river. Orph jumped in ahead of him. The water was cool and the current gentle.

Jake swam out into the center, which was about eight feet deep. Hundreds of those same silvery fish from the creek surrounded him. They dodged his every stroke.

He emptied his lungs, let himself sink to the bottom, and lay face down on a bed of smooth pastel stones. The silence soothed him. He didn't come up until he absolutely had to, until his only need was air.

He dove down again and played tag with the fish.

When the shivers came he got out of the water. He lay on a big warm boulder, on his back, and looked at the single white cloud in the deep blue sky. Orph jumped onto the boulder. He made sure to get close, and shook hard. Jake didn't mind the extra wetness. The sun was already drinking it up. Orph curled up next to him and let out a doggy sigh.

A few minutes later, about to fall asleep, Jake remembered the main reason he'd come to Palenque. He got vertical, got dressed, and went looking for Ben, finding him outside his camper.

"I was wondering," Jake said. "You know where to hunt for magic mushrooms?"

Ben was likely in his forties, but wrinkled his face to make it look much older. He slumped his shoulders, gave an evil squint, and rubbed his hands together. "Oh yes," he said with a creaky voice, "in fact, I do." He paused, stared at Jake, then slapped him on the shoulder. "Uh, Boris Karloff."

"Got it, Master."

"Good, very good...*a fresh, willing soul.* You want to come with us tomorrow?"

"Can I bring my dog?"

"Sure," Ben said, dropping the act. "Long as he doesn't chase other animals."

"Orph doesn't chase anything. Bad case of hip dysplasia. Plus, he's a coward."

A woman came out of the camper. Her dark hair was in two long braids. She was attractive in a simple, solid, no-nonsense way. She smiled and said, "Hi, I'm Kate."

"The better part of us," Ben said, hugging her to his side.

180

While the three of them were talking, a woman about Jake's age, or at most thirty, came up from the river. Her hair was short, bleached silvery-blond, and glimmered in the sunlight. She introduced herself with a strong French accent.

Jake, caught off-guard by the silver hair and turquoise eyes, missed the name. "I'm sorry," he said, "I didn't—"

"W...I...S," she spelled, her petite hand shaking his. The hand came from a long slender arm attached to a short curvy body. "It pronounces like geese but wis a W."

"Weese," said Jake, imagining her naked. "Pretty name." He smiled, told her his, then turned and shook Ben's hand. "Uh, thanks again, man. So, what time tomorrow?"

"Dawn," Ben said. "I'll wake you."

The call actually came before dawn. Dawn was the estimated time of arrival at the mushroom field Ben had heard of, a twenty-minute drive uphill toward the ruins. They went in Ben's camper, also a Volkswagen. But this was a '74 Westphalia (one of the new, heavier, pop-up types) with a propane stove, a fridge, a bunk above the foldout bed, and lots of other extras. Jake was aware that these fancier models lacked a big enough engine to haul the added weight, and tended to blow cylinders trying.

Ben was doing his best to coax the beast up the mountain. He patted the dashboard and whispered sweet nothings as it growled through the dense wet fog.

Jake said, "What are we looking for?"

"An old wooden gate," Ben said. "The guy who—"

"You have by now passed sree," Wis said, in the midst of lighting her second cigarette. She'd been pissy from the start, asking why it was "so importantly necessary" to "rush off in zih black of night wisout a cup of coffee."

She was also miffed by the panting dog. She tossed Orph another disdainful glance. Clearly not offended, he shifted and re-settled beneath her feet.

Jake saw that Wis was straining to keep quiet. Her skin looked as white and smooth as a blanched almond. She seemed delicate, yeah, but this was a woman accustomed to getting her way, and willing to fight for it.

Ben explained that it was a "double gate" they were trying to find.

Wis laughed and made a silly face, like she knew better. "Oh yes," she said, "whatever zat is, I am convincing zair must be only one of zose."

"Well," Ben said, "that happens to be true. It's a two-sided gate, to be more specific, and hanging from one of its posts is a broken metal sign that says *PROHIBIDO PASAR.*"

"Huh?" Kate said. "NO TRESPASSING?"

"You cannot be serious," said Wis.

"It's a very old sign," said Ben, as if to frightened children. "The guy told me not to worry."

"Just maybe pear-haps," Wis countered, "zih land-ownairs of zis place are not in agreeing."

Ben downshifted from second, hunting for first, metal teeth grinding in the darkness. Time paused like a bird shot in flight until the motor once again whirred into action. "Look," he said while laboring up the hill, "the guy told me no one cares."

"If no one is caring, why must it be a matter for us to go zair in zih dark?"

"Why?" Ben said. "Because the guy told me that dawn is the best time to find mushrooms. Why? Because it gets crowded later. Why? Because no one pays attention to the NO TRESPASSING sign. Why? Because, like I said, Wis, the owners of the land don't give a crap."

"Ah," she sighed, smiling to herself, apparently deciding that his foolishness deserved no further comment.

"Bingo!" said Jake, pointing to his right.

Ben saw it too. He pulled off the road and up to the long horizontal gate of cracked, sunbaked wood. The two sides were locked in the middle with a rusty chain. The metal sign, its once painted warning half-peeled away, drooped from one of the rotting posts. Ben drove under the branch of a large oak tree. He turned off the engine.

182

"Wait," said Wis. "I am not certain of zis. I am sinking your idea here is bad."

"We're going," said Ben, staring back at her over his right shoulder. His voice was sharp and without any doubt. "I mean I am. Okay? Everyone else can do what they want. It's less than an hour's walk to camp."

He got out of the van and slammed his door. Kate got out too. Jake, from the bench-seat they'd been sharing, slipped past Wis with a tender bump. Orph followed.

Ben opened up the rear hatch to get their packs. "We're going," he repeated to the back of Wis's head.

"I will wait until you are returning," she said.

She sat stiff, not budging, as if the slightest hint of movement might suggest a change of mind.

"It could be awhile," Kate said.

"This will be okay," Wis said. "How long?"

"I don't know. Three hours, maybe more."

"Oh…well…what will you say if I drive myself to camp? I can stay zair sree hours and—"

"No," Ben said.

"And why? Why is it? Why can you not?"

Because you're a selfish bitch, thought Jake. *Because no one trusts you. Because you have no damn clue that you're asking something crazy.*

But he decided not to say it.

"Listen," Ben said. "It was your choice to come. Well, here we are. I'm locking up. We're going. Whatever it is you decide to do, Wis, right now you need to get out."

With abrupt movements and a dramatic groan, she vacated the camper and stood there looking miserable. She glanced at Kate, perhaps hoping that the rude man's wife might defend her.

Kate, following Jake and Ben, said, "C'mon Wis, grab your pack."

Getting past the gate was easy: dog under, humans over. They hiked the eroded dirt road, up hills and down, crossing and re-crossing a shallow muddy stream while the sun rose slowly above the faraway mountains and lit the fields of scattered cows, goats, and sheep.

Orph stayed close to Jake's side.

"Good pup."

It occurred to Jake that nothing much had changed since the ancient Maya lived here.

Did they eat magic mushrooms too?

Sure, why not?

What a mysterious and beautiful place, a joy for everyone but Wis, who kept stumbling along behind, her sighs gradually turning into moans as the crickets started clattering and the heat began to build. It was no surprise when she stopped and threw down her pack.

"Wait," she said, "where is it we are going? Because if you cannot say zis to me, I am ready to return."

Ben set his pack on the ground. He grabbed his bottle of water and took a long deep drink. Then he eyed Wis. "The guy told me to look for Brahma Bulls, all right? That's what he told me."

"Haven't seen a one," said Jake.

"Yeah," said Ben.

Wis stepped forward and planted herself directly in front of him. "Tell me, Ben, for once and ever, how much more time we are bozzering to look?"

Kate put a friendly hand on her shoulder. "Please, you need to think of it as an adventure."

"I am tired and hot and not in zis mood. I would like to choose what are my adventures, not have zem to be piling on my back, you know? You know what I mean?"

"There," Kate said, pointing beyond Wis's head.

The rest of them turned and saw a Brahma Bull grazing on top of a nearby hill.

"Well, hello," Jake said.

Ben said, "Cowabunga."

Wis followed as the others climbed toward the bull. He moved on. As the humans arrived at where he'd been, he

184

was cresting the next hill. When they got to the next hill he was still walking away, now joined by a few other bulls, maybe heading for some distant cows.

"Hold it," Ben said. He sat down on the grass. "Something's wrong."

"Yes," said Wis.

"What?" said Jake. "Those are Brahmas, right?"

"Yeah, well, it's not the bulls that matter, man. What matters is their shit."

"Shit?" said Wis.

"Cow patties," said Kate.

"Shit," said Ben. "Shit is what makes them grow. I'm seeing lots of that now but not a single mushroom. Which is weird because it rained a couple of days ago. The guy told me this should be the perfect time. I don't get it."

"I do not get any of zis, zis shit," Wis said, kicking a dried-up patty with her boot.

"Whoa," said Ben. He crouched down, grabbed a stick, and poked at what was left of the pile. "Didn't expect them to be underneath."

Jake saw the small whitish dome. Ben gently uncovered the mushroom. After plucking it from the crumbled patty, he took his bottle of water and carefully washed it off.

"Wait," said Wis. "Seriously, Ben, you are sinking zis to be a magic one?"

"Don't know yet." He cracked open its stem. A few seconds later the insides began to turn a greyish purple. "Yep, see, purple. That's the psilocybin being activated. All right, sports fans, here we go."

He held it out to Wis, who grimaced and shook her head.

"Hey, girl, you're the one who found it."

"No, Ben. I would not eat zat shitty zing."

"Okay," he said, and popped it into his mouth.

Wis winced, squealed "Oooh," and clenched her teeth.

Ben closed his eyes and chewed. Everyone watched. Wis showed an impish grin, perhaps with a secret hope that he'd start puking. Or, better, turning purple. Ben smiled at her and swallowed, then went to a different patty. He spread it out with his stick and found another mushroom.

"Boom," he said. "Guess I got the radar now."

He cleaned it well and handed it to Kate, who opened her mouth and took it in.

Wis squeaked out a nervous laugh and sat on the grass.

The rest of them kept looking.

Not every patty had a mushroom. Kate found the next one and handed half of it to Jake. He got the other half, too, after Wis waved it away.

Soon the mushrooms were easy for Jake to find, sometimes coming two or three at a time. He quickly filled a plastic bag. It felt more like the mushrooms were finding him. "What's a good dose?" he asked. He'd eaten the two halves, and two wholes, before the thought occurred.

Ben said, "Oh, yeah, sorry man. The guy told me no more than two. Says the fresh ones are really strong. What's left we can save for later."

Jake smiled and gobbled down another.

Really strong was what he wanted.

By the time they started back, around noon, he'd stashed four big plastic bags in his pack. On the trip home, neon Brahma Bulls wandered through his head.

The next morning Jake cleaned the remaining mushrooms, all sixty-five of them. Then ate six. For many hours he lay on his big warm rock, naked under a towel, staring at the river. He was thinking of his childhood, remembering the sweetest memories, his mind wandering from one amazing experience to another, from one dear friend to another. He could see his parents smiling down at him. He must have been very young. Even his father was smiling, which did not happen often. He could feel his mother's arms around him, holding him close. His father said, "Upsadaisy." He lifted Jake to his shoulders, then carried him around the house, his mother laughing and waving.

He barely believed his eyes, and could not block the tears.

At some point Wis wandered over in a black bikini. She wanted to talk, and didn't seem to mind that Jake just listened. She told him about her ex-husband, Brad, an Englishman she'd met on a vacation to Indonesia. They married back in London, their marriage annulled after three months when "His addiction, you know, for zih beer and zih rugby, zih fish and chips and sex was way too much." She wrinkled her nose at the awful memory and said how happy she was "to be free of zis man who is not appreciating me."

Jake wanted to be alone. It was difficult to look at her. The skimpy bikini seemed a kind of armor and he knew she wouldn't take it off.

Even if she would, he didn't want her to. Not anymore. He didn't think it in a mean way, or say a single critical word (in fact was grinning like a fool), but every syllable he uttered ("Oh"…"Uh-huh"…"Yeah") was an effort.

After a few minutes he stopped responding and turned away, refocusing on the ripples.

She left.

Orph also grew bored and disappeared.

When it started to get dark, Jake went looking. He found his dog three camps away, playing with a red setter. Orph refused to leave. Jake grabbed his collar and dragged him home.

The following day Jake ate ten. Too bad for Orph, because the setter and his people had gone. From time to time the dog checked in to see if his master might want to play. He didn't. "C'mon, boy," Jake said, and got Orph to lie down beside him. Then Jake went back to gazing upwards.

The towering tree he lay beneath had wide green leaves, and long red flowers puffed open like parachutes, their stamens like skinny yellow legs dangling below. The fathomless blue sky peeked at him through tiny swaying windows in the foliage. The tree had a thick white trunk, here and there visible among the many branches. He thought of the fabled beanstalk. Jake imagined climbing it, then realized he already had. He'd traveled a lot, knew what it meant to be in unknown lands, and here he was again. He felt grateful that there was no angry giant to deal with. Unlike poor Jack, there was nothing he wanted and nothing to be feared.

A gentle wind rustled the leaves. Sunlight warmed his face. Jake was full, completely full, of peace.

Is this what enlightenment feels like?

On the fourth day he decided to eat the rest. Forty-nine of them. How else would he know?

He started at eight in the morning, after a breakfast of two oranges and a cup of mint tea. He had plenty of purified water set aside, along with a bunch of bananas and a big bag of almonds. He had filled Orph's bowl to the very brim.

All was well.

No, he thought, *it's perfect. Everything. Perfect.* It was going to be another clear hot day and the river was right there whenever he or Orph needed it. What could be better?

One after the other, Jake chewed and swallowed the first ten mushrooms. He followed them down with another cup of tea. He could sense the drug pulsing through him, adding to what was already there.

Like a reluctant fog, the once thick curtain of his protective mind dissolved into brilliant sunshine.

He took out a brand new journal. At the top of page one he wrote MAGIC MUSHROOM TEST, and below that the number ten. Assuming his thoughts would evolve toward wisdom with each successive dose, he began:

To begin with, he wrote, *I'm sick of the constant ups and downs. How many times do I have to fool myself with some dumb-ass plan (or, worse, a good one, something I am confident and passionate about) only to learn, again, I'm missing what matters.*

Then, thinking I've learned what matters, I come up with another plan!

Does this shit ever end?

He stopped writing. Enlightenment, he'd figured, first meant facing his sacred cow ideas and behaviors, but now he was questioning that. What was the use of trying so hard to figure things out? What did that even mean?

Jake worried that being so worried about the proper way to live had a lot to do with fearing death and the petrifying prospect of everlasting nothingness.

Better to distract himself, right, by thinking of all the ways, the infinite ways he was not enlightened.

Ah, what an excellent distraction!

He picked up the journal. *The best plan of all,* he wrote, *would be to stop planning altogether. Is that even possible?*

How could he let his plans go? Others, of course, had tried. He was a freshman in high school during Kesey's infamous "Acid Tests." They'd happened and he'd never known. He'd not yet read any Sartre or Kafka or Castaneda—was totally clueless—every day wishing he could play sports with the other boys; every day confounded by pretty girls and wet dreams and fears of rejection.

No wonder he knew so little of the sixties. Except for The Grateful Dead. He knew they took part in Kesey's tests. That, by itself, was good enough for him.

Jerry would not be Jerry, he wrote, *without doing psychedelics. Risks must be taken to free us from the prisons of our mind!*

He could hear how simplistic that might sound to someone else. Fuck it, he didn't care. At least it got him thinking like he should, moving in the right direction. And sometime during the next ten mushrooms, all judgmental voices disappeared as his need to explain the wonder of life, even to himself, became less and less necessary.

Mushrooms twenty through thirty bounced him back and forth, up and down, between the multi-layered complexities and interconnections of sex, birth, natural selection, human nature and chemistry, impressionist painting and dead sea scrolls, air, politics and religion, addiction and reincarnation, fast-food restaurants, traffic signals, international time zones, science and fate, the divine right of kings, decomposition, *and*—as Jake knew Vonnegut would say—*so it goes.*

At number thirty-five he detailed, in crisp illegible shorthand, exactly why the concept of God (which neither proved nor disproved the existence of God) was a necessary creation for death-fearing humans (his analysis a sort of undercooked Kierkegaard with a side of stale Nietzsche).

He wanted Orph's opinion but the dog was gone.

No problem, they could talk about it later.

By mushroom forty-five his notes were diminished to isolated words and jagged lines squiggling between them. By then, Jake had no doubt that all forms of life (which for him included stones and dreams) were intertwined by celestial threads invisible to the human eye, inconceivable by the modern mind.

There was nothing more to it than that, but that was a lot.

Across the way, on the other side of the river, a car pulled in, its tires crunching over loose gravel, its Ranchero music blaring. He heard doors slam, and the sound of screaming children. The trees blocked sight of any details.

A woman yelled in a frantic voice, *"Cuidado! Cuidado!"*

Jake groaned at his curiosity.

He got himself upright, slid into flip-flops, and wrapped himself in a flowery white sarong—adequate coverage, he decided, for the quickest of peeks.

Two small boys were on the opposite shore, throwing rocks into the water. The woman, presumably their mother, was trying to keep an eye on them while spreading out a blanket near the car. A plastic cooler sat off to the side. Beside it was a cardboard box.

The father walked off, sipping from a bottle of Coke. He gazed around as if this land, all of it, were his—like a mighty lord perusing his endless kingdom. The man's fat brown belly protruded from his opened white shirt like something trying to get away. Not once did he give a glance toward his wife or children. He stopped and spit. Then, after downing the last of his Coke, he flipped the bottle in a high arc toward the water. It shattered on the rocks right beneath the surface.

Jake lunged forward beyond the trees and stepped out onto a big flat rock. The man saw him. Their eyes locked. Though nothing could be done to change what had happened, Jake felt that something must be said. He lifted his hands to demonstrate extreme frustration. *"Por qué?"*

Though the man clearly understood, he gave a quizzical look. *"Por qué?"* he said, questioning the question.

Having not spoken for two days, and a beginner at Spanish, Jake wondered how to voice his complicated feelings. Sure, the loud music was a drag, and the screaming kids, but that was nothing compared to the danger of broken glass. It was the unconscionable carelessness of this guy he could not understand.

Jake took a deep breath. Obviously the man did not know any better, *stupid shit,* and must be forgiven.

Yeah, okay, Jake would try…if the stupid shit would only make it a tiny bit easier, like losing the nasty sneer that made Jake want to swim across the river and grab his greasy hair and stuff his head underwater until he found every last fucking shard of glass and swore he'd never do it again!

The guy was smiling at him now, like at a child for making a silly fuss. Though Jake wanted to be tolerant, kind and compassionate, this jerk was not worth the effort.

"I don't understand WHY!" Jake yelled in Spanish.

The guy laughed. Then, solid on his wide flat feet, he stared with bold defiance. He lifted his arms and gave them a feeble wiggle, mocking the gringo, laughing at his distress.

"PORQUE PORQUE PORQUE," he said.

Ah, thought Jake, so that's WHY he threw the bottle in the water. "BECAUSE BECAUSE BECAUSE" he could.

Because I felt like it, you dumb-ass gringo!

Comprende that?

Unable to tell this fucker off, Jake retreated back through the bushes. He turned upriver along the path and walked away fast. His rage, his sense of powerlessness, trailed close behind. He passed the old *palapa man*, who lay naked to the universe in what seemed a state of absolute surrender. *Yeah, well, fuck him too!* Jake hurried past, through high willowy reeds, then up a steep hill. Several minutes later he emerged onto an expansive tract of dirt.

Though the path ended there, he could not stop walking. The fat Mexican was now just a bad memory, but impossible to forget. His spiteful voice rattled on inside Jake's head. It said, "This is my country, gringo." It said, "If you don't like how we live, go back to where you came from!"

Jake was panting. Exhausted. The air had turned hot and thick, as if trying to hold him back.

Then he heard something strange, and hearing it made him stop. He plopped down onto the soft warm earth. He closed his eyes. While the Mexican's insults continued to loop on, beneath them there was something else, a high melodic hum, like a breathless chant.

He bent his ear toward the earth and listened. It sounded like tender voices, barely audible, were calling to him, trying to get his attention.

Though Jake had been a realist his entire life, he suddenly thought of angels. *Wow, angels, really?*

No, he thought, *not really.*

But there was no reasonable explanation for those voices he was hearing. And, he reasoned, not all things could be explained. *So yeah, sure, why couldn't it be angels?*

Besides, thinking about angels might lighten things up. *If angels do exist,* he decided, *this is how they'd sound.* Again he was struck by all the things he did not understand, would never understand. Maybe angels had always been in his life? Maybe now he would always hear them?

He opened his eyes and saw something coming his way. It was a strange sort of slithery movement, a short wavy line shimmering vertical in the waves of heat.

He shielded his eyes from the dazzling sun. The wavy line got bigger. This was no angel. It looked like a human being, with arms and legs floating below a faceless head.

Some sort of spirit? Was Castaneda telling the truth?

Anyway, whatever was coming, Jake felt no fear. He wiped at his eyes and squinted, trying to clear his vision.

His heart beat with anticipation. His mouth was dry with awe. It looked like a short middle-aged man moving toward him. *Could this be my Don Juan?*

The thought made his feet tingle. Or maybe they were falling asleep. He shifted his position, calmed himself, and waited for whatever might happen next.

The man stopped. A dirty white sombrero clung to his head. He wore dirty white pants and a dirty white shirt. Worn-out tire-tread sandals wrapped around his dirty feet. He nodded and stepped closer, his body now blocking the sun to allow Jake a look at his face.

It was a lined, sun-beaten, ancient face, as if carved by a machete from a block of stone. It reminded Jake of the Palenque glyphs, and of that face in the creek staring him in the eyes. This man's gaze was also full of hard-earned truth.

Jake smiled up at him. *"Hola,"* he said. *"Buenos días."*

"Hola," the man said. Then he said something that Jake couldn't follow. Apparently confused by the gringo's confusion, the man pointed to where Jake was sitting. *"Señor,"* he said, his droopy eyes furrowed with concern, *"por favor."*

He made a gentle motion with his hands, a sign for Jake to please get up.

Intrigued by the man's intensity, Jake stood. Could it be, like Castaneda, that he'd wandered onto the power spot of some evil *brujo?*

Could this farmer be his spirit guide?

Could Jake be on the verge of a mystical way of life never before imagined?

Excited, he looked down to where the man was pointing and spotted something small, hardly noticeable, flattened in the dirt.

It was a…a baby plant.

Jake blinked, then looked around and saw the many baby plants everywhere around him. He'd been sitting in a field of newly sprouted seedlings. Beans maybe? Zucchini? He didn't know. He focused on the tiny plant sprawled out at his feet. Saw that he had crushed it.

Jake dropped to his knees and touched the severed stem. *Dumb-ass gringo.* He closed his eyes and listened for angels, but heard nothing.

He picked up the dead plant. Held it in his open palm.

Eyes spilling tears, he looked up at the farmer.

The man looked away, plainly uncomfortable with the stranger's uncontrolled emotion.

Jake could do nothing to change that either. He could not remember how to say he's sorry. Could not remember how to say anything.

The farmer turned back to him, about to speak. For Jake, it was as if his entire existence depended on what happened next. The man's eyes were steady and insistent.

"Mira," he said, *"está bien."*

"Look," the farmer was saying, "it's all right."

And Jake knew exactly what he meant: It was "all right" because it had to be. Because there was no other choice. *Because you are a foreigner,* the man was telling him, *and understand nothing of a poor farmer's life, I forgive you for coming into my field, for killing my plant. That is what you did, gringo. That is what happened. It happened, it is done, and there is nothing either of us can do about it, so why make things harder with your useless tears?*

Look, the man was saying, *the best you can do right now is go. Just go away.*

And next time, please, watch where you are walking.

194

SACRIFICING GOATS

Though a mere foothill of the Himalayas, the mountain rising behind Ram Jhula was referred to in his guidebook as a holy place. Intrigued by that, Warren asked Roshan, owner of the Krishna Inn where he was staying, if someone could show him the trail. Roshan seemed pleased by the question. "Yes, yes," he said, "why not?" He smiled and waved off further discussion, jumped on a motorcycle and sped away.

The next morning, at breakfast, Roshan came to Warren's table, shook his hand, and ordered a pot of chai. "My treat," he said. "It is good you want to know our holy mountain." The conversation then shifted to the small piece of it that he and his partner owned. They planned to someday build a meditation center. "With a healthy restaurant," Roshan said, "and perhaps a spa."

Warren sensed that the man might go on and on, so steered him back to the mountain itself.

Roshan said, "Ah, the mountain, yes. Perhaps we will climb the trail to sometime see it?"

"I would be honored."

"Good. Then certainly it will happen," said Roshan. He checked his watch, apologized, and again hurried off.

Warren felt blessed. Though almost sixty, he had remained an avid hiker and loved the idea of climbing a holy mountain, with a local guide, for what must be a spectacular view of the Ganges River. An extraordinary opportunity!

But as the days continued to pass, with Roshan perpetually busy at running and maintaining the inn, the best Warren got was a passing wave.

Then, while sitting in the garden one late afternoon, he saw the man veering toward him.

"Come, come," said Roshan, and led him to a far corner of the property. "You see," said the innkeeper. He pointed at what looked like an old storage shed, its stucco walls on the verge of crumbling, its warped door hanging by a single rusty hinge. "My special project."

"I see," Warren said, smiling, wanting to be polite. "What is it?"

"This dirty shack, once filled with rats, will soon be for Ayurvedic medicine."

"Well, congratulations."

Roshan smiled and shook Warren's hand. "Thank you. I am a new innkeeper. Not yet two years. I want to give what tourists want."

Warren saw his chance and took it. "Do others want, like me, to see the holy mountain?"

"Not yet," said Roshan. "That, I hope, is coming."

"Does it have a famous temple?"

"No, nothing like that. It is just a holy mountain. It has always been that way."

"You and your partner must feel lucky to own land there."

"Oh yes, we are lucky." Roshan laughed. "And soon, if gods are willing, we will find it."

"You don't know where it is?"

"We have never looked. I am hoping, Warren, you can someday come to help us."

"Yes, of course, I'm ready any time."

"Good," said Roshan. He smiled, patted Warren's shoulder, and disappeared into the shed.

The next day a truck arrived with a stack of lumber. Two days later another arrived with a pile of sand, a roll of chicken wire, and bags of cement.

Roshan stayed busy. A week went by.

When Warren asked if he still wanted help finding the land, the innkeeper stopped a second and said, "Most certainly, my friend, I am working on that. Yes, why not?"

The American nodded and moved on. He did not want to look like some anxious, needy foreigner. While waiting for the hike to happen, he kept himself occupied by roaming around town, visiting its many ashrams and temples, paying to see the villa that the Beatles once rented.

Another week had passed.

At his wit's end, yet trying to be civil, Warren told Roshan to total up his bill, that he needed to leave the next morning.

The innkeeper looked puzzled. "I am planning for us to find our mountain land."

"I wish I could have helped," Warren said, "but I truly have to go."

"Oh, yes, no problem," said Roshan. He grinned his biggest grin and said that their climb was "one day meant to happen." He said that life was "full of miraculous times, full of big surprises." He gave his guest a few tender slaps on the back and headed for the motorcycle.

Warren hated dwelling long on disappointment. Instead, he salvaged a vague feeling of hope. Though he would probably never return to India—its poverty and disorder too unsettling—he appreciated the idea, the offered possibility, of some day climbing a holy mountain. He joked with

197

himself that the idea might be preferable to reality. As an idea, the mountain remained a pure and intriguing mystery. It was, as well, quite easy to forget.

In the morning (his backpack leaned against the breakfast table, his journal opened to a fresh blank page) Warren felt exhilarated, as he always did when it was time to leave. Even more than getting to know a place he loved moving on to the next. His plan was to lounge for a couple of hours and write a few notes. Maybe he'd email his son, who he hadn't spoken to in months. Well, no, maybe not.

At noon he would catch a bus to Haridwar, and the following day a train to the vast deserts of western Rajasthan. Beyond that he had no clue. Exactly how he liked it. He was sipping hot masala chai, browsing a book by Osho, feeling alternately attracted and repulsed by the famous non-guru: *a man so insightful,* Warren wrote, *and at the same time, like many Indians I have met, presumptuous. Inscrutably wise and unbearably arrogant.*

He saw Roshan hurrying toward him. This was not an arrogant man, but presumptuous? Oh yes. Warren felt relieved that the time had come to say good-bye.

"We are ready for you coming with us!"

Warren blinked. "Where?"

"To find our land!"

"What, you mean today?"

"Now. Right now."

Warren smiled. *Talk about presumptuous!* He explained that he was on his way to Rajasthan.

Roshan said, "Yes, no problem, plans can change."

"My bus leaves in an hour."

"You can go tomorrow. Today the gods have chosen you to see their holy mountain."

A short stocky man stepped up to the table. Roshan looked tall by comparison. Like Roshan, the man was in his mid-thirties. Like Roshan, he grinned from ear to ear.

"Meet Diggu," said the innkeeper. "Diggu, my good partner, is main owner of our mountain land. His family's land. He is also wanting you to come."

"Maybe next time," Warren said.

They were joined by another man (younger, shorter, stockier) who carried a large pack. Roshan pointed at him with glowing enthusiasm.

"Meet Vijay, our number one guide."

"Good days!" said Vijay with a thick accent. Then he looked at Roshan. The innkeeper slapped him on the back and nodded his head to confirm the proper words. It was clear that the guide spoke no other English.

"Vijay carries the chapatti," said Roshan. "And our mountain gives plenty of water."

"That's great, it really is, but—"

"If problems we do not see," Roshan said, his eyes wide and bright, bulgingly optimistic, "problems we do not have."

My god, thought Warren, what incredible wisdom. As usual. He'd learned, after five months in India, that its persistent and excessive problems had created a culture where they were rarely seen, where only the gravest of catastrophes were noticed. Whatever else that was wrong, or not working as it should—defective, illegal, unjust, or in some way dangerous—was regarded by Indians as an inevitable consequence of life, a karmic and therefore necessary inconvenience that must be accepted, without question, in the present moment. Nothing mattered except the present moment. And in any present moment there was little that could not be tolerated or ignored.

In other words, *no problem.*

Today, seeing it would get him a free-guided trip, food included, up a holy mountain, Warren had no great problem agreeing. He went to his room, opened his pack and dug out his hiking shoes. In his journal he wrote, *Yes yes, why not?*

Though a strong hiker, Warren felt challenged by the climb, much of it steep uphill through a dense pine forest on a narrow rocky path. Equally narrow paths shot off at sharp angles. Vijay looked pleased to be the one who knew where to go.

As they walked, Roshan said that for a long time he had wanted to help Diggu find his family's land. Until now, he explained, two things had continued to confound them. First and foremost, both he and his partner were in terrible shape. Roshan especially, which he seemed happy to admit. He panted and grinned, patting his soft belly, blaming it for his shortness of breath.

Warren got the hint and suggested that they take a break.

"Yes," said Roshan. "Good idea."

The second reason for delay was their scant knowledge of the land's whereabouts. Roshan, between gulps of water, said that Diggu's father, on his deathbed, tried to explain. "The old man tells us we will see a fountain rock, and below it a wishing well. That, he says, is the eastern corner." Roshan laughed and took another drink. "But even if we know what he means, town boys can never find it. Lucky we have a number one guide." He smiled at the younger man, who smiled back. "Vijay lives with family on the mountain, and speaks the local tongue, *Garhwali.* When we first ask him to take us, he sees problems." Roshan looked over at Vijay, saw he was not watching, and grimaced. "He goes like that, like a frightened little boy. He is not pleased."

"Why?"

"He worries our directions can cause trouble with gods."

"Because of this holy mountain," said Diggu. "Because land is sacred, Vijay says we must be careful."

"Yes," Roshan said, then smiled. "He does not want angry gods or curses. Because of that, because our directions for him are not convincing, he avoids us for two years." Roshan's smile had turned sardonic. "He says no to our good fee. Oh no, he says, not good enough. It takes many pots of chai and much serious talk, but he does not agree."

200

Warren saw that the town boys were amused by the whole business—a silly but necessary game. They seemed to regard themselves as men of the world, beyond the peasantry's primitive superstitions.

Roshan patted Warren on the back. "Because of you, my friend, and your interest to see the land, his fee is doubled. We also take an oath to never anger gods. When on this holy mountain, we promise, Vijay is our leader, our number one guide."

Diggu coughed. He appeared a bit nervous, perhaps worried that the number one guide might suspect their sincerity. Coughing again, he stood, ready to go, and shot a cold glance at Roshan before saying to Warren, "Today we go for looking, just for looking on this mountain."

"Oh yes, yes," Roshan agreed. "Only just for that."

After hours of climbing, with many breaks—many chapattis and plenty of water—they saw some goats. Roshan brightened at the sight. "This means we find a village," he said, like a child trying to impress grownups.

"Yeah?" said Warren. "There is a village way up here?"

"Yes yes, why not?"

The village amounted to a small gathering of mud-brick huts with grass-thatch roofs. Out of nowhere came a bristly-haired dog, its teeth bared, rushing toward them. Vijay made a loud clicking sound with his tongue. That managed to stop the mongrel shy of Warren's ass, where it stood its ground, hackles up, and exploded into a fit of high-pitched yelps, its bony frame rattling with vile intent, frightening no one but the foreigner. Another click from Vijay and the beast retreated. Slightly. Reduced to a low growl, it remained within striking distance.

Vijay pointed at the largest hut, then babbled like a tour guide describing the Taj Mahal.

"He shows us this village school," Roshan said.

"Also a special meeting place for troubles," said Diggu. "And for putting in potatoes."

The dog's growling continued, increasingly more vicious as Vijay ignored him.

"And for funerals," said Roshan. "And marriage."

"Oh, yes, good," said Warren, smiling and nodding while watching his back.

As Vijay engaged the villagers in talk, Warren made eye contact with a small boy. The child must have seen the stranger's fear because now he walked over to the snarling devil-eyed monster and slapped him hard on the snout. Warren winced, afraid of how the animal might respond. The child grinned, then laughed, then dealt the dog a brutal blow that sent him off whimpering.

Other children followed as the boy stepped up to Warren and held out a hand. The tourist, with a sad-eyed grin, made a few gestures to show he had nothing to give, which was, as the children apparently knew, a lie. Warren's money belt was strapped around his waist, but he was not about to whip it out and pay this kid off.

The small boy's pockmarked forehead furrowed with determination. He grabbed hold of Warren's pant leg and tugged. It was not the plaintive kind of begging the tourist had grown accustomed to. It felt more like a demand.

Vijay was busy translating between the innkeepers and the villagers, thus forcing Warren, with boy attached, to step closer, and closer, until there was no choice but to notice him. Roshan looked startled by the foreigner's face staring into his.

Warren lifted his eyebrows, trying to show discomfort.

"Yes, this is not easy," said Roshan. "Vijay asks who knows our fountain rock. Of that there is much opinion."

Warren saw that heads had begun to *waggle*—a strange kind of horizontal shudder. He watched with his usual confusion. While Westerners might see it as a form of nervous tick, for Indians the waggle is a primary mode of communication.

Often, it indicates some level of agreement. But not always. Depending on variations of the motion (subtleties

202

that Warren was unable to decipher) it could mean anything from "Yes" to "Maybe" to "No Bloody Way!"

In a crowd this size, with such extensive waggling and many voices speaking at once, it was difficult to even guess what was happening. The boy kept tugging on his pants as heads vibrated at various angles and varying rates. Fingers pointed in a wide range of directions, in sum suggesting a multitude of possibilities as to where the mysterious rock might, or might not, be.

Warren looked hard at the kid, which did no good. He tried to pull away from the hand, which then strengthened its grip. What was he supposed to do, deck the little bastard? What would the gods think of that?

The boy tugged again, and again.

Suddenly, as if mandated by Vishnu Himself, Vijay bent down to face Warren's tormentor. He made a sound similar to that used earlier on the dog.

The kid let go. He waggled his beetle-browed head, shuffled awkwardly backwards, and snuck off, sulking, out of sight.

Warren saw that the talk, as well, had ended. Villagers shook hands with the strangers and went about their business.

"This mountain," Roshan said as they walked off, "has many big rocks."

Diggu said, "Perhaps we do not find our land."

They continued up one trail, then another, for an hour conspicuously silent, partly due to dwindling hopes and partly to conserve energy for the climb.

Warren lost track of time, of place, of purpose. As sweat poured down his face, soaking his shirt, he entered that zone of consciousness he loved like no other—his one true connection to Indian culture—a state of body and mind where he was ever-focused in the present moment on simply one thing: walking up a mountain: this mountain: now.

Diggu gave a shout and pointed. At the crest of the hill, towering in front of them, was a huge reddish boulder, an aquamarine stain creasing down its center as if carved over centuries by a steady stream of water. At its base, encased by a circular jumble of stones, was a shallow pool of leaves.

The perfect image of a wishing well.

Diggu said something to Vijay, who said something to Roshan, who said something to Diggu. It seemed to Warren a forced politeness, the kind of conversation he was used to having with his son. Ray was a grown man now, with a family of his own. He had little interest in what his father thought about anything. Hadn't since he was a teenager, and maybe never truly did.

Vijay put his arm around Roshan's shoulder and walked him up the path.

"Yep," Warren said, relieved that the climb was over, "sure looks like a fountain rock to me."

Diggu said, "Vijay is warning we must be certain."

"What, this isn't certain?"

"To know this rock is ours we first must go to seeing what is west." The next landmark, Diggu explained, was an ancient banyan tree close to the northwestern corner.

They followed Roshan and Vijay off the trail, up the sharply pitched slope to the less daunting side of the boulder. Their number one guide scrambled the final eight feet. He signaled the rest to come.

Warren, last to arrive, held onto Roshan's shoulder for support and gazed out at a long wide field, its grasses swaying in the wind. In the distance was a small house on a hill. The ridge behind it was thick with pines. But most interesting, he now saw, was a majestic old banyan tree about a hundred yards ahead. Vijay waggled in its direction, and kept waggling. He seemed aware that the innkeepers were waiting for him to speak. When he did, Diggu answered back in rapid staccato, like a return of enemy fire. Both then looked to Roshan, as if for needed reinforcement.

"What's the problem?" Warren asked.

"Vijay tells Diggu that perhaps what we are seeing is a different West."

A different West? Warren located the sun, above the banyan tree, arcing toward the distant ridge, which left no need for a compass.

"I don't understand," he said. "What other West is there?"

"Exactly," Roshan said.

Vijay made another statement.

"He warns us to look beyond what we want to see," said Roshan. "He warns us to not be angering gods."

Diggu said, "Never mind that, I am feeling this. Here we find my family land."

Vijay waved at something in the distance. Warren, squinting, saw a man waving at them from under the banyan tree. A flock of goats emerged from its shadows.

The number one guide hurried his people off the boulder, onto the path, and led them to the stranger, whose name, they were told, was Chori. The two mountain men laughed like old friends, speaking Garhwali. The stranger's head looked too large for its thin muscular body. He kept eyeing the innkeepers and asking Vijay questions. After several minutes, the number one guide announced that they'd been invited to eat at Chori's house.

Roshan politely declined. Chori, however, insisted, and headed off with Vijay. The others trailed behind, surrounded by the flock of goats. The meadow smelled of lavender, mint, and something else that Warren recognized but could not name.

They'd just crossed the wide expanse of swaying grass when at once the fragrant air turned rank. The goats, perhaps thirty in all, were put in an enclosure barely big enough to fit them. Next came a stall of yak; a pen of pigs; a rickety wooden cage of ducks; another of chickens.

Then, beyond a narrow band of woods, uphill from a thickly planted garden, they arrived at a mud-brick hut.

A woman emerged to greet them. Her eyes were nervous. Her smile was full of crooked teeth.

Because there was not enough space in the kitchen, the men climbed a ladder to eat on Chori's flat metal roof. How, Warren wondered, could this possibly shed water, or withstand the yearly snowfall? It felt too thin, creaking as they walked. He worried that their weight was causing damage.

Not his problem, no. And best he not mention it. He sat along with the others and concentrated on the steaming bowl of dal in his lap. The wife also brought chapattis and a large pot of chai. For a while no one said much, their occasional chatter sounding to Warren like common social pleasantries. He was glad for the time to himself; glad for the food and the spiced milky tea; glad to look out over steep descending hills at the Ganges River, far below, winding its way like a mighty snake from the snow-peaked Himalayas. This was the place to admire its pristine beauty. By the time it reached Varanasi, hundreds of miles east, the water would be full of pollution, a vast depository of toxic waste— agricultural, industrial, animal, human—including its world-renowned funeral pyres: a defilement of mother nature for the supposed sake of spirit.

Warren shook his head at the cost of superstition. It was painful for him to know that this glorious river would die, unable to sustain a single fish, long before reaching the Bay of Bengal.

Chori raised his voice. It seemed a meeting had begun, and their host did not look happy.

What could have happened?

The sheepish look on Diggu's face suggested it was he who'd said something wrong.

Chori pointed at the gigantic banyan tree, its top visible in the distance. Since he spoke only Garhwali, Vijay translated his words to Hindi.

Roshan, glancing sideways at Diggu, then said in English, "Chori tells us that good tree begins his land."

Their host glided his palm down and away from the tree in a broad sweeping motion to the right, as if skimming over the ground itself. After the barest of pauses, his fingers spiked up, lingered at a precipitous angle, then fell to a decisive stop. Vijay translated to Hindi.

"He tells us," said Roshan, "that fountain rock is where his land ends."

Roshan now stared at Diggu, who was already staring at him. Both waggled knowingly. Neither of them said a thing. Chori, sitting cross-legged, guru-style, also said nothing. Vijay sighed.

Sensing the tension, Warren decided on small talk. He gestured toward Chori and caught the man's eye. "I know about milk and cheese," he said to Roshan, "but does he eat the goats too? Is that why he has so many?"

Chori leaned toward Vijay and whispered something. Vijay whispered something back to him.

"Goats can be selling for sacrifice," whispered Diggu.

"Oh," whispered Warren, wondering why everyone was whispering.

Chori, perhaps wondering the same, cleared his throat and made a long loud speech. The translation never reached English. Warren tapped Roshan on the shoulder and gave what he thought was an excellent look of confusion.

Roshan looked at him with obvious irritation, his forehead crinkled, his brows bristled. "A story is coming of land and gods," he said. "I must listen, yes?"

Warren nodded, sorry for his impatience. He watched their host, fascinated by the man's theatrics (his eyes and hands darting here and there), when abruptly Chori looked at him, made a dramatic waggle, and pointed.

Vijay translated. Diggu mumbled something in response.

Chori kept waggling, kept talking, kept pointing at Warren, who said, "Roshan?"

"Because you are with us, says this Chori man, you need to hear his story."

Warren said, "Yes, I would like to hear it."

207

"Diggu says no. He says you are a foreigner, a guest of ours, and—"

"Tell Diggu that—"

"Chori says…he says you are also drinking chai, eating dal on his good roof."

"Yes, I—"

"Says you *must be included*."

"Please!" said Warren. "Tell Chori I am your friend. Tell him I am happy to be here on his good roof. Tell him, please, I want to be included."

Roshan sighed. Then did as he was told.

Chori smiled and waggled.

"Thank you," said Warren.

Christ, he thought, *how simple was that?*

"Now," Roshan said, "a story is coming."

Warren was aware of the honor he'd been granted. He was proud that he'd had wisdom enough to change his travel plans. This, he felt certain, was a story he would tell for the rest of his life.

Due to the difficult double-translation, it went on for well over an hour. The story began with a man from the nearby town of Rishikesh. He'd come a few days ago, said Chori, to purchase five goats: two for himself and three for his mother. The man's mother was a rich Sikh widow. Also from Rishikesh, she owned a number of income properties in its district. One was upriver from Ram Jhulla, on the outskirts of another small village called Lakshman Jhula. A month ago she'd decided to confront a *sadhu,* a *holy man,* who was squatting in that house.

"Oh yes," said Diggu. "I know of this. A quite mysterious man. Some people, they sing his praises, say he has a godly light. Others are not trusting who he is."

Chori waggled at the translation, then said that nobody knew where the sadhu had come from. The widow, he said, confident in both the wisdom of her years and the deserved privilege of her caste, laughed at those who felt awed by the long-bearded, loud-mouthed stranger, believing only idiots could be fooled by such a shiftless fraud. Their host halted his story to make the point (making sure everyone, including Warren, heard) that the widow was not as certain of the man as she should have been.

Diggu said, "Chori is saying that she mistakes her belief for truth."

"That," said Roshan, "is different than being certain."

"True," said Warren, believing he understood, and consciously waggled with the rest.

The widow was shocked, Chori said, when the intruder refused to budge. "Since you left the house vacant," the sadhu told her, "it has become what it was destined to be: a property of spirit, subject to neither the paltry laws of men nor the selfish whims of a greedy widow." As a holy seeker, a servant of the gods, his duty was to obey their demands and convert it to a temple.

She ordered the sadhu off her land.

He replied by closing the door in her face.

When she showed up with two policemen from Rishikesh, the self-acclaimed prophet warned, then cursed, then went into a trance.

Unconcerned, they took him to jail.

Locked up in a tiny cell, in the lotus position, he vowed in high volume, in what several witnesses identified as the voice of Kali, to unleash the gods of wrath upon them.

The next day both policemen died. A Brahma Bull, coming around a blind corner, had failed to anticipate their speeding jeep. The bull died too. And the widow was struck down with some as yet un-diagnosed illness. She lay comatose, day after day, her mouth moving without a sound. After the best doctors in Delhi could find nothing physically wrong, the son discussed the situation with a famous shaman from Rishikesh.

It was an expensive discussion, Chori noted, and he was quick to point out that the son had never before believed in sadhus or shamans.

"Like magic the son changes his belief," said Roshan. "That is why he comes for goats."

"You mean for sacrifice?" said Warren.

"For sacrifice, yes."

"For angry gods," said Diggu, his face and tone quite serious. But when seeing Warren's bewilderment he was unable to block a smile. "For tying to a stake," he said, "in our sacred Ram Jhulla forest."

Roshan smiled too. "Do not worry, my friend. Gods, in their infinite wisdom, never keep goats waiting long."

"Neither do wolves," said Diggu.

Chori cleared his throat. Their host looked upset by the smiles and English talk. He clapped his hands and gave a shout.

His wife, shadowed by two small daughters, emerged to gather the plates. Chori had closed his eyes. He rubbed his thumb up and down his nose. No one said a thing.

Warren realized that the story had ended. "Wait," he said, "what happened to the widow?"

Diggu stared at him.

"She, like a holy miracle, is saved," said Roshan. "Please, Warren, no more questions."

Vijay pointed at the sun as it crested the western ridge. The guide's meaning was clear: they must be leaving soon. Chori reached out, took hold of Vijay's arm, and pulled him close. The two had a short discussion in Garhwali.

The number one guide, frowning, translated to the town boys, who looked taken by surprise.

"What?" said Warren.

Diggu stiffened. "He tells us to be choosing ours."

"Ours?"

"*Yes*," Roshan whispered like a sigh. "Because we ask about this land he claims is his, he says we must buy goats."

"Huh?"

"Huh, yes, huh!" said Diggu. He jumped to his feet, as if ready to fight, pushed off Roshan's efforts to restrain him, and fired a blur of words at Chori.

Their host, with saint-like calm, waited for the translation before standing. His hand on Vijay's back, he spoke to the number one guide in a soft but persistent voice. He waggled, shrugged his shoulders, moved around the fuming Diggu and climbed down off the roof.

Vijay made one quick comment to Roshan, who did not answer, and again pointed toward the vanishing sun. With that, he also took his leave.

Diggu's face was slick with rage. Roshan walked away, and from the edge of the roof gave an occasional glance at his partner. After a few minutes Diggu called him over. The two conversed in low tones. They eyed the graying sky, which seemed to hurry their deliberations.

Roshan turned to Warren. "We agree to be buying goats."

"Why?"

"Because..." said Roshan, and then he paused to think it through. "Because we know our mountain has other big rocks and trees. Perhaps Diggu is not certain enough. We are sorry, Warren, for you to be included."

"I don't care. That doesn't matter."

"Oh yes," grumbled Diggu. "This Chori man says you are also cursed."

"Whoa there now, wait a damn minute."

And wait they did, in spite of their obvious hurry. Both listened to Warren with extreme patience. They waggled with wet-eyed sympathy as he appealed to their sense of justice. When he was finished, they explained that justice, at times, was beyond human understanding. The trouble, they said (and yes, they conceded, a legitimate problem), were angry, vengeful gods.

"Come on," said Warren, "neither of you believe in gods!"

"Not believing does not mean not careful," said Diggu.

Roshan said, "Not believing also means not certain."

"Well yes, that's true, but—"

"This Chori man," said Roshan, "he may have special powers, and knows we are not certain."

"Okay," said Warren, "okay, I understand. But don't you see what's happening? He's trying to intimidate you. *Scare you.* He wants to *scare you* into giving up your land."

"Yes," said Diggu, as if in full agreement. "The way it is looking, that is no good. Another day we come to be convinced, to see other rocks and trees."

Roshan said, "For now it is best we buy goats."

"I don't believe this," Warren said.

"No problem," Diggu said. "You can change your believing."

Roshan patted Warren's shoulder. "One goat for you is plenty. Two thousand rupees—thirty dollars. Which may seem a great sum, I know, but—"

"No, no way, I will not sacrifice a goat, Roshan! That is not going to happen!"

"Yes, I think it must," he said, moving toward the ladder.

Warren took off as soon as they started negotiating goats. He sloughed off Roshan's protests, headed down the mountain, and within an hour reached the tiny village. It was cooking time. Acrid smoke seeped from the huts. Fathers waved, restraining dogs, as small children ran up with their filthy bare feet, their little solemn faces tinged with what looked like hope. As if he were sacred, they reached out and touched him as he passed.

Warren left the village farther and farther behind. At last he found the spring he'd been waiting for, water gushing from a crack in an otherwise solid face of granite.

In spite of the darkening sky he felt safe. On all fours, like a wild animal, he slurped in the glorious liquid.

Yes yes, he thought, humoring himself, *a holy mountain must have holy water, and now I am full of it!* The idea made him choke. Cold wet divinity spewed from his mouth, his nose, his eyes. Removed from the absurdity, he laughed at what happened back there.

212

Curses, for godsakes! *SACRIFICING GOATS!*

About an hour to go, Warren figured, and quickened his step. But twenty minutes later he was confused not to find another expected spring. He walked faster as the narrow path kept narrowing. Then, instinctively, he stopped.

Wrong trail!

He turned and went back. How could that have happened? *Calm the fuck down*, Warren warned his agitated mind. *Calm.* He slowed his breath and imagined his room, his waiting bed. He willed a smile and convinced himself, because of crossing tree roots and patches of slippery clay, it was best not to run.

BE HERE NOW! Warren remembered. He nodded to an ethereal Ram Dass and was soon rewarded by the sound of barking dogs, proof of his proximity to Ram Jhulla.

He kept walking, his step blessed with new bounce, his mind laser-focused on staying *present*, and he failed to detect that the path, once again, was getting far too narrow.

A branch slapped Warren's face.

Three dogs rounded the corner ahead and sprinted toward him, each of them scruffy and fierce. He tried to make Vijay's clicking sound. That instantly made them fiercer. Terror-stricken, he pretended to throw a rock. That stopped them for a couple of seconds. They shifted their attack to short lunging spurts, pushing him backwards. Again he threatened to throw his non-existent rock. Again they stopped. Again they lunged forward.

His falling, he would come to realize, may have been fortunate. During that ever-so-present moment, however, it was total horror as he crashed down through the clawing undergrowth, over a series of pounding drops from ledge to ledge. He must have gone unconscious because now it was dark. Trees, strong and gnarled, were being swallowed by the murky sky.

Feeling around, instead of broken bones he found lumps, bruises, and minor scrapes. Minimal blood. It was too dark to be sure of anything else. Also too dark to move, since he had no idea where he was. Warren spit out grimy dirt, wiped his mouth and closed his eyes.

He tried not to feel scared, but could not block the tears.

Later he awakened to an invisible world. He touched his head as if to make sure it was still there.

Then he heard them in the distance. Dogs again, lots of dogs, but different from before.

No, not dogs. Not barking, no, it's howling!

Wolves?

Wolves...yes...wolves...howling from all directions, calling to each other. Warren shuddered, straining not to budge. They seemed to be getting closer.

Most frightening was when they stopped their wails, their clamoring yelps, and he envisioned their secret movement. The slightest sounds were amplified in his mind, demonized by his imagination. His body shivered beyond control. Afraid that tears would pinpoint his location, he squeezed his eyes shut against them.

He brought his hands over his mouth. *Please, dear gods, forgive me.* He repeated it in his mind, like a mantra, a silent chant that went on for hours. Though the American had no knowledge of Hindu gods, he hoped there must be one that could save him from being eaten by wolves. As if he'd been doing this his entire life, Warren prayed with a devout sincerity he would never have thought possible. He made lengthy internal apologies for his self-indulgent ways; for not staying with Roshan and Diggu; for his arrogance, his selfishness, his fault in ruining so many things, including his family, the love of his wife, and especially his relationship with Ray, his son, his baby boy who was now a grown man, who he saw less of each year, who he wanted to know but did not know how. At last Warren whispered, "What am I supposed to do? *What...please...what?*"

While blood continued to drip from his nose, and his head ached, and the stiffness in his lower back became a steady throb, what concerned him above anything else (a regret far greater than the pain in his body or the estrangement of his son) was how he'd laughed at the idea of curses.

Can such ignorance be forgiven?

Praying for their mercy, he promised the gods his daily devotion, his constant praise, and was soon surprised by a nearby rooster's COCK-A-DOODLE-DOO!

From that moment on, Warren's life was changed. He now believed that everything happened for a reason. Every single thing. He knew nothing of the many gods, but would never again deny them. Each step, no matter how difficult, was gratefully taken: *forward into a brand new world!*

As Warren slowly limped up the Krishna Inn driveway he spotted Roshan, head down, sitting alone in the garden. The innkeeper glanced to see who was coming. He gasped, jumped to his feet and came running.

"You are alive!" he shouted.

"Yes," said Warren, holding him off.

"Please," said Roshan, steering him toward a nearby bench, "you must sit and rest."

"I would rather lie down."

"Soon, yes, soon, your room it will be cleaned like new."

"No problem," said Warren as he turned toward it, "I'm tired, I need to—"

"No," said Roshan, and his face darkened. "I am sorry, Warren, sometimes I do not think well and...and because I cannot know for certain you are coming, I say yes when a man is asking, this morning, if I have any—"

"You rented my room?"

"Do not worry. If this man does not take his money back, you can stay, for free, in the Ayurveda salon!"

As Warren groaned, the Innkeeper helped him to a bench. They sat, and Roshan looked closer at his guest's condition, sighing with what seemed heartfelt anguish at the torn and bloody clothes, the swollen lip, the purple bruises and oozing cuts. "This is a terrible sadness," he said, "but we must be thankful for our holy mountain."

215

"I was lucky," Warren said.

"No, not lucky. Not this, no no no."

Damn, thought Warren, rattled by his urge to be sarcastic, bewildered by how quickly he'd forgotten the gods. He hunted for some way to redeem himself. "Lucky," he said, "and blessed by the holy mountain. "

"Blessed, that is right, my friend, blessed. It is good I buy you a goat."

"What?"

"To change your bad believing! The wolves, it is beyond all wonder how fast they come. By sunrise every one of our goats is gone!"

"You sacrificed a goat for me, Roshan? You actually did that?"

"No problem, yes?"

"Yes!" shouted a grimacing Warren. "Yes!"

The Indian looked worried. He probably wondered why the American looked shocked. *Was shocked.* Warren needed to say something, but his head was pounding, his ribs were screaming, and the effort to explain his feelings would at that moment be too painful.

"Please," said Roshan, his voice sounding apologetic, as if the words he was about to utter might cause his guest even greater discomfort, "you will pay for the goat two thousand rupees?"

"Of course," said Warren. And with a smile that must have looked like a scowl, he put his hand on Roshan's shoulder. "Thank you, my friend."

"Oh, yes, good," said Roshan, returning the gesture. "Yes yes, why not?"

MAMA LAO

The only way of getting to Muang Ngoi was by the Ou River, a main tributary of the Mekong. Small private boats could be hired from a larger village downstream. Usually they carried supplies, but today it was just Jyl and a boatman for the hour-long ride.

Naked brown children waved at them from the shore. A kingfisher, spreading its blue plumage, puffing out its bright orange belly, stared from a large white rock.

Chee! Chee! Chee! it screeched, as if looking for a fight.

They glided onto a narrow beach. Jyl handed her backpack to the boatman. He carried it through the shallows and she followed, up to her knees in the cool green water. The man set the pack on the sand, then ran back to his boat. She wanted to give him a tip but he was already pushing off.

She put on her pack and walked up the obvious path. It led to an ancient Buddhist *stupa*, then paralleled the river, became a narrow dirt road and entered the village.

She passed a water buffalo harnessed to a cart full of produce. A man stood in the back of the cart (a melon in one hand, a papaya in the other) haggling with the villagers gathered around him.

Jyl went looking for a place to spend the night, what in Laos is called a "guesthouse." Though the communist country had been opened to tourism since 1990, there was, eight years later, minimal development in remote little Muang Ngoi. Fine with Jyl. She had researched the place, and hoped that the lack of electricity would keep most travelers away. But this was clearly an opportunistic village, its residents having thrown up small bamboo huts on their land should people ever decide to come.

She checked out three of the makeshift guesthouses. Each had many huts, packed closely together, for one dollar a night. That was the going rate, which seemed fair since they were equally dark and dingy.

"No extra charge for rats," said a guy with a strong French accent. He was lying in a hammock outside his hut as Jyl peeked inside the one next door.

"Oh," she said. "Good."

The guy had a trimmed, graying beard. "It is not so bad," he said. "You learn to not leave food in your pack. I once forgot a banana and I have the hole to prove it."

"You've been here awhile?"

"Three days. I am leaving tomorrow. You can have my rats."

"No thanks."

"Can I buy you dinner tonight?"

"No, thanks."

"Pity," he said, a fake pout blossoming into a full-on grin. "Okay then, maybe a bit of advice. My name is Adrien and you will find no man nicer in this town. And the nicest place to eat is at a restaurant called Silent Moon. And the nicest place to stay is at the end of the road." He stopped and pointed. "That direction, I think. By the creek. I do not know the name but I found it today. Too bad I did not find it, and you, before."

"Thanks for the advice," Jyl said as she walked away, "maybe I'll see you later."

She could hear Adrien laughing.

"Oh yes," he called after her, "unless you hide!"

True, the guy gave her the creeps, but he did know the best place to stay. The Sunrise Guesthouse was a ten-minute walk, just beyond the eastern edge of Muang Ngoi. The five huts were as small as those she'd seen, but not crowded together. Jyl chose to think of them as cabins. Each sat on the hill overlooking the water. Below one, somebody had piled logs in the creek to make a dam. The resulting pool was sprinkled with bright yellow ducklings, their mother gathering them together—a protection, perhaps, should Jyl become a problem.

The sun was beginning to set. A rippled view of white tree trunks, orange leaves and red bushes, reflected across the bluish sheen. Jyl felt the beauty like a hug. She walked down and sat on a large flat rock. The ducks, apparently, did not mind.

"You want stay here?"

She looked back at a young Lao woman standing on the hill. Her face was noticeably round, like a luminous chocolate moon. "Yes," said Jyl.

The young woman pointed at the cabin directly above the pool. "You come see."

Jyl climbed the gentle slope to join her.

"Me Veeliepone," the woman said. Her lovely round face showed a wide and generous smile. She was older than Jyl had first thought, perhaps in her early thirties. Her upper body was thin, like Jyl's, but her hips were wide, and the slits on either side of her shiny tapered skirt showed thick muscular legs. "Papa own here," said Veeliepone as she stepped into the cabin. "Come inside, lady. You like?"

"Yes," said Jyl, though there was really no difference between this and the other huts. *Cabin* was far too romantic a word. "What does it cost for a night?"

"Ten thousand *kip*," said Veeliepone. "For you American lady, one dollar."

How did the woman know she was American? Jyl would ask later. For now, grateful that they took dollars in Muang Ngoi, she set down her backpack, retrieved the knapsack inside it, and found her money belt. She pulled out one dollar and handed it over. Her plan was to stay a week but she decided it best to pay by the day.

Veeliepone looked at the single bill, apparently surprised, perhaps confused. "You stay long time," she said like a disputed fact.

"I don't know. We'll see."

Veeliepone smiled and said, "You no go." Then she ran off. Jyl took that to mean she should wait. After a few minutes the woman came back and gave her a lock and key. "You American lady, you need lock up."

"My name is Jyl."

"Welcome," said Veeliepone, shaking her hand. "We happy, Jyl, for you be with us."

Jyl unloaded her things. She spread her sleeping bag out on the cot, grabbed her knapsack, locked her rickety door and walked back into the village. It was starting to get dark. She pulled the mini-flashlight from her vest pocket and switched it on. Kerosene lanterns were also being lit, and there were occasional household murmurs coming from inside the huts.

A cow passed by. A few bats swirled overhead.

Jyl smiled, surprised at how safe she felt in this strange place—how peaceful—until the quiet was shattered by what sounded like distant machine guns.

She stopped and looked around, hearing far off explosions and people screaming. None of it made sense. She saw, to her right, a couple of young lovers sitting on a stoop, kissing as if the rest of the world had ceased to exist.

But the gunfire and explosions and screaming continued. The screaming of small children.

Then she saw it, that familiar glow beyond the short bamboo fence of the Paradise Guesthouse.

A television!

Disgusted, she stepped closer. There was a man, another tourist, standing by the fence. Jyl nodded hello and stood next to him. Together they watched a troop of green-clad soldiers charge into a village. A village similar to Muang Ngoi. The soldiers looked like the villagers, except they wore uniforms and were gunning down unarmed men, women, and children.

Also watching this atrocity were a group of small Laotian kids. They sat and stared with haunted rapture, their attention glued to the screen. They held onto each other, sometimes screaming, sometimes giggling, and behind them were adults, perhaps their parents, equally enthralled by the horrific images.

"What's going on?" Jyl asked the other tourist.

"Movie night," he said. "They do this once a week."

"They let their kids watch this stuff?"

"They say that's why they do it, for the children. To connect them with the outside world. A man told me they'd watch every night if they could, but running the generator is too expensive. The movies come from Thailand. The other one I saw wasn't this bad, but quality doesn't matter. Entertainment, that's what they're looking for."

"Entertainment?"

"For them it's a show. These people were never in an actual war, so must think this stuff is all made up. The last one was a monster flick. For them, I think, there's not much difference."

Jyl moved away, unable to look or listen another second.

"Sorry," she said, "I can't do this."

She found the Silent Moon restaurant: six small tables on an open deck under a low bamboo roof. Each table had a candle, but as of yet no people. She sat at the one farthest from the entrance and ordered curried fish, which came with rice and a fruit salad. One dollar. She chased her meal down with a glass of the famously cheap, barely drinkable "Whisky Lao."

She swallowed it, winced, and ordered another.

Jyl was in Muang Ngoi because of her older brother, Pete, a pilot in the Vietnam War who had flown missions from Bangkok to Hanoi. He'd written one letter to their parents.

Can't say I'm having fun, he wrote. *On the way back to base we get rid of our extra bombs over Laos. Too bad for the villages below. Our captain says they aren't part of this war. I've heard otherwise. Either way, no one asks our opinion. We do what we're ordered.*

Though the letter went on for pages, that's what stuck with thirteen-year-old Jyl.

It was 1972, in Kansas, where she did not want to be. Her kind of curiosity was not a good fit. Or her idealism. And now this! Up until that letter she had always idolized Pete. He'd been a good brother, gentle and kind. So why would he drop bombs on innocent people? How was that possible?

Pete died a few months later. Because he could not explain what he'd done, the fact of it kept gnawing at her. In junior college she studied psychology. *What makes a person do something he knows is wrong?* That's what Jyl needed to know, but the answers were too vague.

At Berkeley she switched to Asian Studies and focused on the Vietnam War. She learned that random villages, like Muang Ngoi, were bombed because generals believed there must be "collusion" between Laos and the Vietcong. How else to explain why the mightiest country on earth could not defeat an army of peasants? Though a great deal of the logistical information was classified, she discovered that between 1968 and 1974 her country dropped over two million tons of ordnance on Laos: what averaged out to be a bomb every six minutes, all day long, for six full years. She wondered how many of those bombs had been Pete's.

Human Rights organizations estimated that thirty percent of them did not explode. They lay hidden somewhere in the mountainous terrain and might detonate without warning. Hundreds of people, mostly children, died each year. Others were maimed for life.

Her doctoral thesis: *A War On Reason—How Wrong Becomes Right.*

Jyl, now thirty-nine, was an assistant professor of history. She was on a tenure track at UC Santa Barbara, and being pressured to write a book. "Listen," said Doctor Baldwin, the department chair and her enthusiastic mentor, "with Laos open to tourism, you could do first-hand interviews. A perfect time to make your mark!" He then mentioned that her student evaluations had been "slipping." What a nice way to put it. "I would approve of you taking a sabbatical," Baldwin said. "The trip, I believe, will do you good."

Jyl got the waiter's attention and ordered another whiskey.

Things had come to the point where she no longer wanted to make a mark. The last thing this world needed was another fucking mark.

She'd decided to take an unpaid leave of absence. She needed to get away. And not just to escape the hamster wheel of academia. Her two-year relationship with Miles, a theatre professor, was also a twirling, senseless mess. She knew it was her fault. Though usually a happy person, her drifts into cynicism came too often. Miles should not have to endure her dark moods, her continuing need for personal time and space.

"It has nothing to do with you," Jyl told him on the day she flew to Bangkok.

"I know," he said, "but sometimes it feels like we're in some damned soap opera, Jyl…like no matter what I do you won't believe that I'm the good guy."

"Oh, honey," she said, holding him close, fighting back tears. "I'm sorry, Miles, I really am."

But it felt like she'd been freed once they said goodbye.

Jyl knew that her bouts of depression were because of Pete. She'd confessed it to herself, to her therapist, and finally to Miles. The purpose of going to Laos, she wrote on the necessary forms, was to research her proposed book. At the time she thought that a necessary lie. She might as well have told the truth. She had no intention of writing a book, was probably finished at the university, and didn't care.

She was in Laos to make peace with her brother. Jyl had picked this village because it lay beneath what she'd determined was his flight pattern.

The next day at breakfast, again at the Silent Moon, she was reading a book of poems by Mary Oliver when Adrien sat down to join her.

"Oh," he said, "what a pretty sight after a night of rats."

"You sure know how to charm a girl."

"I like to please. You would see I am good at that. But my time has run out. Where do you go next?" He looked away from her and waved, like an old friend, at a couple of young tourist women walking by. They saw him but ignored his greeting. Seeming not the least bit bothered, he turned back to Jyl. "After this I mean. Where can I find you?"

"No, I'm staying here."

"Here? In this tiny place?"

Jyl was also surprised by the way she'd said it, as if staying in Muang Ngoi had been decided. "I think it's beautiful."

"Beautiful, perhaps, if there were nowhere else. Do you not know Luang Prabang?"

"Famous for great French bakeries."

"Ah, you have been. Good. And what about the south, the four thousand islands?"

"Some other time," she said. "This trip I'm staying in the north."

"But why?"

"I'm researching the Vietnam War."

"You poor Americans, you cannot ever let that go."

"I'm trying. It's complicated."

"No," said Adrien, showing and then hiding a sarcastic grin. "It is quite simple, my dear. *You lost.* That is what happened. We French lost as well, but for certain we know when to give up."

"I hope that's true," she said, re-focusing on her book, "because now would be a perfect time."

"Oh?" he said. "Already you are tired of me?"

She turned another page. "Exhausted."

Adrien laughed and got to his feet. "Well, *Ma Chéri*, I see you are not worthy of my effort." Then, as he left, he said something else in French. From the sound of his voice it was not nice.

"What a dick," she heard from the table behind her.

Exactly what she was thinking. Jyl turned and saw the tourist guy from last night. He looked to be in his mid-thirties—unshaven yet handsome in a tall, thin, gawky way.

"Excuse my French," the guy said. "I've wanted to punch that jerk for days."

"You don't know he's the nicest man in town?"

"Oh yeah, I did hear that. From him. His line to any decent-looking female tourist." The guy blinked and his eyes softened. *"Oops,* that didn't sound right."

"That's okay, I'm tired of things sounding right."

He reached over and shook her hand. "Hi, I'm Nathan."

"Jyl."

"You're American?"

"Yes," she said. "And you?"

"Canadian."

"*Oops*, that's what I meant to say. I'm Canadian too. Safer to be Canadian."

"Agreed," said Nathan. "Welcome to Muang Ngoi."

"Thanks. I take it you've been here awhile."

"Eleven days."

"You must like it."

"I do. I like to hike. I've found six smaller villages in the mountains." One, he said, was an hour away. The farthest

225

was a six-hour hike on a steep curvy trail, which meant starting off at dawn. "There are also bamboo forests, and hillsides of tiered rice fields. There are miles of limestone karst, a few waterfalls, and a spirit cave!"

Jyl liked the calmness of this guy's voice, the kindness of his eyes. "Have you seen any bomb casings along the way?"

"You're kidding, right?"

"What?"

He pointed across the road at the bamboo hut on stilts. A bunch of children were gathered underneath, playing some sort of game with sticks.

"What's holding up that house?" he said.

The casings had been painted black, but were easy to identify. They stood out like burnt fingers.

"How on earth could I miss those?"

"Yeah," said Nathan. Then he pointed down, behind her, at the flowers in the yard next to the restaurant. "Or those." She looked at the two split shells that served as planters. "I've seen them used for fences," he said, "and troughs, and culverts. In some of the rice fields, people stand the casings up and paint faces on them, I guess to scare away the crows."

"Can I go with you sometime?"

"Where?"

"Hiking."

"Oh," he said. "Yeah, sure, whenever you want. How about now?"

"Now?"

"I'm on my way."

They paid for their meals, bought some bread and fruit, and walked to Jyl's hut. She took the poetry book from her knapsack and replaced it with a camera. Veeliepone, in the garden area by the river, leaned on her hoe and waved as they were leaving. The path ran past the guesthouse, along the creek, then meandered for half an hour through a dense wooded area before coming to a steep rock face.

226

Nathan stopped by what looked like the entrance of a cave. Water poured from its gaping mouth.

"The *Tham Kang*," he said. "*Tham* means cave. *Kang* means spirit water. This is where your little creek begins."

"Have you been inside?"

"Yeah. Once. People believe it's a holy place. The water, they say, comes from the god of mountains. You like caves?"

"Uh, no," she said, backing away.

"I wasn't offering, only wondering. I went with a guide. There are markers along the way, what us Canadians, as you should know, call *ducks.*"

"This a joke?"

"No, for real. A 'duck' is a kind of cairn—a few stones balanced on top of each other."

"To mark a trail."

"Yeah. And this cave, other than bats, has plenty of nice ducks. I think I could have managed it on my own, but the guide said that tourists once got lost inside and died. Hard to believe. Anyhow, if you change your mind, I'll show you where the water comes from."

"No chance. I hate caves."

"Me too," he said. "Usually. This one I liked, but I admit it's strange in there."

"Why?"

"Hard to explain."

"No, come on, what?"

"Okay. I don't believe in ghosts, okay, but I felt something. Nothing bad, but definitely strange. Like I was crawling back through time. Who knows, maybe I was. Except for a few unlucky tourists, this cave saved lots of people's lives. This was where they hid out during the war, while you Americans were dropping bombs."

Though Jyl knew he didn't say it to be mean, she felt her same chronic grief. It was time to tell him about her brother. They walked as she quickly summarized her life, from a thirteen-year-old idealist to an expert on the Vietnam War.

Nathan stopped and looked at her. "Why were you surprised by the casings?"

"I wasn't."

"But in town you couldn't see them."

"Yeah. It's weird. I guess I still haven't quite accepted that bombs were dropped on innocent people. Maybe that's why I'm here. So I have to."

For the next few hours they hiked around craggy green mountains to the hamlets of Bana, Huay Bo, and Huay Sen. Jyl saw what Nathan had described, including the metallic scarecrows. As they left Huay Sen she was startled by the sight of an intact bomb. Her heart raced. It lay next to a bamboo hut, well secured by a heavy chain that was wrapped around one of the hut's posts, and padlocked.

Jyl hesitated, then got out her camera and crept up for a closer look.

A small girl came running from the hut. "Photo!" she shouted. "Photo!"

A man followed the girl outside. "You photo?"

"Yes," Jyl said, and snapped a picture of the bomb.

"Two thousand kip," he said.

"Okay," she said, and handed him the notes, the equivalent of twenty cents.

"Good," said the man, as she took one last look at the bomb. "Hey lady, you want buy?"

Nathan laughed. "Yeah," he said, "a bomb. Exactly what we need."

The man laughed too, then looked away, distracted by something off in the distance.

"They sell them for the metal," Jyl said. "I'll bet he has no idea this could be live."

"Yes, yes," the man said, his interest returned, "live bomb, lady! Many danger! You buy live!"

My god, why would he think she'd buy that? Who in their right mind would want such a thing? *Maybe the U.S. government?* She knew there were munitions experts trying to find and safely detonate the bombs. Maybe, with entrepreneurial villagers like this, Americans had to pay to perform the service. What an appropriate irony that would be, but how could she be sure? Unfortunately, Jyl had never studied Lao. She did, however, know the word for *who*.

"*Phuthi?*" she said, lifting her hands. "*Phuthi* buy?"

"You," said the man. "You good army lady."

"No," Jyl said, shaking her head. "Sorry."

"Photo!" said the girl, smiling, pointed at herself. "You, good lady, photo me!"

She was five or six years old, a beautiful child whose glowing innocence distracted Jyl and saved her, for the moment, from thoughts of Pete, above, pressing some evil button. "Yes," she said, "okay."

"Okay!" the girl squealed, "okay okay!" and crouched in front of the bomb.

"Not there," Jyl said, turning toward the path, directing her to a spot by the trunk of a towering palm. She took a few pictures of the girl, then gave a slight bow to show she was finished.

"Two thousand kip," the girl said, holding out her hand.

Jyl was certain it would end up in her father's pocket, to be used by the family. She handed the girl a dollar.

"Five photos," Jyl said, holding up her right hand, wiggling its thumb and fingers.

The girl giggled, took the money, ran into the hut.

Jyl and Nathan got back to Muang Ngoi late that afternoon. They walked through town and down to the river. Like the locals, they stripped to their underwear and dove in.

Villagers laughed, giving them a *thumbs-up*.

"*Di rai!*" they said. *Very good!*

After swimming, Nathan went to the Sunrise. Jyl wasn't hungry. She walked back to her hut, put her knapsack inside, and went to sit on the big flat rock. The mother duck decided it was time to leave. She led her wobbly band out of the water, beyond the dam and down the shore.

"You have good today?"

It was Veeliepone standing on the hill, holding a swaddled infant. Jyl could see, by the way the woman snuggled the child, she must be its mother.

"Today *di rai*," said Jyl. She mimed the snuggling. "Yours?"

Veeliepone nodded and kissed the baby's forehead.

Jyl patted the space next to her on the rock. She felt certain this was where the young mother sat when tourists weren't around. "Come, please, come."

Veeliepone walked down the hill and stood close by, perhaps uncomfortable sitting next to the American lady. For several minutes neither of them said a thing. Then, a total surprise, Veeliepone handed her the child.

"Oh," said Jyl. "Yes?"

"Yes," the mother said, and sat beside her. Together they laughed at the infant's squeaky sounds and funny faces. "Halia," said Veeliepone.

"Halia," Jyl repeated. "Halia."

As if hearing herself called, the baby looked up into the stranger's eyes. It was a probing look that held Jyl close. She felt immediately drawn to this tiny being. Connected.

Or perhaps you just need something to connect to?

That was her mind admonishing her heart, as was its habit, for making too much of vague sensations.

"How many months?" Jyl said.

The young mother held up six fingers.

"Really? But she's, she's so...*aware.*"

Veeliepone gave her head a slight twist—obviously confused.

"You know," Jyl said, opening her eyes wide, like Halia's. "Aware!"

Veeliepone lit up. "Yes, this girl *sees good!*"

Sees, thought Jyl. The perfect word. Yes, that was it, Jyl felt as though she'd been truly seen.

Oh, for christsakes! Where is this stuff coming from?

Then the baby's eyes snapped shut. Her lips crinkled and she burped up some milky-looking drool. Jyl laughed at the unsightliness of reality. She fingered clean the tiny face and wiped the slimy residue on her shorts.

"Good," said Veeliepone. "You good mama."

"No," Jyl said, shaking her head, "I never had a baby."

Veeliepone kept smiling, kept patting her shoulder. "You good Mama Lao."

Sweet, thought Jyl, but it was definitely time to give the kid back.

For the next two weeks the pattern stayed the same. In the morning she met Nathan for breakfast at the Silent Moon, then they hiked to somewhere different, together finding another four villages. In the late afternoon they swam in the Ou river, and as sunset neared Jyl said good-bye.

Once she tried to break that pattern by offering to buy him dinner. She wanted to show her gratitude, to thank him for his dependable, undemanding friendship.

He declined, saying he liked evenings to himself. "No offense," he joked, "but even from you I need a break."

"Understood," she said. It was a load off her mind that nothing would happen between them.

Veeliepone and Halia were always waiting at sunset by the river. The three of them would sit and watch the colors fade…watch until the stars began to show. Then, to extend their time together, they'd go to her father's hut, which always smelled like fish. Pang, her father, a small wiry man, would be waiting with a bowl of carp from the creek. "Ah!" he'd say, as if their coming to his hut for dinner again were a huge surprise. Pang's face was as lean as his body. Except for the generous smile, he looked nothing like Veeliepone. She must have gotten the roundness from her mother.

With fish each night was sticky rice. It came from the large enamel pot that sat, like a permanent fixture, on Pang's table. The pot was covered by a thick metal lid, to keep away rats.

Jyl could see it had been made from a used-up bomb.

At one of their first meals, after serving the rice, Pang had pointed at the cold sticky goo, then at himself.

"Luk khao niaow," he said.

When Jyl looked confused, he said it again, slowly.

Veeliepone laughed and made a funny face. "Papa say we rice people."

"Oh," said Jyl. She pointed at the rice and patted his hand. "Good! Good!"

Though sometimes the fish came raw, in a watery herbal sauce, like ceviche, the normal fare was bony fried carp atop a gob of sticky rice. At each meal, once the baby had been nursed, Veeliepone handed Halia to Jyl. While going for her bowl of food she often looked at her father and said, "Good Mama Lao."

Pang would laugh and nod his head.

One night, after the expected hand-off, Pang looked at Jyl and started talking, first pointing at the baby, then at his daughter. Whatever he was saying, it upset him. He recovered and continued. A single tear dripped from his left eye. The old man shook it away, gazed for a few seconds at Veeliepone, then rose and left the hut.

Jyl turned to her. "What?"

"Papa say sad story. Say I baby when mama die."

"Oh, no," said Jyl. She wanted to hold her new friend, to stroke her hair, but instead snuggled Halia close and kissed the baby's forehead.

Veeliepone, now sobbing, said, "Baby need good mama."

Jyl thought of her own mother, who she missed. "How did your mama die?"

The young woman wiped away tears with the back of her hand, her fingers thick with sticky rice. She pointed upward and whispered, "Bomb."

The next day, when Jyl and Nathan reached the cave, they stopped by its mouth, took off their packs, and, as usual, sank their sweaty heads into the stream. Jyl kept hers down a long time. When out of air she came up panting.

"You okay?" Nathan said.

"I want to go inside."

He looked surprised. "Sure?"

"Yes. Please."

Nathan dug out his headlamp, Jyl her little flashlight, and he led her in.

Soon as they were a few strides past the mouth, darkness came. It was a darkness Jyl had never experienced, like the day was being swallowed. They flicked on their lights and kept walking. The path narrowed. Around the first sharp corner it opened up again, for maybe ten feet, and there were two tunnel-like openings in the rock. Three carefully balanced stones marked the one to the right.

"Nice ducky," said Nathan.

They had to crawl on hands and knees to make it through. The air was thin, Jyl's breathing fast and shallow. On the other side, a few feet away, the path split again, a duck instructing them to go left. There, dripping with stalactites, was a high ceiling. The passage smelled musky, probably from bat shit. Jyl saw the backs of shiny dark bodies huddled in the upper shadows.

They moved through another tall narrow passage. She thought of the word *black*. This was the literal meaning of that word—far darker than a lack of light—a darkness so thick and intense that her small mechanical torch proved a foolish toy. If ghosts did exist, this was where they'd be.

Nathan came to a sudden halt. "Oh," he said, "I forgot."

Aided by the beam of his headlamp, she looked past him at a fissure running from wall to wall. She guessed it two feet across and ten feet deep. On the other side was a duck.

"Forgot?" she said. "How could you forget *this?*"

"It's okay. An easy jump."

"No." She'd wanted to go all the way, but couldn't.

"In ten minutes," he said, "things open up. It's awesome. There's a landing, a cathedral ceiling, and a clear deep pool.

People do rituals there, to honor the dead. There are candles and matches. I thought we could light one for—"

"No," she said again, this time with urgency, "I can hardly breathe." How wrong this was. How stupid. Climbing around inside a cave would not bring Veeliepone's mother back. "I'm sorry. I have to get out of here."

Thank God, Nathan didn't say anything else. Talk would only suck away more air. She let him lead her out, out into the daylight, and the sunshine was miraculous, transforming her darkness into a kind of blurry fog, then floating it away.

Color, in its overlapping hues and shades, greeted her like a friend. This was her world. This was where she had to stay.

Another three weeks passed. They were hiking the same known trails to the same known villages, and didn't do much talking, both content with the friendly silence between them. That was what Jyl needed—silence, a friend, and lots of walking. That helped dilute the darkness of her thoughts, but it was always there.

Veeliepone's story had opened up something inside her: a view into the actual flesh and blood of this place. She could now imagine bombs exploding, villages blown to bits, people dead and dying in unspeakable ways. Before, though she knew the relevant statistics, they had never seemed quite real. The many casings proved that bombs had dropped, but not the damage they had caused. Facts did not show the thousands of innocent people devastated by America's war. They did not show the face of Veeliepone, a motherless child, whose life was irrevocably altered. Now Jyl saw the woman's stoic despair. She recognized it, every time she looked, in faces throughout the village.

It made Jyl viscerally aware of what her brother had done.

The single fact that stuck in her mind was the suicide rate among Vietnam Veterans, an average of twenty-two a day. Some soldiers, after following orders, could not rationalize the harm they'd done as *duty*. Maybe other wars had been different—*maybe*—but with Vietnam, because of the draft, many young men became soldiers against their will. They felt forced to go, forced to tune out the protests back home, forced to endure their doubt as they displaced poor villagers, destroyed homes, and killed anyone—at times women or children—who got in the way. Jyl thought of the napalm, the Agent Orange, the permanent scars of that horrible, unjust war. The suffering they had caused seeped into some of the soldiers' minds and could not be forgotten. There was no way to undo it. No way to accept it. And, for some, no way to live with it.

Jyl believed that Pete would have been one of those, which made her feel worse.

Perhaps the hardest thing to face: she was one too.

She knew it. Could not deny it.

She was lost, like a frightened soldier in a dense unknown jungle. Walking helped, lots of silent walking, but there was no way to escape the darkness.

Then Nathan announced he was leaving. Jyl, never surprised by bad news, felt her normal, expected distress. Since childhood she'd had an unreasonable reaction to good things ending. Like her favorite movies. It seemed unfair when the final scene went black and credits started rolling, as if she'd been tricked into caring about something that was not real.

She tried to joke. "Finished with me, eh? Off, I suppose, to find someone better?"

"Off to see my guru in India."

"Oh," she said, and laughed. "Guess I can't beat that."

"Odd, don't you think, that we never talked about our personal lives."

"You and I aren't talkers."

Nathan shrugged—an apparent agreement. They were both quiet hikers, both quiet people in regard to their personal lives. Jyl bent forward, as she'd been wanting to for weeks, and kissed him on the mouth. Nothing romantic, but she needed him to feel her love.

"Ooh, well, maybe I'll change my mind," he said with a big manly voice.

They paid the bill, he bought bread at the bakery, and she walked him to a waiting skiff.

"Thank you," Jyl said, "for being my friend."

"Good luck with your brother," Nathan said. He handed her his headlamp. "I want you to have this. With that toy of yours you'll just get lost."

They hugged and said good-bye. She waved as the boat puttered off. She was on her own.

Jyl tried to smile that thought away, but it did make her anxious. She walked back to the Silent Moon, ordered a cup of tea, and began another letter to Miles. This was the third. She'd never finished the others, fearing what she had to say.

Dear Miles, she wrote, *First off, I have to tell you that I'm staying longer. Something is happening, I don't know what. I have to see what it means.*

Then she tore it up. A letter like that would not help. She needed time to figure things out, that's all.

In a few days she'd try again.

But she didn't. Jyl decided she wasn't ready, and for the next couple of weeks stayed close to her hut. The land had begun to feel like home. Each morning she fished with Pang at his favorite spot on the creek. They used hand-held nets. He knew where the fish hid out, under the larger rocks, and showed her how to sneak close, how to block their escape, how to scoop them up.

"Di rai!" he would say whenever she caught one.

Back on his property she helped him lay electrical line: a long, half-inch thick, plastic-coated bundle of copper wires. It ran from the dam, from the turbine thing he'd bought, to a large battery in a shed next to the communal toilet. From the battery went individual strands, one to each hut. Jyl realized that this was why he'd built the dam—not for ducks but so that his could be the first guesthouse with electric light. The finished system gave each hut a single low-watt bulb, which stayed lit at night for a couple of hours. It didn't help much, but was a big deal for Pang. She pointed at hers and said to him, *"Di rai!"*

On afternoons Jyl often worked with Veeliepone in the garden. Aside from weeding, that meant hauling buckets of water from creek to plants. She loved the work. She also loved helping out with Halia. She only went to town for needed supplies like matches, kerosene, cooking oil and toilet paper. While there she bought other things too...special treats...like passion fruit, pastries from the bakery, or, when his bottle was getting empty, Whiskey Lao for Pang. The old man loved his Whiskey Lao.

Jyl insisted on paying for the bulk of it, as thanks for him feeding her each night. Though she spent ten times what the fish and rice were worth, it showed how appreciative she was for having been treated with such kindness.

Tourists came to rent the other huts for a day, or sometimes two, but Jyl befriended none of them. She had no need. At sunset she sat with Veeliepone and Halia on their big flat rock. They would watch the ducks, wait for darkness to settle over the world, then go to eat with Pang.

One night he was clearly not himself. He smiled, as always, but there was no joy in it. Jyl looked into his eyes, touched his hand and said, "You okay?"

Pang pointed at his chest. "Me. Trouble."

He seemed angry, and close to tears.

Jyl looked to Veeliepone.

"Papa owe man, he pay for light. Have trouble is shame."

"A man is trying to shame your papa?"

"No," said Veeliepone. "Papa shame for not pay back money."

"How much does your papa owe?"

"Four hundred thousand kip."

"But that's, that's forty dollars," said Jyl. "I want to help. I can give him the money."

"You give?"

"I give," said Jyl.

Veeliepone beamed at her father and spoke in rapid Lao.

The old man turned to Jyl, now with tears of joy, and said, "No trouble! No trouble!"

The next morning she handed Pang two twenty-dollar bills. He looked at them as if they might not be real, then looked back at her. His expression did not change.

"Okay?" he said.

"Okay."

He nodded and walked off. Suddenly he stopped, turned toward Jyl, and pointed at the ground. With wide happy eyes he said, "You, here, much good home. No trouble, okay?"

Jyl got the feeling that "much good home" was Pang's way of saying how grateful he was, and that this, his home, was her home too.

She smiled and said, "Yes, okay."

After he left she grabbed her knapsack and walked through town, down to the river. Her extended visa was nearly up. She would soon have to leave, and knew she was not ready, aware that her time with Veeliepone and Pang had softened her heart, soothed her sadness, and helped her mind accept its occasional darkness. But to get another month meant a three-day trip down the Mekong to Vientiane. And she might be denied. The communist government, unaccustomed to tourism, was suspicious of foreigners who stayed too long.

Jyl dove into the river and floated on her back. She gazed up at the empty azure sky. Then, on an impulse, thinking this might be her last chance, she decided to get a view of Muang Ngoi from its opposite shore. With bold confident strokes she propelled herself out into the flow.

She was a good swimmer, had won medals during high school, but now felt instantly outmatched. It felt like she was being dragged away. The other bank was beyond her reach. Struggling, she turned around and swam her hardest, fighting the strong current, shocked by how long it took to escape the steady pull. At last out of danger, Jyl dog paddled slowly to a sliver of beach. She was a few hundred yards downstream from the village.

Exhausted, she lay on the warm soft sand. Her cold skin tingled from the sun's welcomed heat. She closed her eyes and waited for her breath to calm. She dozed off, was holding hands with Miles, gazing at the vast Pacific Ocean when roused by something. She didn't know what. Jyl sat up and looked around. She saw men at work on the hillside to her right, and could hear the sound of handsaws. Oh dear, she thought...more guesthouses?

Chee! Chee! Chee!

To her left, on the tip of a rocky promontory, was a kingfisher. It looked like the one she'd spotted her first day. That felt like years ago. She'd come here to make peace with Pete. What did that mean? Though he sometimes crossed her mind, he no longer seemed connected to this place. She had come because of him, but he was not here.

She thought of Veeliepone. Whenever the young woman called her Mama Lao, Jyl felt a gentle tug. The name, the way she said it, sounded natural, like a sister's hello, a loving invitation. How happy Veeliepone and Pang would be if she stayed. And yes, she could. *Yes, that is possible.* She could take a boat down to the Mekong...could take another upriver, a couple of days away, to the border of Thailand...could cross over for a few days, then get a new three month visa for Laos.

Or maybe there was some way to stay longer?

She imagined what it would be like to live here full time, to make this village her home. The idea made her heart beat fast. She was down to her last three hundred dollars, but there was a thousand stashed away in her Santa Barbara apartment, and five in the bank, and nineteen in an IRA she's paid into while working at UCSB.

In Muang Ngoi, if she was careful, even with an occasional trip to the states, that money could last thirty or forty years. Maybe for the rest of her life.

Yes, this could be her world. She could be a part of this. She pictured Pang's smiling face, and imagined seeing it every day. *Much good home.*

She whispered it out loud, "Much good home." What a beautiful way to express her hope, her wish for a different life. In Muang Ngoi she sensed the possibility of inclusion, of belonging, that was missing for her in America, where she'd always felt foreign.

Miles would never understand. Or her parents.

Jyl didn't care.

She swam upstream to where she'd set her knapsack. It was exactly as she'd left it. People did not steal in Muang Ngoi. A woman washing clothes wished her a good day. A man, working on his boat, smiled and waved. She waved back. Jyl dried herself off, pulled on her shorts and cotton blouse, put on her socks and boots, and walked up to the *stupa*. She kneeled and prayed: for release; for courage; for trust in whatever happened.

Yes, she would live here, as poor as the rest. She would learn a simpler way of life.

She felt strong and whole and full of peace.

There was an old cardboard box in front of her hut. What could that be? Was Jyl supposed to open it? Not sure, she decided to wait. She set her knapsack inside and walked down to the big flat rock. The ducks, accustomed to her presence, swam by unafraid. They hardly looked like babies anymore. Before long they'd have ducklings of their own.

Oh, wow, how naive is that? Jyl laughed at herself. These, she knew, were not wild ducks, they belonged to a nearby neighbor and would soon be plucked and grilled up for the tourists. Not ideal, but true.

This place would make her face the truth. The villagers of Muang Ngoi were no different from anyone else on the planet. They, too, wanted things: bigger and better boats; concrete houses; generators and televisions. They did not

240

romanticize poverty. They were rice people because, up until now, they'd had no other choice.

Jyl sensed her coming darkness but could not stop it, could not quiet its brutal honesty. Of course they would keep building guesthouses. They would greet the coming tourism with open arms. She could almost see the alluring restaurants, gift shops, and bars (especially bars) littering the riverbank. "Happy Hour!" the tacky signs would scream. And rock'n'roll would blast at night. There would be a dock, and a constant cloud of smoke from idling motorboats. The water would be streaked by gas and oil.

Or maybe not. Maybe, instead of boats, there would be a clanging metal bridge across the river, a parking lot next to the Buddhist temple, and a tourist bus arriving every hour.

And every room of every fancy guesthouse will have its own television!

Why on earth was she thinking this stuff? Was her cynical mind revolting because she'd decided to live here?

Jyl looked up at the sky, at a bank of clouds moving in from the east. She'd dealt with this voice in her head before. She didn't need to listen.

Much good home! What about that? The old man wants more huts on his land, that's what he wants!

"You have sad today."

Veeliepone was standing right behind her. How had Jyl not heard? She dried her eyes and said, "Yes, today I have some sadness."

The young woman sat next to her on the rock and held her hand. They sat that way for a long time.

At last Jyl felt uncomfortable…felt the need to walk. It didn't matter where. She would go back to town, buy some bread, and maybe her own bottle of Whisky Lao. She squeezed Veeliepone's hand, thankful for the kindness.

"You no leave," her friend said, as if worried that Jyl were never coming back.

Jyl stood. "I'm going for a walk."

"You need stay," said Veeliepone. Then her troubled eyes lit up, like a child with a secret she wants to share. "You come, I show."

The young woman took Jyl's hand and walked up the hill.

Jyl let herself be led.

They went to the box lying outside the hut.

Veeliepone picked it up, pushed open the door, set it on the floor and opened it up. "You see!"

Inside was some kind of fabric. Veeliepone spread it out on the bed, on top of Jyl's sleeping bag. It was a hand-made quilt with hundreds of squares, each from a different color or pattern of skirt. There were no two squares alike.

"For me?" said Jyl.

"Yes, for you."

"My god, how gorgeous!"

Veeliepone knelt down and pulled a traditional Laotian skirt from the box. It was strikingly similar to the one she wore. "I make for you," she said. She pointed at her own skirt. "Like me, see?"

It reminded Jyl of a Japanese kimono: beautiful, yes, but far too formal, far too tightly bound.

"Yes," she said, "I see."

"You like?"

Jyl smiled and nodded.

"For thank you," said Veeliepone, full of joy. "For much good home."

Jyl felt her hands get clammy.

"You dress," said Veeliepone, holding the skirt out toward her.

Jyl took a step back. "I like," she said, "but I can't take so many gifts."

"You take," said Veeliepone. There was a glow of expectation in the young woman's smile. "This you, Mama Lao."

Jyl felt pressured. Trapped. Though this was what she'd wanted—to be included, to be welcomed like a sister—the look on Veeliepone's face made her nervous. She could not

242

imagine ever wearing that skirt. She would not give up her shorts or blouse or boots. "No," the American lady said, her voice sharper than intended, "me no Mama Lao."

Tears welled up in both women's eyes.

Veeliepone sat on the bed, the dress in her lap, and Jyl sat next to her. She reached over and held the young woman's hand. "I'm sorry," she said.

Veeliepone lay on her side and put her head in Jyl's lap. "Sorry for me, I need."

"That's okay," Jyl said, not knowing what else to say.

"You stay," said Veeliepone. "You need stay."

Jyl stroked her hair. It needed a good washing. "I'm glad," she said, "that we are friends."

"You not friend."

"Yes, I am your friend," said Jyl.

Veeliepone sat up and looked in her eyes. "No. You not *see!*" The Lao woman's hands were gripping hers. Apparently this was different from simple friendship. "You not *see* Mama Lao."

Oh, dear...should Jyl have known this was coming? Had she been kidding herself? Was it possible that the thirty-year-old woman actually wanted her as a mother? No, no way, there'd never been any hint of that. She felt certain that *Mama Lao* meant something else to Veeliepone. What was going on? "Please," she said. "I want to be your friend."

"No, Jyl, friend not stay with rice people. Friend need go. You Mama Lao. You money people."

Money people? The sound of that gave her a shiver.

Yeah, okay, Jyl wasn't stupid. She knew that Veeliepone and Pang believed she must be wealthy. How lucky, right, that this person they liked and trusted, who they'd taken in and shared meals with, was a rich American lady: able to vacation for as long as she wanted; able to eat breakfast in a restaurant; able to donate supplies for the house, and extra treats, and give away forty dollars—*No trouble!*

Jyl leaned over and kissed the young woman's hands, then got up from the bed.

Veeliepone looked about to cry. "Please, you not go."

Jyl touched Veeliepone's shoulder. "Don't worry," she said, "I'll come back."

She grabbed her knapsack and left.

At the main path she turned away from town, toward the mountains, walking along the creek and into the woods. Jyl knew that her connection with Veeliepone and Pang was real, they truly cared about each other. But the money thing bothered her.

Maybe it shouldn't.

Maybe that's why she was here, to make these sweet people her family, to help them any way she could.

And hey, if it didn't work out, she was free to leave. There was nothing holding her. This was all her choice.

My choice, that's right, and I can change it any time.

Jyl thought of that as she walked, of her freedom to go when and where she pleased. It made her think of Pete. Pete and his bombs, his airplane zooming over and away.

Though there was no logical connection, there was also no denying how she felt. She didn't trust this kind of freedom. It seemed too easy.

It seemed wrong.

At the cave, thirsty and exhausted, she tossed off her knapsack, dropped to her belly, and drank from the stream. Jyl knew she wasn't thinking right. Her sense of guilt—guilt for Pete's undeniable crimes, for her own undeniable privilege—was stronger than she'd believed, and too harsh to be fair.

She felt lost again. Alone. It struck her that she was missing Nathan. Nathan more than Miles.

She sat by the cave's entrance and looked into the sunlit forest. The creek carved its way across the earthen path, then through tall yellow grass and off into the waiting trees, their whitish trunks like keepers of the layered greens, violets, deepening blues and purples.

Oh yes, she loved Muang Ngoi. This was where she needed to be. But for her, even here, like anywhere she'd ever been, there was something missing.

Jyl thought again of Pete, of when they were kids. She remembered him crouched down next to her, behind some bush, during a neighborhood game of hide and seek. She was a small girl at the time. He was nine years older, and would tell her when to run for the apricot tree on the other side of the cul de sac. "Go, Jylly, go!" he'd say, and off they'd sprint, her in front and him right behind, until both of them tagged the trunk and yelled, "Olly olly oxen free!"

She had no idea what that meant or why they had to yell so loud, as if their lives depended on it.

But they did, every time, and every time, while panting for breath, he hugged her close and she felt safe, like he would always be there to protect her. Always.

Jyl went for the headlamp, put it on, and walked into the darkness. If there was a place to say a prayer for them, she'd find it.

STRAWBERRIES

It was mid-July, and an unusually warm day on the northern California coast. Brady was naked in his backyard, smoking a joint, wandering among the flowers while his daughter and ten-year-old grandson were off at some Disney matinee. Brady and his wife, Ellie, used to get naked in the garden on such gorgeous days. In honor of her, he took another toke. He had an hour to remember where he'd left his clothes, and nothing better to do than contemplate the single puffy cloud floating above his apple tree. That's when he heard a scream, then another, from Tucker's side of the fence.

No—from inside Tucker's house.

Hard to tell if it was something to bother with. He assumed not, and paid it no attention. Like he paid no attention to sports, or the latest Hollywood movies, or the daily news. A waste of his precious time. Re-focusing on the cloud, the perfect poetry of it, he hoped to transcend his tendency to fret. Having topped seventy, and finally retired, Brady's job, at last, was to have no job. No longer a teacher, other people's problems were no longer his. Since losing Ellie last winter he felt no need to be a responsible citizen. Brady knew he could not fix a thing. Whatever the hell happened *out there* was beyond his diminishing control.

The cloud began to dissipate. That didn't bother him either, his mind content to endlessly ponder nothing…except there it was again, the screaming. Then he heard what seemed to be slapping.

Or maybe someone being spanked?

Not his problem, no, but he could not deny the force of it.

Brady began to sweat. A spark of cold flashed through his chest and down both arms. Maybe he should call the police? Though not wanting to get involved in a family squabble, he could not look away if someone was being hurt.

He went for the house, for the phone, but stopped himself, turned around and stared at the Tucker's asphalt roof. The police would not act on a mere complaint.

Besides, what would he say?

What proof did he have that there was any real problem?

Brady clenched his jaw, angry at the deeper truth. More than anything else, he was afraid of making unnecessary trouble, of looking like some old fool. He needed a better idea of what was going on.

He inched up to the fence and heard a woman's voice. He couldn't understand what she was saying. Soon he heard her panting, a kind of fast-paced moan. A few seconds later came a spank.

She cried out, "No! No! No!" when what she clearly meant was Yes! Yes! Yes!

Brady was breathing hard, caught off-guard by the sound of kinky sex. Not a chance that this was Fred and Carol Tucker, both of them limp as old carrots. Brady guessed it had to be their son, Dale, rollicking with some girlfriend. Dale was maybe sixteen. He'd probably volunteered to stay home and *take care of the house* rather than go on the family vacation. Brady remembered him as a short skinny blond kid in a Little League uniform. With hair in his eyes, and a pimpled face, he once knocked on Brady's door, asking for a donation to send their all-star team to play in Sacramento.

Christ, that was what, a few years ago?

"Oh My God!" the girl screamed.

The spanking got harder, the screams more frequent. Anyone within shouting distance knew this was her idea of a good time. The whole deal was crazy, but Brady saw no reason to get police involved. *So what am I supposed to do?* He felt an unwanted sense of personal obligation, his mind demanding that he somehow make this end, keep it away from his daughter and young grandson.

Yeah, right—he was lying and he knew it. They wouldn't be back for at least an hour. That could not explain how upset he felt right now.

Was it about the kinky sex? Though he'd never understood the appeal of spanking, or anything else remotely S or M, he used to love his sex with Ellie. She didn't mind getting wild at times, assuming it was consensual and stayed private.

That's the problem, the blatant publicity of this!

Righteously upset, and wishing he weren't naked, Brady retreated from the fence. He tripped over something and stepped on one of Ellie's strawberry plants. Ripened fruit oozed between his toes. Twisting to regain balance, he lost it completely and fell headfirst into the bed, crushing several more. Strawberry slime stuck to his chin, his chest, his stomach.

He scrambled to his feet. Juice, like blood, dripped down his leg. Brady stifled a scream, stormed to the deck, and scraped off the sticky mess, astounded that his penis had stiffened, a sensation he hadn't had in months.

He found his shorts and gingerly pulled them on, zipping with extreme care to a steady stream of spanking, the young woman alternating her breathy commands between an encouraging "YES!" and an encouraging "NO!"

Brady sighed and groaned and paced the yard like a prisoner. Like a caged and starving de-clawed beast.

Helpless. Totally helpless.

When the ordeal ended, a stoned eternity later—his mouth dry, his knees trembling—it was as if he'd survived an aggravated assault. He sat on the deck and held his head, soothed by the silence. His anguish slowly dissipated. He sent his torturers a soft whisper of thanks.

He retracted it with vengeance the next morning, waking to their moans, their gasping sighs. Covering his head with a pillow, Brady cursed the horny deviants to a hell he did not believe in. And they got louder! Luckily, his grandson slept like a log. Luckily, his daughter took extremely long and early walks. When it happened again that afternoon, however, there was no escape. He was startled by each shriek, stung by each slap, stupefied by the rising repetitions of "oh my god Oh My God OH MY GOD!"

His grandson, Bo, apparently unperturbed, went to watch television. That the child watched so much of it explained why nothing shocked him. Megan, Brady's daughter, was the one he needed to deal with. She asked if he had their phone number. Brady told her no. Either of them could have looked it up, or screamed over the fence, but didn't.

Megan was flustered. She acted as if it were his fault. "Really, Dad, this shit has to stop."

"What am I supposed to do?"

Her face went blank, like the blood had been drained away. The look reminded him of her awful smart-ass teenage years.

"Gee," she said, "how about, you know, *something?*"

He brought a boom box into the backyard and turned up the music.

"What's that," Megan said, "the soundtrack?"

She and Bo left the following morning, cutting their visit a week short. He couldn't stop that either. And by late afternoon the kids were back at it.

His curiosity, Brady was ashamed to admit, had morphed into obsession. He tiptoed to the fence and put his ear to one of the slits between the boards. What he heard was straight-ahead, high-energy intercourse, the girl moaning in a way he recognized, building toward an orgasm.

Brady hunkered down and leaned his back against the fence. Head bowed, he listened. Like a youngster hearing it for the first time. Like a widowed, lonely, getting-old man, hearing it, perhaps, for the very last time. Or, he realized, like anyone of any age, because these are sounds that no one ever gets used to—sounds that bypass the brain, penetrate the flesh, rattle the soul—sounds that recall the sweetest of all journeys to a place so sacred that we must be banished, tossed from the pearly gates, within seconds of arrival. No wonder we scream, we moan, we slobber what cannot be said. Sounds spill out of us like seed from a fallen flower. Painfully beautiful sounds. Sounds that, if we're not in the center of them, surrounded and swallowed, make us feel afflicted, lost, abandoned.

Oh God, I miss my Ellie.

He never heard the boy say a thing. It was just the girl, calm and emphatic.

"No," she said, "please Dale, not like that."

Like what? What?

"Stop, Dale, I told you to stop!"

Then it was quiet for several minutes. Brady pictured the boy's red face, the girlfriend disappointed with his performance. He felt sad for the kid. He knew that feeling. Ellie was different than the others, was never like this demanding girl. She'd always made him whole, no matter what, and he hoped that's what was happening now for Dale. Maybe there were tears being shed...gentle touches given... kind words spoken.

Or maybe she'd up and left?

Tired of them consuming his thoughts, Brady's mind wandered elsewhere. He considered getting up on the roof to finish his shingling job. He checked his watch, it was after five o'clock, and he considered turning on the Giants game. He considered getting stoned.

"See," the girl said, surprising him with a lusty whisper, "this way, baby, see."

She wanted it softer, she said. Slower.

Then faster, harder.

Brady imagined one sliding on top, then the other, a fleshy undulating blur, writhing against every surface in every possible position.

He went inside the house, grabbed some beers from the fridge, hurried upstairs to his bedroom and turned on the TV. He lay on the bed, put on headphones, and watched a movie so idiotic that he was unable to laugh, drinking until he finally dozed off. At four in the morning he got up to pee, then turned off the fuzzy screen. He heard the girl moaning.

As if personally threatened, Brady snuck back into bed, pulled the covers over his head, and groped for comfort, squeezing and stroking himself with utter self-pity.

Disgusted, he ripped his hand free.

He stuffed little foam plugs in his ears.

Eventually he fell into a fitful, haunted sleep.

When he woke around noon they were cooing like doves, then grunting like pigs, then howling like werewolves.

"You're too big!" she cried.

It sounded to Brady like some sort of weird sex game, her complaint meant to bolster Dale's ego, excite him into giving what she was claiming not to want.

"God," she yelled, "you're huge!"

Him, huge? How had that scrawny kid finagled his way out of Little League?

How did itsy bitsy Dale find a hottie like her?

Brady drove to the hardware store, walked up and down the aisles, and bought, he realized on the way home, the same extra-grip roofing nails he'd bought too many of last week. When he got back, to his bewilderment, they were going as strong as ever. *Huh? What kind of drugs are these kids on?* And he couldn't do any shingling because he didn't want to look like a peeper.

He did dishes instead. He scrubbed toilets.

He wanted to run away, to never come back. It felt like when he was a kid, like that time the big carnival had come to town. Thinking of that, then, at least stopped him thinking of this, now.

It was in Fresno, California, where his parents used to say that nothing ever happened. "Well I'll be damned," his father said, clearly happy with the music, flashing lights, and half-naked tattooed ladies selling tickets.

Brady had just turned five. He didn't know what a carnival was, and could barely wait to see. He held his mother's hand as they walked by people with strange clothes and painted faces.

The whole thing felt like a dream.

251

His parents sat him and his twelve-year-old brother, Wes, on a first-row bench inside a big white tent, each with his own Coke and cotton candy.

"We're going for something," his father said, "which cannot be shared with children."

Brady knew that meant drinking, but didn't worry because Wes was with him. Wes had promised their mom they'd stay put on the bench and wait.

A man came out. He bowed, twirled a wand, and pulled a rabbit out of his big black hat. And a goldfish. Other things too. Brady liked that. Then dogs went running around in circles, barking and jumping through hoops.

Brady was fine until a midget lady with curly yellow hair tried to get him to dance with her and the dogs. The midget's lips were painted a glossy red. She had crooked brown teeth, hair on her chin, and wouldn't leave him alone, making pretend-sad faces while tugging at his hand.

"Go on," said Wes, giving him a push, "she wants to dance with you."

That got the midget lady tugging harder, which made Brady piss his pants. When she and Wes laughed, and others started laughing too, he ran from the tent, out into the crowded darkness. He was lost for what seemed a long time. He sat alone, in the dirt, crying.

Then came lots of hugs and kisses when his mother found him. "I'm sorry, honey," she kept saying, "I promise I'll never leave you again."

He would find out that was a lie, would know it long before gin became the only thing she cared about.

Now trying to get her out of his head, Brady went to the garage, got on his bike, and rode like a demon to place after place he didn't want to be. The plaza was packed with begging vagrants and their hungry-looking dogs. The marsh was full of high school joggers. He headed out into the bottoms, through fields of oblivious cows and run-down barns, and ended up at the ocean. Its hovering fog felt ominous, like a gaping white mouth.

He peddled back home with aching thighs, exhausted, the blue sky being swallowed all around him.

In the backyard there was still a bit of sunlight.

What he thought he heard was not what he expected.

Brady hurried to the fence, to make sure, and peeked between the boards. Yes, *thank God,* it was him, Dale, a baseball cap turned backwards on his head, baggy pants halfway down his skinny ass, and he was mowing the lawn!

Which must mean the parents were coming home!

Which meant this thing was over!

At last, finally, over!

Brady went inside the house. A golden glow burned through a gap in the thickening fog and lit up the living room. The world again seemed warm and safe and kind.

He heated a can of soup on the stove and made a piece of toast, feeling grateful for the renewed, quiet, uneventful rhythm of his life.

Hah! He could hear Ellie laughing, surprised at how tame he had become. Loud horny teenagers would bother her too, but she'd never have let them freak her out.

"Let's show 'em!" she'd have said, pulling him down on top of her.

He remembered, before getting together with Ellie, how suspicious he'd been of anything out of the ordinary, anything he did not understand. She'd convinced him to take a leave of absence from teaching and travel with her to Germany. They walked the streets of Munich, they went to castles, they rode bikes through the Bavarian countryside.

He was hooked.

Each summer after that, they went somewhere different.

Random images now flashed through his mind: their bed in Montepulciano; buying bottles of water at a convenience store in Taxco; the abrupt ending of a trail in the Bitterroot Mountains of Idaho. He'd gotten them lost. They'd run out of water and had to sleep, hungry and thirsty, cuddled together in the cold on a steep rocky hillside.

253

Brady sat on the couch, in the last orange glow of sun. He thought of the summer they'd toured big cities in the United States. Ellie's idea. Not something this country boy would have chosen. *Talk about being lost!*

On day one, in New York, a middle-aged black man stopped them on the street. He appeared well dressed, but then Brady noticed his un-ironed slacks and scuffed-up shoes.

"I can see you folks are not from here," the man said. He had a soft voice and big friendly eyes. "Listen to me," he said. "Because this can be a dangerous place, I'm giving you advice."

Brady glanced at Ellie, who was smiling.

"You listening?" the man said to him.

"Yeah."

The man looked around, as if to be certain that no one was watching. His eyes seemed to get bigger. Brady saw streaks of thin red veins edging their milky whiteness.

"Brother," the man said, "you need to know how to keep out of trouble, okay?"

"Okay."

"So I'm telling you, no matter what, don't you make any kind of contact with people on the street. Don't you look into anyone's eyes."

The man kept staring at Brady until Ellie cracked up.

Then he turned to her.

"Mercy, woman, you're not scared?"

"Terrified," she said, and they both started laughing.

Brady felt left out. He was confused, looking back and forth between them.

The man slapped him on the back. "For peteysakes, relax," he said. "Take it easy, friend, nobody gonna eat you."

Ellie had no fear of people like that, or of the places, like inner city neighborhoods, that Brady thought should be avoided. Back home, she worked on weekends at a food bank in Eureka. Ellie said she missed that.

254

She suggested that on their city tour they volunteer, a few days in each place, at food banks in New York, Boston, Chicago, and St. Louis.

At first he resisted, then reluctantly went along. He may not trust those places, but he did trust her. He felt lucky to have Ellie in his life. He needed her to know that.

One early evening, after work, they went to the free public zoo in St. Louis. They were heading for the entrance when a little boy came walking toward them with his parents. Brady made eye contact with the kid, and as they passed each other, without a word, both simultaneously lifted their hands and slapped palms.

Ellie loved that moment. "That boy saw the magic in you," she said, snuggling close.

She and Brady shared plenty of exotic experiences he might remember—like hiking to Machu Picchu, or the "Holi" day water fight on the streets of Delhi—but what came to mind now were the common daily moments…like that boy at the St. Louis Zoo…like sipping coffee at a shelter in Chicago, handing out plates of food, laughing and chatting with people he would otherwise never have met. He remembered Kyrie and Leticia, Malcolm and Mohammed.

Feeling Ellie close, Brady went to bed early, fell asleep, and dreamt of them on a bus somewhere, driving at night through an unknown, unseen landscape.

It was peaceful. Quiet. Absolutely quiet.

Then came the slaps and moans.

Brady bolted to his feet. His mind felt stuck like an ant in honey. He stood there in the dark, naked and shivering, listening to self-indulgent teenagers flaunt their insatiable desire, their unyielding sexuality. He simply did not get how these kids could keep going and going and going.

Please, Ellie, what do I do? What?

But he was beyond any reasonable advice.

Who knew if the parents were ever coming back?

Who cares!

He charged to the open window and screamed into the night. Not words, it wasn't words that came out, it was like a growl, low and angry at first, then rising in pitch, stretching into a long anguished howl! He gasped for breath and howled again as tears streamed down his face. His voice cracked and he squeezed out a wheezing sort of cry. Other than that, there was no other sound. It was just him, panting with utter torment, defeat, surrender.

He saw a light go on in their bedroom below, then in many of the surrounding houses.

The morning was sunny and warm, another a vibrant blue sky. It was unusually quiet too. Brady remembered what happened last night, the depth of his despair, but he felt good, as if all his fears had been flushed away and there was nothing left to hide.

The backyard looked fresh. Welcoming. It was like seeing it with Ellie's loving eyes: the plum tree, its fruit ready to pick; flowers in full bloom on the many perennials she'd planted.

Without Ellie he would never have become a gardener.

He kept things growing because of her.

She guided him to the far side of the apple tree, showing that the potato vine had once again invaded its lower branches. He was the one who'd wanted the hardy climber. Still did. He loved the way it covered their western fence with delicate white flowers. But she'd warned him, and was right, that it would try to take over the tree.

"As usual," she'd say, joking as each summer he worked to keep the rascal under control, "you don't listen to reason."

Brady laughed as he walked to the shed for his ladder and shears.

After a few minutes of clipping back the vine he said, "See, honey, no problem."

"You're the problem," she said, her lips against his cheek.

Brady took off his clothes, lit a joint, then quickly put it out. Getting stoned could be a bad idea. What, was he nuts?

256

What if those kids start up again?

"No!" he said, low and hard, clenching his fist, angry that he'd let them sneak into his peaceful mind. He should have known that would make Ellie go. He tried to calm himself but could already feel her, gone.

He sat cross-legged on the deck, letting his eyes wander from wrinkled skin to carrot stems, from lettuce to elephant garlic and back to wrinkled skin. It seemed this was a test: a time to admit his persistent loneliness, and face it. Would that bring Ellie back?

Then it hit him—her strawberries!

Brady rushed to the mangled bed and dropped to his knees. He might have saved a few of the broken plants if he'd gotten to them yesterday, but he saw it was now too late. *Oh, Ellie, I'm so sorry.* The best he could do was to dig out the dead ones, like small fragile bodies, and carry them to the compost pile.

He lay them tenderly onto a scattering of kitchen scraps.

He covered them with dry brown leaves.

He went back to the bed and worked his fingers down into the loamy soil.

It's the feel of you. The feeling I can't forget.

"C'mon Brady…snap out of it."

"I don't know what to do."

"You need to get out of here."

"What?" he said. "Where?"

"I don't know. Someplace new."

"I don't think I can."

"Of course you can. You have to. You need to go, honey, someplace you've never been, and see what happens! It doesn't matter where, just go!"

FINALLY
-a fable for tomorrow-

Coyote, because of his transmogrifying nature, must at times admit his attraction, even affinity, to humans. Just last night he used their word "finally." He remembers thinking, *The moon finally set beyond the mountain,* whereas nothing of the sort could have happened since "finally" means, well...*finally*. It means that the moon will never again rise or set. It indicates an ending, a permanent outcome.

Such a definition, he understands, is far too literal. Or is that just what humans would say? He can hear them in his head. "Lighten up," they snicker. "The word," they claim, "is spoken every day, and therefore must have merit."

Nevertheless, Coyote has finally stopped believing in finality. As this thing becomes that: like day to night or fall to winter—like river to ocean to clouds to rain to river—life goes on in one everlasting flow. Humans are great at separating things, at naming things, at applauding those they like and dismissing those they don't. Perhaps they should become more appreciative of how one reflects the other. Perhaps they, like he and every other animal, should accept the inevitability of change.

258

As the cliché wisely states: *When something ends something else begins.*

The wonderful thing about clichés is that they often tell essential truths. That's why Coyote uses them whenever possible.

The only reasonable response to life, he believes, is expressed by the once popular saying, *Will wonders never cease?* That the answer is a question, he insists, is key to life's elusive lock.

For Coyote, who has nothing personal to protect, actual locks and keys are not of any interest. Metaphorically, however, he struggles every day with an instinctual need to preserve sacred spaces. That is his life's work. No, it isn't easy. And now he is concerned for his own home.

He and Rabbit live in the spacious entrance of a cave. Its other entrance, far below, at the base of the mountain, has been discovered by a group of spelunkers. Each day he hears their voices echoing through the labyrinth of twisted tunnels. Each day he hears them getting closer.

Someday they will make it up top, and there is no way to keep them out.

Under normal circumstances that would be no problem. Coyotes and rabbits are adept at quick adjustments to civilization's relentless progress. Unfortunately, these are not normal times. They both feel vulnerable because Rabbit is big with child. Or, more likely, children. In a week or two there will be lots of Coyote Rabbits romping through the desert, but for now she needs a safe place to conserve her strength, give birth, and nurture their young.

This morning, early, Coyote went out looking for another home. While still a grumpy creature at times, his coming fatherhood and deep love for Rabbit has softened him and renewed his faith in life. Though old and worn, he feels as strong and confident as a pup.

So far he's found no new suitable place for them to live. He searched the nearby ridges. All of the caves were occupied by others: foxes, bobcats, mountain lions.

He drops to the back of a slender box canyon, a delightfully private spot, and finds the most extraordinary thing: an old Volkswagen camper. How it got there he has no idea, since there is no road of any sort—just boulders, cactus, sagebrush, and a scramble of dwarf junipers.

He approaches the vehicle slowly.

With people, Coyote can never be too cautious.

After several minutes, sensing no one else around, he opens the metallic door, goes inside, and is soon convinced by the thick stale air, devoid of human odor, that the camper has been abandoned. Perhaps this person got lonely in the middle of nowhere. Or ran out of food.

Or was eaten.

Coyote lies back on the thin foam bed and looks the place over. It's not as big or nice as their cave, but will have to do until they can find something better.

He hurries back and tells Rabbit.

"Good," she says, pointing toward the descending tunnel. "I think they're almost here."

Sure enough, he hears muffled, not-too-distant grunts and groans. "All right," he says, "let's go."

But as they exit the cave, Rabbit stops and stares at him. A look of wonder covers her face.

"What?" he says.

"It's coming," she says.

"You mean now?"

"Yes," she says, her eyes full of light. "Could be any time."

"Okay then, Sweetheart, it has to happen here."

He gently leads her back into the cave.

She curls up in the corner and he joins her, cupping her with his body, breathing in her soft, earthy fur. Every few minutes he strokes her lovely ears and nuzzles his nose into her neck.

She brings his paw to her beating chest and whispers back to him, "Bless you, Sweetheart."

That is their name for each other—*Sweetheart*—the only name they know.

As time passes, Coyote falls asleep. He dreams of fenceless prairies. He dreams of air falling like water from a silent, empty sky.

He's awoken by Rabbit squeezing his paw.

"What is it?" he says.

"It feels like...like a whole new world being born!"

"Good," Coyote says. "Stay calm, Sweetheart."

Right then he smells the coming humans. He turns and watches the first of them arrive—a white-faced, dark-haired woman. She crawls into their living room, sees the sunlight shining in, and turns off her headlamp.

Then she spots the animals.

Rabbit, turned away, panting and puffing, has no idea they're being watched. She moans like the buzzing of a thousand bees, her body tingling with mild, mystical convulsions. She laughs and looks back at Coyote.

"It's coming!" she screams with joy. "It's coming now!"

The woman looks down the tunnel and holds out her hand. "Wait," she says to whoever is behind her. "Shhh."

Coyote looks at her and smiles.

She smiles back.

Rabbit gasps as a tiny body emerges between her legs. She hands it to Coyote, then fast returns to wait for the others.

The woman gasps too, as if she were also giving birth. She's begun to cry. She puts her hands over her mouth.

The proud father holds his child up for her to see. He makes certain to show its sleek coyote snout, its tiny sharp teeth, its floppy rabbit ears.

The woman looks amazed. Tears fall from her glistening eyes, down her smiling face. "Oh my," she says, without a trace of doubt, "will wonders never cease?"

www.ingramcontent.com/pod-product-compliance
Lightning Source LLC
Chambersburg PA
CBHW020742250626
47155CB00003B/886